I0680431

Probable Pillo

Probable Pillows

The Collected short stories of Frank Goodman

FG Publishing
2020

First Printing: 2020

ISBN: 978-0-244-86649-5

CONTENTS

NOT THE REAL SEA

It had been Eamon's idea to go to the seaside. 'We deserve a break', he said, washing his hands in the kitchen sink. Eamon always washed his hands the first thing he got into the house like a surgeon washes the germs away before an operation - meticulous, unhurried. Maire, who disliked habits of any kind, had always found irritation with the precision of his ablutions, found it more so now that there was no dirt, no day's toil to remove.

'We'll go by way of Canterbury then on to Margate and eat in a restaurant there'. Maire looked at him, smiling, washing, as carefree as a schoolboy in the new joy of his idea. It would be good to get away for the day though, the meal would take the place of the pair of pale blue slingbacks that she had seen in Dolcis window, but they needed the break. It was a good idea she had to admit, charming in its simplicity, after all what could be nicer than a family day out by the sea. 'Let's hope the weather holds', said Maire, looking out the window at the late afternoon sun that beat on against the brown straw that had once been their lawn, it hadn't rained for weeks. 'It'll be just our kind of luck that it pisses down'.

The next day was the same however, flat and hot and they loaded up the car with beach type things and eventually Becky and Sam once they got them away from the T.V. then they were off. Eamon was full of high spirits but Maire was reserved, holding her happiness back until she was sure the call to joy was justified. Too much had happened over the last months to enable her to embrace happiness that easily. Sorrow was like a cloud inside her, greying out the patches of blue.

Eamon drove fast along the A2 talking about the past, about when he was a child. Maire had heard it all before but he told it well and she found herself half listening. 'Before this road was built there was just a little road, you can see a bit of it over there', Eamon pointed, Maire looked at the patch of crumbly edged tarmac. She tried to imagine an England where all roads were no bigger than that one but could not. It belonged to a time of horses and carts and people for whom a trip to the next village was a lifetime adventure. She could only hold thoughts like that for so long then lost them in a kind of universal sad feeling that one got for things that had gone forever. Maire had been told that all change was for the better but remained unconvinced. How could it be good if it made people unhappy? 'The traffic jams along here were really something then', Eamon continued, 'My old man hated them, we'd go for miles out of our way to avoid them, I must have seen every back road between here and Margate at one time or another'. Maire smiled, she too remembering the endless squabbles of the childhood Sunday drive, the hours spent on the road and the all too fleeting moments by the sea.

In the back, Sam played grimly on his GameBoy, vanquishing cartoon dragons in an as yet vain attempt to save the princess from a terrible fate. Becky sulked and breathed on the window, she would miss Neighbours and Home and Away, everyone else's parents at least had a video so you didn't miss things. She wrote the word 'Jason' in the condensation twice. Eamon drove swiftly in and out of the traffic, pointing out things, explaining things. He was in control and he liked nothing better. It had been hard on him these last few months and she knew she hadn't helped, but a hard knot inside her, the stubborn knot, fought back against him. She had stood in opposition to his belief in pride, his sense of dignity simply because she had feared the worst - and now the worst had happened. Deep down a silent corner of her heart bled for him, but she couldn't stop blaming him.

'Will we be there soon' asked Becky in her disdainful voice. 'No, not for a while' Eamon replied. 'I'm bored' she whinged 'Why don't you read your New Musical Express or something', he said. 'It's Smash Hits actually' she pointedly waved the magazine under his nose to confirm his stupidity. 'Don't do that when your father is driving,' said Maire sharply and Becky slumped back in a sulky heap, staring dourly and unimpressed at the passing countryside.

Canterbury had changed, Eamon said, except for the bit around the cathedral. Certainly around the old castle walls where Maire imagined there had once been a moat was a large and very busy dual carriageway, it certainly had the same effect as a moat for those trying to cross it on foot, for sharks read Volvos, she smiled to herself. Typically enough at the moment she felt her spirits lifting she sensed Eamon's begin to drop. 'They've made a right mess of this place,' he said bitterly, as they jostled through the Thursday morning shoppers. It looked pretty much like any big country town to Maire, the old sitting incongruously by the new, half-hearted pedestrian precincts, full of all the familiar shops. But she knew Eamon took it as a personal insult and each Arndale centre or flyover imposed on his past symbolised in some way the oppression of the peoples.

'I've seen worse' said Maire cheerily but the look he gave her made her heart sink, the day was as good as lost already. How often had she seen that look over the last months, how often had it numbed her heart, it was her fault it seemed to say, her fault after all, perhaps she too had become a symbol of oppression.

Having dragged Becky from the Next and Sam from Virgin Games, she was only too glad to be back in the car. It took them a long time to rid themselves of the traffic congested, ring road and Maire could feel Eamon's anger slowly mounting, even on the best days it was never far from the surface now, she breathed a sigh of relief when they finally began to drive freely again. They reached Margate without speaking, Sam was on the third level of Dragons Lair and Becky had gone to sleep. Maire bit her lip to stop the tears from forming. Why did they always have to make difficult things worse? But she knew why of course, knew what was happening, why did she keep avoiding it?

Margate was busier than they had imagined and they had to park far back in the town, which set Becky and Sam moaning at having to walk. Eamon strode ahead, his hands in his pockets Maire noticed suddenly how purposeless he looked, like those people you saw standing on street corners just staring, or sitting side by side in pubs with nothing to say and their hands on their beer. Work was a funny thing, it pressured, offended, tired, you cursed it, swore you were glad to see the back of it for the day but when it was no longer there you felt purposeless - because whether you liked it or not you were work. It was only work that gave you any real status any sense of being there at all. Maire was lucky, motherhood changed all that, her focus had changed, her reason for being established.

Despite their parking problems the sea front was not that crowded and the beach held only intermittent human flotsam. 'They're all in the theme park', suggested Maire. 'or in the pubs' said Eamon. 'Can we go there now' said Becky. They strolled up toward the pier looking in the shop windows, most of which were amusement arcades. Sam was kept out of them with difficulty. Maire let him go in just the one in the end. Becky went with him while she and Eamon waited on the pavement. 'Are you enjoying yourself' said Maire pointedly. Eamon smiled at her humorlessly, 'it's nothing now compared to what it was in its heyday, it's a shame'.

'Everything disappoints', said Maire.

'What's that supposed to mean'. He didn't look at her but she saw the muscles in his jaw tighten waiting for the reply.

'Oh I don't know' said Maire 'I don't know why I said it'.

'Another of your little digs is it' he rubbed his hand nervously on his forehead.

'Not really - it's over now Eamon, it's all done with it really is and I'm not going to keep on talking it over and over'.

'You still don't understand do you', he wagged his finger at her, the teacher's lecture, 'why things had to be this way'.

'Oh I've always understood why you do what you do Eamon', Maire looked beyond the finger to the man, the boy, 'It's a shame your choices aren't more beneficial to your family.'

'We can begin again,' He said, but his voice was too soft, like he said it without really knowing how.

'You can begin again Eamon, I can begin again, but there is no we to recover.'

She could see Sam running from arcade machine to arcade machine watching the display then pushing the buttons and levers as if they were responding, as if he had put money in, the concentration on his face reminded her of Eamon, eager, intense, full of brash certainty, but it was a certainty based on nothing, a certainty that crumbled easily when struck against the hard edge of the true world.

'I owed it to a lot of people, you know I did,' Eamon said finally. 'Yes I know', she said. 'I know but I can't forgive'.

He lifted his arm and gave her a squeeze 'Try' he said as if that act could make it all right, like lets shake hands and be friends, something so male child about it, as if you could do that. Perhaps that was the problem really, men played at living, deep down it was still all a game. Real life played with the same gusto. It was a brave thing for Eamon to do, side with the strikers for a better deal. Viewed from one perspective he was brave and admirable, a veritable foolhardy David in Goliath's path. High on the traditions of his forefathers and the rhetoric of struggle, he had struck his blow for the freedom of peoples everywhere, keeping alive the memory of all those honourable failures before him, whose efforts had been legendary and whose place in history had been stolen from them. But his stone, when thrown of course had had no effect, and now he was just an unemployed man in an unemployed world and the hard bitter price of his bravery would now be paid - paid by them all. The breeze picked up and stung her face with a light flurry of sand, she winced for a moment. Eamon reached out to help and she instinctively took a step back. She saw how much she had hurt him with that gesture but couldn't help it, her pain turned to anger before she could control it - there was nothing left in her to stop it.

The restaurant Eamon chose was not really to her taste. She would have preferred something with a bit more style but Eamon no longer took criticisms of his judgement well and she let it pass for the sake of some meagre harmony. It did have a good view of the sea though, facing out from the first floor. 'I like the sea' said Sam filling his mouth with chips, 'it never stops moving'. 'Of course, it's not the real sea' said Eamon. 'It looks real' said Sam puzzled. 'What I mean is that its technically part of the Thames Estuary, the real sea begins on the other side of the North Foreland'. The word technically made Maire dig her fork hard into her skate, it was a word redolent with the pedantry that seemed to twine around the root of her frustration but she said nothing, for now there really was nothing more to say. She looked at them all, her family, not a bad bunch really. A normal family on a day out by the sea, a family that would soon cease to be a family and therefore begin to be less normal, less happy forever, this was their father's legacy. She looked out at the sea doomed forever to impostorship now by Eamon's technicality; it still rose and fell as it had before spraying its invigorating discharge over happy screaming children. She watched a family splashing carelessly in the foam, the father holding the son by the arms and swinging him into the white water, the mother holding the little girl's hand protectively at the sea's edge. Next week they would take her home away, men with papers and apologetic smiles flanked by other bigger unsmiling men. Then she would be back living with her acidic told you so mother as if she had never left, as if she were a schoolgirl again. Then there would be the jobs, in Tescos or the DHSS and the tiredness, the soul destroying tiredness that would clutch at her capacity for motherhood. She was glad that Eamon would not be there, there where she could blame him every day and begin to hate him. He still hadn't accepted this but he would soon, she would make him. He raised his glass and said 'Cheers, here's to us', in a wan sort of way, exuding pathos, inviting comfort. Maire ignored him and returned her attention to the sea.

BILL REMEMBERS HIS CHILDHOOD

In a small flat in London, Bill Johnson pounds on a typewriter and tries to wrest some ounce of meaning from the surge and counter-surge that floods through his brain and that he calls experience. Outside in the warm July street two women argue, jaws set, fingers wagging, their shopping bags held tight in their well-worn hands. Three boys watch them from the other side of the road. They like to see adults fight; there is something comforting to them about adults acting foolishly. As the fight reaches its verbal crescendo they nudge each other and giggle. Suddenly, simultaneously both women turn and walk away.

In the flat, Bill tries to remember his youth, tries to remember what it felt like, tries to remember those highs and lows and how you got through growing up just because you didn't realise it was happening. Bill finds it difficult to reach back that far, Bill knows his time was another time and though not yet old cannot imagine childhood now, Bill belongs to a time when things were in black and white. Bill remembers trolleybuses and bomb sites.

Bill stops pounding as there is no more coffee in his cup, he stares at it disconsolately; he once had a t-shirt that said 'this machine runs on coffee' on the front, he may have it still somewhere in the stale recesses of his cupboard. In the kitchen Bill finds an empty coffee jar - disaster, Bill knows he must go to the corner shop or his childhood will not be recovered today.

Marina Alexandreou leaves the Eagle pub where she has just finished her lunchtime shift. She is happy that it is warm, though she feels quite tired - peoples' needs make her tired, the Eagle pays well but is very popular. She walks along the High Street gathering in the summer, the traffic is thick and loud as usual but she pretends not to notice, her time is her own until seven tonight when she must go back to the Eagle. Till then she can do what she likes but will probably just go home and try to sleep for a bit. Marina sees a poster in the travel agents window, a stark white windmill above a blue, blue bay, Marina's never been to Greece but still regards it in some part of her being as home, she imagines being there walking past the whitewashed buildings, along harbour front streets that run right to the sea, Marina feels the boats tug at their moorings in the afternoon breeze, she wonders if she'll ever go now, she is twenty eight and already she senses the fragility of opportunity, but she remains optimistic in all things, her thoughts drift on.

She realises that she has no milk at home and turns towards the shops, she thinks about her tiny flat and sighs, living in a small way is getting to her, making her smaller. She knows that she's putting more and more of her hopes on something coming from the business course that she is taking, that it will somehow miraculously elevate her, but also she knows that it is not usually that easy, never that easy. Experience counts for so much in this life they say, but the experience you get is never the one they want somehow. She smiles at this and a man passing hoping the smile is for him smiles back but Marina does not notice. Marina reaches the Patel stores - it's more expensive than Sainsbury's but she can't face the thought of all that bustle and crush.

Bill Johnson hears the shop bell but he doesn't look up as he is between buying filter or ground and readying himself for the decision after, that between continental dark roast or Colombian. The aisles of the shop are small; goods leap out at you from every corner in a fanfare of packaging. At the counter an old man tells Mr. Patel the shopkeeper 'I'm 77 you know,' then stands back a little like it amazes him too. Bill decides on filter - though he always gets in a mess with it, he feels he deserves it. Bill moves along the aisles to find some filters and not looking forwards but sideways, bumps into a young woman who has arrived silently at his side, 'sorry' he mutters automatically and looks to see if she is annoyed. "s OK', she says and smiles, Bill notices her black curly hair and her eyes, A moment later Bill finds he is looking at her eyes again. They are deep brown, almost black, and something shines in them, even when she's not smiling, as she's not now, staring intently at the wall of goods trying to find whatever it is she needs, it's a glorious light happy and kind, it makes Bill feel warm just knowing it exists.

Marina is aware that the man who bumped into her is looking at her. This is not new - she is used to men looking, knows they find her attractive but since that realisation either makes them aggressive or coy the fact does nothing for her, but this man is a bit different, not thrusting forward or drawing back he is just there and he looks, She turns to look at him and he does not look away, he is, she thinks, in his forties perhaps but he dresses like a younger man and can, his body looks hard and slim beneath his t-shirt and jeans. She smiles at him again, he says 'I can never find anything in this place can you?' Marina wonders if he is married, his hands are empty of rings and his t-shirt is badly in need of a wash but things like that don't always tell you. Marina thinks she might go with this man should he ask her, an instinct, but not if he is married, married men are too much trouble, they never come alone but bundled up with the bad news their families have become. The 77 year old man leaves, carrying his amazement and 4 tins of catfood and Mr. Patel calls out 'can I help you at all please' and breaks the moment. Bill waves to Mr. Patel to say 'its ok' and waits for the girl to answer, waits to see if she will 'what is it you're looking for' she says her lips remain parted as she finishes speaking half smile half question, her eyes are all question. 'Filters' says Bill lamely and feels he's missed an opportunity. Marina points them out for him and takes her milk to the counter. She does not look back, perhaps she was wrong about him, perhaps he was just fantasising. Marina shrugs, She's at a time in her life when she's not sure that a man is exactly what she needs. Bill pays for the filters quickly, 'She's going, you fool,' he tells himself, though a part of him is already resigned to the fact. When he turns round the shop is empty and moments later on the pavement she is nowhere to be seen.

Friday night 7.00pm. The good weather has held all through the week and the stored warmth remains, the evening air feels soft to the touch. Bill leaves his flat and walks along towards the river, the street is deserted except for a group of teenagers lounging artlessly by the chip shop, their collective boredom surrounds them like a cloud restless and heavy, reaching out for whatever it can suck in. They look at him contemptuously, Bill stares back, they snigger conspiratorially on cue, Bill smiles at them and ruins their game. He hears them swearing at him as he turns the corner. Bill spends most Fridays in the Spotted Horse;

14

like many single people he is careful how often he goes to the pub, knows how easy it is to go there every day. The Spotted Horse is a drinkers pub', no loud music, no large T.V. screens, no restaurant, Bill spends his time there talking to people he knows well, though he does not know things like where they live, their marital status or even their last names, he knows them well. After a week away he looks forward to their company.

Marina arrives at the Eagle pub at 7.00 sharp, Chris the landlord greets her with a friendly leer as always. Chris still occasionally tries to get her to sleep with him, usually around Christmas time but he is never upset that she says no and probably won't mention it gain for a whole year. Chris doesn't know that last time she nearly said yes.
There's more to working in a pub than just selling drinks,Whether you like it or not, each pub has its social function, each pub is a little community with its own rules and hierarchies, each is an homogenous world into which you will have to fit. Marina knows it is her job to be pretty and attentive, to take all but the downright aggressive or crude with a giggle and a smile, to ignore the trailing sweaty hands and the whistles when she bends down, she no longer feels afraid of these men. She knows the sadness that lives within them, senses the inadequacy that makes them so angry. Even so she still does not like it when they touch her and she is careful not to go too close when collecting glasses.

The pub is unusually empty for a Friday night. Being close to the river but not on it means that on a night like tonight the riverside pubs, terraces will be spilling with drinkers all wanting something from the extra magic of the reflecting water. Chris grumbles, Marina is glad of a quiet night.

Bill stands outside the Spotted Horse and reads the sign again as if on second reading the meaning might change, "Pub closed for re-decoration until 25th. Apologies to our customers".
Bill stands there adrift, trying to decide whether to be angry or depressed. He looks around for inspiration, a decision; he knows the pubs by the river will all be hopelessly full. The logical thing is

to go home but somehow in the wake of what might have been home seems unsatisfactory. He walks off, not the way he came but parallel to the river, drifting in the city night. Bill has not gone far when he finds The Eagle, a pub he did not know existed. Bill looks it over, it seems ok - right sort of beers, no suggestion of Venetian blinds or neon signs, no evidence of designer pretensions. Bill goes in and there behind the bar is the girl from the corner shop, Bill wonders once more about the possibility of fate.

Marina sees the man come in but does not place him at first, just a vague notion that she has seen him before, does not place him until he is at the bar and ordering, then she sees that look and remembers. She smiles, 'Hello again' he says, 'I thought you'd gone out of my life forever'. It's a silly thing to say but she likes it, likes it because he knows about phrases like that and because he's not afraid to say them out loud whether they're meant or not. A regular nearby snorts and moves away down the bar giving him a look of contempt. He doesn't seem to notice, he is only looking at her. 'My name's Bill,' he says.

By the time Bill leaves the Eagle he's got a date with the girl with the laughing eyes whose name is Marina and whose other name is something Greek and ends in U. The very word 'date' seems juvenile and silly but it's the one that comes into his head like perhaps he is going through a second (make that fifth) childhood. Nonetheless he will see the girl with the laughing eyes on Sunday and he feels lighter somehow than he has been for a long time, raised up closer to the starry night sky. He walks home along the river, letting the water sounds calm him. In the distance, across the water, he hears music and laughing. People trying to be happy, he wishes them luck.

Marina wonders about the man who has just left, the man called Bill, She knows that he will be kind but kind men can so often be weak and weakness is a kind of cruelty in its way. She remembers a time when she would give herself unreservedly to a man hungry for their moments together and wishing only to please - but to give in such a way had been a mistake - it made men fearful or scornful. Now she was more careful, she let her love wait. Marina looked forward to the weekend, she dried the glasses slowly building her defences against disappointment.

It is Sunday and Bill is up early and writing; he thinks about the forthcoming evening and wonders about her. 'Marina' he tests the name for resonance, for meaning, wonders if he places too much store on physical beauty, it's been his downfall in the past. The whole of the city littered with painful memories and sad places like a tattered map of the heart, parks, streets, houses, pubs and restaurants all replete with the sorrow of loss or the blank face of disappointment, in each of these places something painful remained, memories no longer raw but haunting. Bill wonders if this will be one more for that scrapbook that lies in his head, past lives with no more than a few fading photographs to prove they ever existed at all. Shaving, he stares at himself in the bathroom mirror, but he can no longer be objective about a face so familiar, can't see what others might see, what she might see. It's a young man's face into which old bits have crept, thinning hair, greying temples a few fine wrinkles under the eyes as if to say, 'you've put me off for a long time now but not for ever here I come'.
Bill laughs, laughs away at the man in the mirror, whose eyes are too serious and sad.

Marina is early, not because she worries about being late but because she never knows how long things take and walks down to the High Street far too quickly. She has a choice now between walking down the road and looking aimlessly in the shop windows or going into the pub alone, though she hates the way people stare at women on their own (and it's not just the men), when they enter. She goes in anyway, people stare. She goes up to the bar and smiles brightly at the barman, 'red wine please', his surly sideways glance becomes attentiveness to her radiance, she knows that she can do this. She does not know how but she knows that she can do it and knows it works. She doesn't really like to admit it, it has been useful to her on more than one occasion but it has got her into trouble as well. She tries to use it carefully but knows she likes the attention it brings her.

She takes her drink and sits at a table to wait, she does not wait long a couple of sips and he is here, smiling boyishly and saying 'I see you've got a drink already'.

In the restaurant Bill can't stop looking at her, while she talks he just fixes his eyes on her face. She's so lovely he begins to get a little scared, begins to wonder why she would want to be with him, He knows women like him but he also knows not always enough, attracting them isn't easy, attention to detail is important, one little mistake and the spell is broken. He knows he's not handsome or charismatic enough to be forgiven again and again like some men, he moves with care, he listens attentively. Marina talks in sparkling waves of anecdote and story. She likes it when he tells her he is a writer, says 'that must be fun' he is relieved that she doesn't say 'how interesting' but a little piqued that she uses the word 'fun'.

'I wouldn't call it fun exactly, it's harder work than that.'

Marina waves her hands in a Mediterranean way. 'Everything is hard work, even failure, in fact' she adds after a moment's reflection 'Failure is harder work because you have nothing to show for it'.

Bill feels this argument is off beam somehow 'Doing nothing can't be hard work though' he suggests.

Marina grins impishly 'Nothing is the hardest work of all and cannot be achieved overnight'.

Bill is about to analyse her view when he realises that she is teasing him.

They laugh.

Marina tells him about her childhood. When she was sixteen her father had tried to marry her off to a fat greengrocer from Highgate. He had been uncomprehending when she said no and even more credulous when having told her that to disobey him would mean that she had to leave the house forever, she left. He never did understand how things had changed. Bill is sympathetic, says he believes in love, believes that choice is important, believes that pleasure is the root of well-being. Marina smiles at this, wonders if it is a clever line but thinks it is so clever that it doesn't matter.

Marina decides that she may sleep with this man, Bill, but not today, though she has desire for him and knows she is not one of those girls who lock their bodies away like some bright sweet to entice, fearing to give, doubting the outcome. She likes to wait a bit, it made it more romantic, less animal somehow. Not long though, God, not long.

Bill and Marina say goodbye and she kisses him lightly on the lips. Bill puts a hand on her waist but does not hold on as she pulls back. Marina likes this part of a relationship, the new beginning, the sweetness, anticipation that fills their actions. Whilst waiting in hope for something, human beings are at their most kind she thinks.

Bill thinks about Marina on the walk home, he is slightly high on drink and excitement, he replays the evening, the way she looks, the colour of her skin, the curl of her leg, the sense of firmness under her clothes, the smell of her body close, the light sweetness of her lips. He feels the currents of life and possibility running through him, that great feeling when hope, that old deceitful dog re-emerges in him, he realises that it has been a long time, now longer between attacks, Yes, he thought, hope comes slower each time.

Marina hopes too but not like Bill, these things are not as simple for her. Things that move one way bring other changes in their wake. Marina has come to be wary of change, for changes are complex things whose implications only arrive with time.

Marina knows that a good thing is about to happen in her life but hopes that it is not at the cost of some other good thing. Back at her flat she begins to tidy, idly humming to herself, She has made it a nice flat, Bill will like it here.

When they meet again it is Wednesday, a light rain drifts across the streets, making wild glistening patterns in the lamplight Bill arrives at Marina's flat with a bottle of Chilean Cabernet and a bunch of flowers. She kisses his wet face as he walks past her into the room and he kisses back harder than before. Marina feels excited for the first time, anticipation finally ahead of anxiety. She opens the bottle and pours two glasses of wine. They sit on the sofa and talk but the talk does not last long, the room is full of their desires, its weight drags on their words, tugs at their actions. Bill takes Marina by the hand and leads her towards the bedroom, thought he doesn't know exactly where it is. Marina does though and, grateful for the boldness of Bill's action for sparing her the fumblings and juvenility of sex on the sofa with her bra round her neck and panties round her ankles, pushes him towards the right room.

Bill likes the look and the feel of her dusky skin, the way she groans lightly, encouragingly as he slips inside her, likes the light in her eyes that tells him she is in pleasure. Marina likes to feel Bill inside her. He is not rough like Mick or sad and apologetic like Salim. She likes the way he holds his body above her, resting on his hands so that there is no weight and the only place their bodies touch is there. His stomach is almost flat like a boy's. She puts her hands on his buttocks and feels the hard muscles beneath. Afterwards he is attentive, comforting, not at all distant or self-absorbed.
Bill's main thought at such times is gratitude, as if he has a debt he must now honour, concerned that in the remnants of desire, there will be no damage.

When he leaves it is morning, he will be late for a meeting with his agent, but it's right that he should, love should be that way.

The days pass, the taste, the sense of each other shapes and changes things, orders their thoughts. Marina begins to think of the future but is still careful. She has been here before, shaping thought futures that did not occur; weddings, husbands and families all neatly laid away in the tissue paper of what might have been. Marina thinks of children more these days but still does not know what to do. Part of her aches and part is scared, not of the pain or the carrying, but of what she might have to become, what parts of her life may be consumed by them. As always when uncertain, she holds back but Marina knows that she can't remain forever on the merry-go-round of men - that one day the ride will be over and she could walk away with nothing, but not yet. For now she still believes, must believe, in the brighter day, it will be hard when she cannot do that.

Bill wants to be with this woman more than anything but then he's wanted that before. Things had a habit of escaping you, the things you really wanted, till it seemed to him like wanting was a form of curse. Even so Bill thinks he might marry Marina, would ask her if only he can think it through, Bill doesn't think about children at all, it never occurs to him that he might ever have a family, live like a family - he's not lived like that since childhood.

September brings the inevitable change in the weather, the days become unpredictable. Sometimes cold, sometimes warm, sometimes wet, sometimes not. Bill and Marina stay in a lot eating pizza and watching videos of old 40's films that Bill collects off the T.V. Marina says she likes Burt Lancaster best because he has good muscles and a big grin - not like those little men with thin mouths who are everywhere in these movies. Bill says she has a Chippendale problem and needs to broaden her outlook. Marina considers this but is unconvinced. 'Why should I change the way I think when it wouldn't change the way I feel.' Bill suggests that she might surprise herself, is about to recommend a course of action but she silences him with a kiss.

Marina prefers her flat to Bill's It's not just the untidiness, the abandoned look of Bill's place, - Marina likes precision, the sense of order, of things going to plan. Bill was not a lazy person but he had some lazy habits that Marina keeps an eye on, waiting to see whether familiarity would make them grow.
Bill watches Marina as she places and tidies, senses an obsessiveness behind her actions , a ritualistic pattern that calms and determines things. Bill suspects patterns, suspects all order as bogus, contrived, knows he must evade this order or be swept into it.
They make love a lot, knowledge of each others' bodies has heightened things, they push at the edges of sensuality, here is

harmony, here they do not question each other lives.

But Marina feels the newness slipping from their love and knows that beyond this newness the path forks, soon they will have to work at the relationship or let it go, soon they would have to learn to accommodate and to understand, to share more than just their bodies and their moments.

This merging was the hardest part for it required dedication, it required generosity and it required trust.

Bill knows that his life does not amount to much but it does exist in a sort of harmony, it's a balance that took a long time to come. When he was young he had been such a romantic, such a believer in the saving power of women in his life. It had been a life lived out between the agony of anticipation and the shame of rejection. He knows he will never suffer such pain again but is wary of his emotions, that those betrayers of equilibrium still lurk somewhere within him awaiting their moment.

One day the street is full of leaves and Bill realises that the summer is over. Soon the days will shorten and the dank grey skies will reign over the city. Bill hates the English winter, the great blot it makes on his soul each year, wonders why he stays on, meagerly feasting on the carrion of Empire. His friends have long since split to warmer, softer climes. He stares idly from time to time at the big atlas he keeps for reference, runs the names of places off his tongue, there's still a lot he hasn't done.

Marina begins to think past Bill for the first time and this makes her sad. She knows herself well enough to spot the small things, the little self-deceits that hide bigger truths. She sighs and closes her eyes and waits for the sadness to pass.

Bill doesn't go to The Eagle much anymore, tells Marina it annoys him to see all those men ogling her and he's quite busy with some pieces on the Italian Renaissance which he's doing as a favour for a friend. Marina tells him she understands.

Marina takes her cardigans and jumpers from the top of the wardrobe, they smell old and stale and will need an air. The flat is getting cold, seems emptier in the bleak flat light of Autumn. Marina hums 'Save the Last Dance for Me' and shakes out the creases.

It is a Sunday, it is the middle of October but as bright and sunny a day as you could ever hope for this far north of those really warm places. Bill and Marina are walking hand in hand across Hampstead Heath, in the distance the city is a set of smudged oblongs. Bill points out some of the recognisable buildings but Marina finds them difficult to spot. The whole city seems compressed, jumbled in upon itself. Bill looks at the clouds churning in the west, he thinks of the half-written manuscript upon his desk, an unread novel by Balzac lying beside it. He thinks 'Perhaps it is time to travel again', he has never seen Prague or Budapest or maybe even to the countries of
South-East Asia where life was simple and mystical.

Yes, it would do him good.

Marina looks at the sky in the east, still pure and cloudless as it had been in the early morning. She would buy herself a new sofa for the winter with big cushions and soft comfy arms and a warm coat with a large collar that she can pull up around her ears when the wind is blowing off the river.

LOOK BACK IN HACKNEY

Sheena is a dancer with some company or other that does those musical shows, you know, the ones with the big cast list of nobody you've ever heard of in but you can singalong with all the songs.

She told me which musical when she came down to borrow some milk, but I've forgotten it now. I guess I wasn't really listening, just watching her. - she had that way of standing, you know, the way dancers do, as if they're just about to launch off into a pirouette. All coiled and sort of ready.

I didn't have any anyway, milk that is, but she stayed for a chat and ended up drinking some wine from a bottle that I had left over from a dinner party of a couple of weeks previously. It wasn't very nice, the wine that is, but anyway while we were talking she told me all about the new writing auditions.

'Angry young man for the Nineties' it was called, though of course women could enter as well. The holders of the competition made that quite clear in the hand-out which I got later from the Albion Theatre down the road.

Now I hadn't written drama for years, hadn't really written a proper play ever but I was trying my hand at anything these days in a sort of 'fuck art let's sell' fervor, so I was definitely interested.

'What's so different about a play anyway?' Sheena had said encouragingly.

If only that was true, I told her, plays had to mean something to be worth a damn, you couldn't end up all style and no product and get away with it.

Sheena thought you could though and said she had been appearing in them for years.

I told her you couldn't get away with that in serious drama. I could see she was a bit offended, she didn't say anything but her buttocks kind of clenched. I told her I didn't mean to be pompous but that I did have certain standards. She gave me the usual 'standards won't pay the rent' stuff and I gave her the usual 'no pain, no gain' reply which somehow helped without actually meaning anything.

The next day I got the form, as I said, and spoke to the man at the box office about the competition, trying to sus out the competition for the competition, if you see what I mean. In his opinion, he said, it was a bit has-beeny, lots of tubby bearded types in chunky knit woolies, lots of broken blood vessels in the cheeks, sort of chaps but the money was kosher, he assured me, five grand for the winner but not to expect to see the media buzzing round like the veritable flies on it, if you knew what he meant. I told him that I'd given up on my reputation and was operating on a cash only basis. He patted me on the arm and told me it was for the best.

I spent the afternoon demolishing the best part of a Rymans A4 to little avail. It wasn't that I couldn't think of anything to feel angry about - Christ knows! It's just that I didn't sound angry enough and when I did there was Jimmy Porter grinning at me from every page, his full contemptuous mouth daring me to top him. Of course I couldn't even begin. I wasn't an angry young man, I wasn't even vaguely upset.

In the end I binned the lot and went down the pub. It was still early but the Marketing crowd from the building on the corner had already made their invisible transition from their office. One I knew called Maurice came up and bought me a pint. I didn't refuse, though I knew the price would be 30 minutes of what a bastard life was and how cut throat the industry had become. Perhaps Maurice should write my play for me but then Maurice wasn't really angry either he was just a wanker.

Things looked up later when Jeff came in. Jeff had a great pedigree of anger, from student union secretary all the way through SWP to Save the Whale with all the other stuff thrown in, Anti-nazi league, CND and the like.

'Tell me about anger, Jeff.' I said, sidling up beside him.

Jeff scratched his bald patch, fiddled in the pocket of his waistcoat for a packet of Rizlas then looked at me schoolmasterly through thin rimmed glasses.

'Anger is the natural state of the dispossessed, Jim and the outlawed and the prejudiced against. If you're not one of these then you'll never know the kind of anger you're talking about, forget it'.

'But you're not one of those Jeff, yet you've got anger,' I queried, hopefully.

Jeff gave me a baleful stare. 'I am dispossessed of my vision of a harmonious world, I'm outlawed from the chance to effect harmony'.

'I could learn to feel like that I'm sure'. I told him. It sounded very playworthy when you said like that, feeling lost and forgotten and all that.

Jeff rolled his spindly cigarette. 'What you need is awareness. Get to know what's going on in the world. Read about what's really happening. You'll soon get anger -. mines a pint of Theakstons by the way'.

I bought.

So I read the paper. There was a lot about the Royal family who seemed to be having a hard time of it and couldn't fart with out someone noting it and turning it in to an issue.

There was a lot of photos of women in underwear, though when I read the story it didn't seem to be about underwear or even about women really.

There was a lot about masturbating & jealousy and people with their heads stuck in railings and cats that could whistle 'Can't get you out of my head.' Also nude parachuting and wiry balding men in leather jackets punching cameramen because they were too close or something and that was about as near as it got to anger.

When I next saw Jeff in the pub I told him that the papers weren't much help. He told me that I'd read the wrong paper and should have chosen something like the Guardian. I informed him that I wouldn't be paying 50p for a newspaper, even for the sake of my art. So he gave me some copies of a magazine he had called 'Third World Watch'.

At first this seemed more like it, it had lots of stuff about black people and poor people being ripped off by all sorts and getting upset about it. Starving ragged women and their moon-headed babies, stuck out in those builders site lands without so much as a Tracker bar between them for sustenance. Sad eyed droopy mustachioed Latins on sun-shadowed verandas recounted tales of murder and intrigue all somehow to do with the CIA. Russian girls with ruddy open faces and closed silent eyes sold themselves in the dark on the bitter streets of Moscow recounting their run-ins with the local glasnost Mafia.

Surely there was something here I could use for anger. I went to work and for a while slightly flat European characters moved across vivid backcloths of deprivation. Looking stunning and being stunned by what they saw; intrigue, despair and a bit of love interest bt it was all a dead end - the calamity of these people was too huge, too alien, it didn't make me angry, just amazed.

Still, I was sitting working on a scene about the failure of the Guatemalan rice crop and the love affair between Giselle, a French nurse attached to the U.N. and Robert a CNN journalist trying to get to the bottom of the issue, when Sheena called. She was off to Leicester to dance in 42nd St. at the Empire there but would be back sometime in the middle of the night as they didn't pay for hotels on gigs less than 150 miles from London.

'How long's the booking then ?'.

'Six weeks' she said ruefully. 'All over the Midlands'.

'You'll be looking even more knackered than usual then I guess'.

She threw a sofa cushion at me, which was a bit unfortunate as it was the one where I'd left the carton containing the remains of last night's meal. Biryiani sprayed the room, a large part of it ending up on my manuscript.

I'm sorry' Sheena said between bouts of hysterical laughter 'Have I messed up your play',

'It was messed up already' I said.

She came over and took a look, 'Quezalfenago, where's that?'.

'Guatemala.'

While Sheena wondered where Guatemala was, I took a tissue and wiped the curry sauce off the pages. Pale yellow Turmeric stains remained.

'These people don't seem to be very angry' she said 'just depressed'.

'You're right' I said 'and so am I'.

Sheena put her hand sympathetically on the nape of my neck. 'Perhaps if you went to some of these places you'd get that edge or whatever they call it'.

'That's a bit extreme just for a few grand don't you think?'

'But you could use it on other things stories and articles and the like,' Sheena described a significant volume of work with her long delicate fingers.

'No', I dropped the Guatemalan thing into the promising but irrelevant pile at the bottom drawer of my desk, 'the more I think about it the more I want to write about something going on here. Something about the dispossessed, the outlawed, the prejudiced against'.

'Oh you mean the immigrants' said Sheena.

I looked at her open-mouthed. Now why hadn't I thought of that. Yes of course and who better to help me understand that than Manweela Ghosh.

I'd met Manweela back in 1991 on a writing course entitled 'Write that Blockbuster' that had purported to give the struggling writer the keys to the scenarios that sold millions. In the end everybody thought it was a bit simplistic and it concentrated a lot on how to do the deal once you'd written the block buster rather than how to write it in the first place. Manweela dropped out after the eighth week but not before she'd been through most of the men in the class, using intimidation rather than seduction to achieve this. Not that she couldn't have used a subtler approach with her italianate curls and big brown eyes and her infectious laugh - It was just that she had no time for such prevarication. Directness was her byword. My turn came about the week seven. As she wrestled deftly with my belt buckle, I told her I always imagined Asian girls to be demure and reserved.

'You've seen too much Satyajit Ray,' she said. 'It's the culture transfer thing.' She pulled downward on the top of my pants. 'You Brits adopted eating curry and pot pourri. I took up screwing and collecting ceramic thimbles.'

Somehow we had remained friends, perhaps because I was not at all put out by being seventh on the list of her selection.

Manweela had temporarily abandoned her search for literary success and was working as a salesgirl in Dolcis 'Not a good place for those who are olfactory sensitive,' she told me. Which is where I caught up with her the following Monday. 'Aiee, Jimmy you still trying to write like Barbara Taylor Bradford?' she asked as she positioned a pair of pale blue Doc Martens in the back of the window display.

'No I'm a playwright now, sort of,' I told her, moving quickly on, 'I'm writing this angry play, in fact that's what I wanted to ask you. Does it make you angry to be discriminated against ?'

'Me!' she waved a brogue in an offhand manner, 'I'm an Indian, for god's sake, we were discriminating against each other when you were still living in sod huts and painting yourselves blue, this discrimination means nothing to an Indian, it is his daily breath. What annoys us is that you do it so badly'. She put down the brogue and flashed those eyes at me. 'You're looking well Jimmy, you looking after yourself I can see.'

I shrugged, 'But it does make you angry?' I asked again moving as inexorably toward my subject as Manweela was to hers. She got there first, her hand cupped my buttock. I caught her wrist. 'Tell me about this Manweela' as her body closed on mine.

'I'm too busy to get angry, you get angry, I guess, when things don't happen, as long as things happen, you happen with them. So, how a bout a quick one for old times sake.'

'If a man had said that Manweela...' I remonstrated.

'Then I hope you'd say no', she bit my ear and pulled me in to the store room.

Later, rising from a crushed pile of empty shoe boxes, as she was slipping into her knickers, she said. 'You should see my father, he is the man who likes to contemplate about deep issues. I'll take you to see him tomorrow evening, call for me here'. Then she went back to serving and left me to gather my trousers under the open-mouthed stare of the Saturday girl.

Professor Ranjit Ghosh was much more my idea of how an Indian should look & act. A small man in a white collarless jacket, his bespectacled face intelligent and serene, very Ben Kingsley, very Alec Guinness.

'Good Evening, What is it you wish to be knowing,' He said with the air of a busy man as soon as Manweela had introduced him. Though she remained in the room it was as if she had ceased to exist for him - there in the presence of men. I told him what I wanted - he screwed up his face - then said, 'This is not for you young man to talk about our anger, our anger is like a cold wind that blows far away yet we can still hear its rustle'.

Manweela snorted.

He continued. 'It is a part of our hearts, our history, it is the energy which enables us to endure. It is not the anger of the white man.' He said it like Geronimo might have and I began to wonder if he was a little odd.

'Understanding brings awareness' I said 'and awareness brings anger'.

Manweela snorted at this too as if to prove she wasn't in any way partisan.

'Immigrants can't afford to be angry, Jimmy, not in the way you mean. This is the anger of the white man who has space and time to contemplate injustice. For the poor man anger will only ensure that his torment continues'.

'So you're not angry then?' I shot a glance a Manweela she smiled and shrugged. 'What you are talking about is not anger but showing off,' Prof Ghosh continued, 'a craving for attention. That's all it does you see - draws attention to the angry person. At first glance this is impressive, this emotion but after a while not so'.

I wrote that down though I didn't quite understand the thinking behind it - but perhaps I could use it anyway.

When I left Prof. Ghosh shook my hand 'You are nice boy Jimmy, can't you do something for this crazy daughter of mine?' Manweela scowled, I found the thought vaguely scaring and just smiled and twitched in that non-committal way that says don't ask. Professor Ghosh nodded sadly and closed his study door. 'Was all of that any use?' asked Manweela as she tugged me in the direction of her bedroom.

'Some, not much - Look Manweela don't you think about anything but sex?'

Manweela narrowed her eyes as if thinking, 'Yes I do but not while there's a chance I can be having it.'

On my way home, considering the weary nature of things from the top of a number 30 bus and trying not to aggravate the scratches on my back, I read through the notes I had taken.

Perhaps it was in the nature of Asians not to get angry about things I thought, perhaps they were as Prof Ghosh had said too civilised for such self engendered emotions. I'd never seen anger as such a complex issue but then I suppose I hadn't thought about it to this degree before. I was almost ready to give up. There was one more possibility; the Afro-Caribbean perspective. Now Black people seemed much more upfront in that respect and if I needed to know more about their concerns then I needed to see Otis.

Otis worked at the Pizza Hut in Islington while he was waiting for a record contract. He was also the rap DJ at the Black House DC, the Stoke Newington club where I'd met him. An awesome figure in swathes of black leather and mirror shades he epitomised black insouciance, that hip flip, stay loose, cool with the dark undercurrent of violence and savagery that made it so compulsive. The next afternoon when I dropped into the hut Otis was looking a little less awesome than that, dressed in his candy striped shirt and red apron, sporting a neat little pill box hat which had 'Spicy hot one' printed across it. He was slicing pepperami and looking sideways at a bank of LED clocks which were all running down to zero like the doomsday bombs in those old spy movies. 'Hey Jimmy man what do you think of this lyric', he tapped the back of the knife on the counter to punctuate the words.

' I'm losin my way
I don't respeck myself
i'm livin my time at the back of the shelf
I gotta get out, gotta make my way, gotta get myself a ticket to the US of A.'

'It sounds kind of angry' I said hopefully 'what are you angry about Otis ?'.

'Hell man it's just a fuckin' lyric', Otis finished slicing the Pepperami as a carillon of 'pings' heralded the arrival of simultaneous zero. 'Usin lots of ace words you know, words that hook, that's the key.'

'Yes I know but isn't it the idea the thing that carries the song and in this case isn't that anger?'

'Course not' said Otis placing the little plastic white tables carefully in the middle of three Cheese Feasts. '14 Arscott Street' he yelled to a helmeted muffled figure sitting at the back 'and take 2 Pepsi Max and a Haagen Dazs Chocolate calypso. You're timed at 3.20 o.k.' He handed over the boxes and the muffled figure nodded sullenly and waddled out . 'It's the music man, the beat, that's what makes it happen.'

'So you're not angry then'? I reiterated, hope fading.

'Angry why that's just bad attitude - I don't need no negative vibes - you want a pizza by the way, no? - I tell you why that is, why man 'cos I'm gonna fuckin make it. There's no way I can fail. Today's catering executive will sooner or later end up with a record contract or with God - like Hallelujah you sinners save your souls with a little l'argent - you know what I mean? Both these things are very loo-crative.' He ruffled through a stack of serviettes as if they were already a wadge of cash. 'The future will be good man. Anger is for losers like that empty shit out there'. He pointed. A shaven headed man with 'fuck off' tattooed across his forehead was walking along Upper Street with a can of Kestrel squeezed into his fist. He looked at each passer by as if he wanted to kill them. He was angry all right, his anger was so tangible that it came off him like sweat but whilst I realised that here indeed was an 'angry' young man, I was disinclined to ask him why, knowing at a glance that even if he could tell me he would surely rather rearrange my teeth.

Back at the flat a dozen envelopes lay on the doormat calling feebly for my attention. Most were bills but there were three rejection slips that some Editors had been kind enough to send for me to add to my already admirable collection.

One was from Bronze, a magazine for the untarnished writer which hailed out of Litchfield wherever that was - they told me my piece on a homeless Parisian artists was interesting but lacked true insight. One from Geezers magazine, a down to earth life style magazine for men who told me that my story of a stock exchange romance wasn't sexy enough for them but didn't tell me whether it was a lack of graphical detail or a shortfall of couplings that was to blame, and finally, the BBC. Good old auntie beeb, told me that the story of two Cornish Tin Miners trapped underground on the day the mine closes but are rescued by conservationists looking to preserve the mine's heritage, wasn't 'aural' enough.

I threw the letters into the binder with the others. It was now quite a tome.

'Fuck them.' I thought. Everyone's got a different reason for rejecting my stuff. It's too long, too short, too personal, not bloody personal enough, not sexy, too smutty, not original, too original and of course that old chestnut, not the kind of thing we are looking to publish right now. Which meant that it hadn't been written by an established author, so they weren't even prepared to consider taking a risk on it. This was, after all, the age of 'not my ass on the line'. Nobody took chances any more, corporate bravery disappeared when the first salvos of mass redundancy made it clear that dispensing with people's services without good reason, always every Company Director's secret desire, had become an institutionaised reality. Being turned down was bad enough but every rejection letter also contained a modicum of advice, a smug little morsel of 'if I were you,' but all platitudinous and vague - none of them were worth a fart.

I kicked the book across the room what did they know about it, what did they know about my work. I kicked at the book again and the letters came out and flew in different directions. I was deciding which pile to follow and kick again when I suddenly realised I was angry! Busting with the stuff - and it was stuff I could use, understand - it was mine. I put a sheet of paper in the typewriter a glorious pristine anticipatory white sheet and began.

'Interior -Day - a small flat in North London' Graham a struggling writer pounds on his typewriter then stops - the door bell rings Graham exits then returns a few moments later with the post........

When Sheena got back from Kidderminster at about three in the morning I was still at it, she looked in seeing the light on, her face was pale and her head heavy with fatigue.

'How's it going ole Jimmy?' She said, rubbing her nose with her hand.

'It's going', I said, typing on, 'at bloody last'.

'You sound angry; she leaned over my hunched frame for a glimpse of my face.

'I do ?' I said not looking round, 'what a relief'.

Sheena went over to the window, she was wearing black ski pants and a pale blue angora sweater, her hair was piled up on the top of her head ballerina style, which made her neck seem impossibly long. She yawned in a big armstretching way then cupped her hands behind her head.

'Stay like that'

'Why ?' she turned to face me but kept her arms up.

'It inspires me'. I battered on syllable by syllable.

'You're not writing about me are you?' she wrinkled her nose at the thought.

'Well no - well sort of - well you're in there somewhere'.

'Oh thanks a lot,' she closed on the pile of completed pages but I waved her away. 'Not yet, soon but not yet'.

'So' she said resuming the cupped hands pose, 'what am I called in this piece'?

'- er Gloria', I mumbled.

' Gloria! she snorted Gloria! Glory be what am I a whore or something, whoever heard of a nice character called Gloria - they're always blowzy, cheery good time girls full of gin and wandering around after their loser gangster boyfriends waiting for the next black eye. '

'You've been watching too many B movies'. I told her, 'anyway it's just a working name. I'll change it if you like.'

'O.K.' said Sheena, 'call her Ethel'.

'What' I spluttered, 'nobody calls anybody Ethel any more'.

'That's why you should do it anyway I'm off to bed'. She left me with a faint aroma of Cacharel and a punk singer called Ethel, oh well - at least it was anti-style.

I'd finished they play in about a fortnight, pretty inspired work for me. Then I got a couple of nice copies made down at 'Pronto Print'. Jeri, the Pronto Reprographics Consultant, told me she'd read it while she was copying it and thought it was very good though she felt it lacked expletives. 'People that angry would swear more,' she assured me. I thanked her for the advice but told her I thought that the use of four-letter words for effect had had its day. 'Suit yourself,' she said and went back to stacking a pile of blue and red sheets with 'Total Quality 'r Us' printed on them.

I sent the play off with the form and the fiver (for administration costs as they always say) and after that felt a bit deflated. Like it must feel when your children leave home.

So, as with most of these competition type things, it's always months before you hear anything if you hear at all so I put it to the back of my mind and got on with the daily grind. There was money to be made by that purple pen of mine even if it was only a fiver here and a fiver there. Captions, adverts, prize letters, pieces like 'What a wacky world!' or 'My favourite curry'. Follow the trends that's the key, whatever gets massaged to the top of the 'that's interesting!' ladder, lock onto it and go. UFOs, Gall Bladder operations, Street Crime (50 ways to foil your Mugger), Tattoos, Hair-do's, Are you a babe? (20 ways to check your megability). Grit your teeth and get stuck in, recycle the phrases on new product (the word has somehow pluralised itself) and keep that roof over your head.

One morning I was looking for a rhyme for Hackney in the rhyming dictionary. From the choices on offer I was trying to decide between agony and appendectomy when Sheena came in with the post. 'Here's your junk mail' she said, 'I just got back from Milton Keynes, the coach broke down'.

'Help yourself to coffee' I gestured to the filter machine and decided on agony. By the time Sheena had poured herself a cup and slumped down on the sofa I had opened the only letter in the pile that looked real and was in a state of vague excitement. 'They've short listed it - the play'.

'How short ? Sheena murmured through sipfuls of coffee'

'It doesn't say'

'Well it might be a hundred'

'Don't be silly a short list is short. They want me to go down to the Albion theatre for a chat'.

'What does that mean a chat ?' Sheena finished the coffee and poured herself another.

'I don't know but that's what it says here look. - on Friday'

Sheena looked 'Hey this letter signed by Jeffrey Alcott'.

'What - oh so it is I hadn't read that far yet - are you impressed?'

'Sort of - it's certainly a step up from 'Chinwag' and 'Which Duvet' and those other things I've seen your stuff in.'

'So you read them do you? "

"Only when you.... ' Sheena went red and studied her coffee cup.

On the Friday I duly presented myself at the Albion Theatre at 10.00am sharp. The man from the box office waved to me and pointed 'Go on through dear, they're all in there somewhere'. I went into the darkened theatre and wondered where the 'there' in question might be; the stalls, the stage, the dress circle. Suddenly a rich thespian voice boomed out from the deep recesses of the stage. 'Mr. Milne is it? 'Yes' I replied in the direction of the voice. 'Put some bloody light on back there one of you.' The voice boomed again. The stage flooded with light and there centre stage was a chunky figure in a blazer. 'I'm Jeffrey Alcott,' the now embodied voice continued, 'I expect you've' heard of me'. 'Yes of course' I simpered, 'I'...He held up a hand, 'there's no need' he said. 'Come up here Mr Milne and we'll begin'. He led me to the back of the stage and off thorough a labyrinth of corridors and staircases, till finally somewhere near what surely must have been the upper rear of the theatre, we entered a large room brilliantly lit by a large skylight that covered most of the ceiling and through which the morning sun was pouring. In the room was a large table around which sat a half a dozen men and a small elfin woman with a clip board. They all smiled at me when I came in. 'Who's this?' growled a rotund man at the far end of the table .'Jim Milne,' I offered.

'Yes, yes but which play?'

'Oh - Slipping Away.' there was a shuffling of papers. 'Ah yes the play about the writer'. The man who growled was called Max Sheffer. He was something of a patriarch of the West End stage and was dragged out whenever there was a TV discussion on the state of English Theatre today. Though I couldn't actually name any of the plays he had written, I knew that they had been a big success at the time, though again I wasn't exactly sure when that was. Of the others I recognised Justin Goodrich, Director and outspoken critic against what he called, the bleary, bleakness of modern drama. He had recently courted public notoriety by referring to a popular tragi-comedy by a well-respected gay playwright as a 'storm in a condom'. The others were duly introduced to me but the names went skipping by, I smiled, they smiled again.

'What's the major theme of your play would you say?' Asked the pale blond man to my left who was called Richie or Ronnie something. 'Major theme?' I said, somewhat startled, 'Well ....anger I guess',

'Yes, of course, but anger at what ?,

'Anger at being rejected',

'But that rejection anger what's at the root of it? Don't you feel that one's reaction to rejection is simply a knee-jerk response to something deeper?'

'No one likes rejection.' I reminded him,

'Yes, perhaps, but not everyone gets angry about it. What makes those who do get angry, get angry do you think ?'

'Lack of maturity ? I offered.

A murmured demurral rose up around the table to punctuate my error. 'You must look for the grandeur in anger, not the petulance,' Goodrich was saying. 'Now take the scene where Graham asks Ethel (great choice of name by the way, Ethel, very resonance free), to go to bed with him and she says she's too tired and he takes it as a rebuff whereas in fact she is just too tired. Then Graham writes a note of rejection to himself and adds it to his book of reject slips. Very poignant but don't you think a little....'

'Pathetic?' offered Richie/Ronnie.

'Certainly not the act of a man angry to his soul.' Goodrich continued, 'Elegiac, yes, but out of keeping with the main thrust of the character.

'We like the way he doesn't swear though' the elfin woman said, raising the clipboard like a child might raise its hand in class.

'Oh yes' Goodrich continued, 'it's very refreshing to meet a playwright who doesn't need to invoke four letter litanies to express frustration'.

'Thank you' I said.

'Jenny's got some Ideas for the third act but of course we won't ask you to consider them unless your play is the one accepted'. Goodrich smiled so imperceptibly I wasn't sure I had seen it, 'So good of you to call, well let you know soon'. With that I was mentally ushered out of the room. The heads closed around the table in fervent discussion and I was left to slink away along the tiny corridors to the exit, which I found eventually with the help of two scene shifters and a tea boy.

But they didn't - let me know that is, the next thing I heard was about 3 weeks later when a lecturer from Tooting, was announced as the winner of the 'Angry' prize with his work 'Looking Back'. Well bollocks to them I thought and they didn't even send me a rejection slip to add to my collection.

Sheena and I went along to see the play. At first I said I wouldn't but the curiosity got the better of me. I wanted to see what the man from Tooting had that I didn't. After about 20 minutes or so I realised what it was, a capacity for plagiarism. It was just more of Look Back in Anger, the same character set, the same concerns, just updated to a Thatcherite landscape where unfortunately the class divisions that underpinned the original stood up rather well. Re-cycle the existing play, now why hadn't I thought of that? At the end Sheena leaned over and kissed me on the side of the head.

'Never mind Jim, I preferred your play'.

'So did I 'I mused sourly, 'funnily enough so did I'.

Still, everything you learn comes in handy I always say and Sheena was very taken with the scene I wrote about the rejection slip, so I think that's worked in my favour. I've not even wasted the stuff I did on those third world folk - oh no. I'm doing this screenplay about the Guatemalan thing - it's light and brittle and just the thing for Hollywood. I see it as an ideal vehicle for someone like Tom Cruise. Full of 'let's do it' in a caring sort of way and maybe Meg Ryan as the nurse, 'cause i'd like to get to meet her but I'd settle for anyone really, after all, you've got be professional in this sort of thing.

It's no good getting angry, is it?

COMING BACK TO CAITLIN

I push my foot down hard.

The bridge pylons come into view, like little hurdles in the distance. I blast onto the bridge doing about 110, the metal hawsers flicker by like the edges of film frame running out of synch. Somewhere below in the pale light of almost dawn the unseen Severn washes its flat salt spaces with an early tide.

The wind screams around the Mercedes like angry birds. Sea winds and land winds buffet each other for the right to batter me. I hold the car steady. I keep the car moving.

'I'm coming home Caitlin,' I say, 'Coming home at last'.

It seems forever and yet no time at all since we sat on that wall, dusty sandals and grubby white ankle socks dangling our short legs over the valley side, watching the town smoke and steam in the July afternoon air.

'The world must be very big' you said as you stood up on the wall straining on tiptoe trying to see across the hills into the next valley. *'This valley is quite big after all'.*

I laughed at her. 'This valley is nothing compared to the rest of the world, it's a little speck, that's all. Not even on a proper map.'

'I can't imagine that'. She sat back down beside me with a thump. 'The very thought of it makes me dizzy'.

'I can', I assured her, 'it's big and I'm going to see it all'

'You never will', Caitlin looks at me warily, the way people stare at strangers. 'There's too much of it, you never will'.

'We'll I'm going to try'. I stuck my chest out daring her to call me a liar but she just smiled.

'You'll have to go somewhere new every day then, every day mind'. '

Perhaps I will then'. I think about this for a while, 'Yes'.

'Everyday mind'.

'That's right'. I said, chin out, full of sudden bravado.

Caitlin made a sad face, 'Then you'll never have time to come back and see me'.

I had thought about this for a moment then come up with an excellent solution. 'You can come with me'.

Caitlin laughed and shook her head violently. 'You won't get me going to all those places with all those horrible insects and snakes - ugh. No you'll just have to come here if you want to see me.'

'I will' I promised her, saddened momentarily by the thought of having all those adventures without her.

'I will'

The motorway curves through into the full light of day, though there's still that sense of something unfinished in the early morning. Travel's just like an hallucination, all those miles, looking back you can't recall a lot, only an impression of distance, pretty much like you remember a dream.

It is thirty four hours since I last slept. Thirty hours since I took the phone call in the sweltering lobby of a Gulf hotel, Thirty hours since I stared out across the palm trees with the sombre Welsh voice echoing in my ear.

Caitlin, I still remember those early kisses, down the alley by the newsagents. In the half dusk of a winter evening, our breath steaming the air in great gulps, my hand underneath your cardigan on your soft dimpled flesh, oblivious to the beating of your warm, warm heart.

You gave me a love bite then cried to see the damage you had done with the simple sucking of your lips but I wore it proudly to school next day and wouldn't tell them who though in that small , small town everybody knew.

I leave the motorway where the hills begin, from here it's just one valley after another, one small town and then a hill. Indolent eyes stare at my car as it passes, I am a stranger here now and these people are as unknown to me as any Kurdish tribesman or Sudanese farmer.

She came to the station to see me off, carrying one of my holdalls. The one with my bright new university scarf tied round the handle. Caitlin in her red check Sainsbury's overall, it's her lunch hour. Standing on the platform with red cheeks, pale, pale face. She looks at me carefully, never taking her eyes from my face. 'First step on that journey of yours boyo, eh'. 'You'll come down to London to see me of course' I say.

'Oh you know I'm not much of a one for traveling going to Neath is OK but any further... it's still too big, you know... perhaps one day'.

'Don't be daft you'll come', I told her, but she never did.

As the train curved away out of the station. I watched her smiling waving figure get smaller and smaller until the tunnel took her from my sight.

'See you at Christmas', she had said but I never did come home that first year what with one thing and another though I wrote her quite a bit. 'You must get your Mum to get a phone,' I told her.

Next July when I saw her she was almost shy, like we were now strangers and would have to begin again, but once we had talked for a moment or two, it was almost as if I had never been away.

She poked fun of my student ways, all the long words I had learned. Even though she found me 'hopelessly posh', she still let me sleep with her that summer, late at night on her mother's settee, as long as I was careful not to make too much noise.

'Caitlin you MUST come to London' I told her as my new term drew near.

'No, I won't' she said, 'Don't ask me again'.

And as I kissed her soft tear wet cheeks I knew that no matter how much I loved her I could never ever come back.

I cross over the last valley and there it is below me unchanged, untouched by the great upheavals of our century. Grey, slate roofed buildings huddled on the valley floor. I begin my descent.

When I got the television news job she said on the phone,
'You're a TV star now then'.

' No' I said. 'I'm only a cameraman, you'll never see me on the screen.'

'But I'll know you're there, won't I and I'll be seeing the world now, you'll show it to me every night on the news'.

'I guess so Caitlin', I nodded at the phone 'I guess you will at that'.

So I'd phone her now and then, at strange times, on lonely, semi-drunken nights in hotels never far from the sound of gunfire, where the plaster shook and the lights flickered. If the phones weren't down I'd steal a few moments to hear her cool Welsh voice, fresh and simple almost dreamlike in its simplicity, cooling me, easing me. So for a moment my eyes could no longer see all that I had seen and I could forget that wherever I went all the world had to offer was death, for there was always Caitlin from the valleys, a sensible voice in the madness.

As I enter the town I am suddenly angry. This town had known her all these years, this town had seen her face afresh each morning while my memories grew stale and dim. I yell, I roar, I make my car roar. I drive up the high street at sixty. Old women bent forward over their shopping turn to look, shaking theirs heads in weary disapproval. I drive fast right through the town and out the other side, right up to the churchyard where I lay my flowers with the others on the bright red earth of her grave.

IT'S YOUR CALL

I hate it when the phone begins to ring.
I hate the sound of it.
I hate the idea of it.
A sudden rude shout followed by the persistent nagging shrill, then the sulky silence following its sudden stop. The final tones hang there in the air remembered, unsettling.
It takes ages for the room to calm.

I stare at the phone after it stops. It's a white phone with grey pastel buttons, some of the buttons are numbers but some are words, strange cryptic words, 'recall', 'secrecy' and strangest of all 'LR'. I've made up my own versions of this, once it was 'Lone Ranger', then 'Last Resort' but now it's 'Let it ring'.

Let it ring.

'It's only a machine', I say. I say it out loud to the empty room. "It's only a machine". I pick it up and hold it in my hand, gingerly, in case it starts to ring again. I know what's inside it. I've seen its electronic guts spilled over the floor before. Just these small inconsequential pieces of plastic and silver all bound up with bright coloured wires, like it was off to some joyful party instead of just lying there on the floor, in bits.
There's nothing to a phone really, nothing to fear, nothing to fear but the voices. The phone was good at voices, the sharp tones of anger, the low tones of loss, the bubbling sound of sorrow.
When the handset is on the floor, when you have backed away from it, all the voices are tiny sounds, like the rustling of crisp packets in a darkened cinema or the scattering of mice under the floorboards.
Now it's ringing again. I know it's her. Each ring sounds just like her voice, her angry, accusing voice. I only have to pick it up to hear the real thing.

I go to the window. It's almost dark, the trees rustle slightly in the breeze. The streetlights have just come on and the bulbs still have that pale pink blush, the blush that will soon harden into a bitter yellow, will soon fill the street with garish facades and etch them deep with shadow. I try to push the ringing from my head. I stare across at the lighted windows of the houses opposite. I study the people there, watching TV, eating dinner. I watch them talking, touching, being. "I'm just like them," I say, "just as normal, just the same", but it isn't true. I don't really believe it for a moment. I know all the time I'm in some other place, a place where the simplest things have a mighty significance, where things like a touch or a sigh are no longer inconsequential acts.

The phone stops ringing then starts again immediately, like it stopped to take a breath. At that moment someone moves in the phone box on the corner. At least I think it's someone. I stare harder while the light goes on fading. There is. I can see the faint movement of a head in the gloom.
Her.
Well she's done that before, just as she's sat underneath my window in her car all night or stood beneath the streetlamp opposite for hours. She's here again. I can feel her closeness, feel her mad determination, her crazy desire. She's getting ready for what's next. Well I'm ready too. I take a deep breath and stare at the shadowy figure in the beginning of the night.
Margie.
Well - Hello Margie.

I don't know what she wants anymore. I used to think she wanted me but I know now it is way more complicated than that, that I'm in some scheme inside her head that only involves the idea of me and not me, not me at all. Of course she knows I'm in. She's waiting for me to crack, to pick up the phone and shout at her or to smash the thing against the wall, to hear the amplified clatter and crash before it all goes dead. I don't do that anymore. I'm learning. I walk away from the window. I cross the shrill room. I turn all the lights out and leave the house, walk down to the corner away from the box, acting naturally. I'm out for a quiet evening stroll, a loaf of bread, a trip to the pub, but as soon as I turn the corner, I run past the garden ends and round into the back alley. Then I'm over the fence and into my house through the back door. The rooms are silent save for the laboured rasp that is my breath. I walk carefully to the window, I'm no longer fit, my breathing's irregular, I'm groping for air, panicking for it. I take shallow breaths till it is easy again. My sense of triumph wears suddenly away. How childish was that? Like a game of hide n' seek in the park. 98...99..100... coming ready or not. So what if she does wander off into the Holland Park night? She knows where I live. I can't run away – I could move away, sure, but I don't fancy that. I'm not that scared of her anymore.

Funny how you can get used to things, things that you can't imagine you'd do, things you can't imagine you'd tolerate but you can. Perspectives get altered and you find that beyond anger there is resignation and that beyond resignation there is something else, something old and deep, something way beneath thought, something instinctive, something to do with survival.

I pour myself a drink and lie back on the sofa, fingering the edge of my glass and watching the car headlights rake the ceiling. When it began I was angry, then I became scared, now I'm not scared anymore and want to become angry again but can't. There's this new feeling, silent and alert, watchful, careful. Like birds are as they edge toward the breadcrumbs on the lawn, careful not to blunder into the moment.

It's been six months now. Margie's intrusions have become a way of life, like milk bottles rattling on the doorstep or the grating of jets low across the sky on their way into Heathrow. Phone calls, letters. Her face at street corners, any street, any time, sometimes sorrowful, sometimes angry, sometimes with words, incoherent and inexact, sometimes silent, this constant shadowy presence in my life.

Sometimes when I sleep, the times when I am too deep down to hear the ringing in my head, I dream of killing Margie. I dream that her ebony hair is thick with blood and her eyes empty and unseeing. I kneel down beside her and lift her shattered face close to mine. I feel neither sorrow nor joy. I feel a strange oneness. Despite the wounds, despite the blood, I start to kiss her and the dream ends.

Margie would like that dream. Margie liked all notions of sex as death. When we were lovers she liked to be hurt, to be bitten and scratched and twisted out of shape, pain close by to the ecstasy. It's that extra she used to say, that extra thrill. Makes you feel you're on the edge of something else, something exciting. I wonder if she actually wants me to hurt her, wants me to take her by the throat and throttle her, to smash her skull in with a lampstand.

Yes it's possible, Margie could just be that crazy. Crazy Margie, but then I guessed that when I started going with her, knew that from the moment I saw her at that party, watched her dance, felt her kiss. That was what I wanted, a crazy woman who didn't care, who didn't give a damn about anything. Hard living and unpredictable, a truly wild woman. It was what I wanted.

Madness.

Oh, there were times that I thought I was in love with Margie, though it's hard to imagine now – it never lasted long, maybe an hour or two just after we had made love and my body was still singing from the pounding it had taken. Then I'd lie back with her crazy head nestled on my shoulder and think about the two of us, together, living out the days one by one. Even so I just couldn't imagine myself married to Margie, Margie doing the groceries, Margie at the dry cleaners. Margie wasn't the kind of woman you married, wasn't the kind of woman you could cope with on a day to day basis.

So I guess it was all my fault. Maybe Margie would have been as competent at the mundane things of life as the next woman, but I didn't want Margie for that. I didn't want Margie that way. Sometimes she'd turn up with bags of groceries and say 'I'll cook.' Then I'd pretend that I'd already made reservations at a restaurant. The thought of Margie in an apron, hands covered in flour bothered me. Wild women don't cook. They don't do dishes. I couldn't explain.

I pour myself another scotch. It's quite dark now, the streetlight casts pale pools into the room. Cut square by the window frame, they fall in strange shapes across the wall, distort the room with little tricks of light and shade till it's not my room at all but some dark anonymous ante room, a place to wait. No more personal than that. I drink, the whisky burns my mouth and gums, stings my throat till it reaches some place where it doesn't hurt at all and becomes no more than a warm sensation. I take another sip and the process begins all over again, my mouth has learned nothing from the warmness in my gut and the fire still burns.

I know I'm to blame for Margie, but I can't help feeling it would have happened sooner or later, that there would always have been a point in time where Margie would have stopped acting crazy and become crazy for real.

Looking back I see things clearer, recognise things, little mannerisms, sudden changes. All I knew then was that Margie wasn't always Margie. That she had these moods. Like sometimes you'd look at her and you'd find someone else looking out from those dark eyes, a completely different person from the one you had just seen a moment before. 'Margie', I'd say, 'Margie are you in there', grinning, kissing the tip of her nose, waiting for her to snap out of it and smile, but she didn't always. Sometimes the other person stayed, looking at me with a painful emptiness, making me feel uneasy and it was this other person, the one I didn't like, that turned out to be the real Margie after all. As time went on she would be there more and more often, blank bitter eyes staring hard, carrying the anger that came up from somewhere dark and spread into the room. Some days she'd shiver with each breath and accuse me of almost everything, vindictive, vitriolic, hopelessly paranoid. I became wary of the other Margie, nervous at her impending arrival, on my doorstep, on my phone. In the end the other Margie came too often and when I told her it was over between us. Then she came for good.

Now she's out there in the street somewhere. Waiting for me to come home, waiting to begin the litany again. The litany of love for god knows what and god knows who. It's a litany of hope, of the despair of hope, of the hopelessness of hope, of the destructive power of hope. A chilly reminder that hope can strike suddenly, at anytime.

I go to the window and look out. She's right there on the pavement looking up. She sees me and for a moment our eyes meet. Her dark eyes are blank, little points of emptiness against the streetlight.
We look at each other like this for a long, long moment. but it's no communion. We are as separate in our togetherness as ever.

She goes back to the phone box. The phone begins to ring again.

As I said beyond resignation there is something un-nameable but beyond that there is something else. There's always something else beyond what we know, beyond what we can contemplate, beyond what we think we can stand.
Always.

I pick up the phone. "OK , I'm listening," I say - and she just hangs up.

THE LOST POTATO

Keith lit a rocket and stood back a little, not all the way back, not grownups back, not light blue touch paper and draw your pension back - no just a little, so the sparks from the suddenly ascending rocket splashed his face. Robbie, standing at a safe distance shook his head knowingly, his pale, thin, serious face disapproving. 'He'll cop it one day', he said to no one in particular, 'one day the bottle'll tilt and he'll get that rocket right up his nose'. ' Don't be daft' said Keith, 'it'll never 'appen, don't be a wimp'. Charlie and Tony looked on grinning, they liked to see Keith and Robbie argue, Tony wiped his nose across the back of his sleeve smearing the grime on his upper lip, and waited on Robbie's reply. Robbie shrugged, 'It's not my face' he said and turned back to the bonfire, he threw a handful of paper into the fire and watched it blaze briefly, brightly.

It had taken them all week to build the bonfire, out on the waste ground in front of the flats. The main struts had been pulled out of the derelict houses up on Dock Road. Eight feet long, and solid with age they formed a teepee like framework around which the rest of the bonfire had been constructed; orange boxes from the market, off cuts from the wood yard, cardboard boxes, newspapers, tree branches, anything that looked like it would burn. When it was finished they guarded it after school in turns for three evenings to make sure that other kids didn't steal bits for their own bonfires or just smash it down out of pure malice. Keith lit a banger, held it in his hand for a long moment as the sparks issued from the fuse and then lobbed it into a group of boys on the far side of the fire, they scattered quickly but nonchalantly as it landed. It exploded immediately. 'If you hang on that little bit longer before you frow it,' said Keith laughing, 'they don't have time to chuck it back'. I watched Keith throw another, this time into a group of girls who stood at the fringe of the waste ground, this time the effect was more dramatic as they ran squealing in all directions. Keith swaggered back exaggeratedly, the cut of his leather jacket, which always seemed too big for him, making him look even more comical. The girls shuffled back like water returns to a puddle after you have stomped in it. Charlie and Tony and Keith stood laughing at the bonfires smouldering edge. I looked at Robbie and saw he was looking at me, I shrugged my shoulders at him as if to say so what ? He carried on looking. Keith pulled out a bundle of bangers from his jacket pocket and peeled off another one. He lit it and held it for a long, long time then threw it into a high arc toward the girls, it exploded in the air above their heads showering them with hot sparks. 'You're bloody dangerous you are Keith Johnson,' yelled Tracy Webb. 'If you don't like it go home,' said Keith turning back and smirking to us. Tracy was often the spokesperson for the girls. At thirteen her parents let her wear make-up openly and she had already developed what my mother called 'a figure', though we had other words for it. Tracy stepped forward a little into the firelight, 'it'd take more than what you've got in your pocket to scare me off'. The girls giggled on cue. Keith shifted uncomfortably as he sought for a suitable reply, he was unable. 'Bugger off you' he said. Tracy smiled, it was a smile that made me feel uneasy. Now it was her turn to swagger back, as she did so she thrust her hands into the pockets of her coat and lifted it so we could watch her walk. The high heels made her legs look a different shape than those of the other girls . We were quiet for a while after that, Charlie threw paper at the fire while Tony poked the embers with a stick. Keith had wandered off to terrorise some people from the next street. I was left with Robbie and his baleful stare.

'Why do you go along with all that stuff', he kicked at a broken brick and made it skitter into the fire releasing a little burst of startled sparks.

'At least Keith's a bit lively,' I said annoyed by his Sunday school attitude, 'things are a bit less boring when he's around'.

'Is that all you want from life,' he snorted, 'to be a bit less bored'.

I thought about this for a minute, it was a question I had asked myself from time to time. 'Yes,' I said defiantly, 'yes that's all I want, yes come to think of it that'll do nicely'.

Robbie looked pained. I thought if he starts on all that stuff about what sensible people do I'll stick a banger in his ear. Luckily he never got the chance.

'Got a light?' Tracy and her friend Helen had detached themselves from their group and stood beside us. Tracy stood with neck arched and cigarette proffered between her red lips. She stood like that for a moment watching me watching her. The cigarette bobbled comically as she spoke, 'what's the hold up?'. I removed a match from the box in my hand and struck it, it lit, I held it to the end of her cigarette and she sucked on it noisily, she took the cigarette from her lips casually surveyed the lighted end and looked at me from under her long mascaraed lashes. 'Thanks' she said and smiled coyly, the way she did it seemed like one of those adverts on TV though I couldn't remember which one. Her friend Helen smiled in the same way or tried to though she didn't offer me any cigarette to light.

'Want one' said Tracy offering me the pack.

'Er - yeah' I said 'sure'. I put the cigarette in the corner of my mouth and lit it. The smoke went straight in my eyes and I couldn't see properly for a moment. I gave Tracy back the pack and tried not to cough.

'Ain't you got any bangers then' said Tracy.

'I've got a few ' I said,

'I haven't' said Robbie, 'they're dangerous'.

Tracy gave Robbie a dismissive look, 'wary of a little danger then are we', she put her hand on the top of her thigh and brushed at imaginary cigarette ash. 'It doesn't do to be too safe you know'. She winked, 'How about you', she turned to me, 'Barry's a real live wire in class' Helen chipped in effusively, ' He's -' Tracy gave her a look and she shut up suddenly. She continued to look at me through black eyelashes and I at her through my pall of smoke, I saw she was waiting for me to break eye contact first - an old school game. So we stood there looking at each other smiling while Robbie said 'c'mon Barry let's go' and Helen fidgeted her shoes in the dust. Eventually I sensed Tracy's anger mounting. It was as if I was attached to her in some way. I could feel it coming up slowly from wherever anger comes from, like what happens when you open a shaken bottle of pop. I broke eye contact then, for some reason I didn't want to see her angry. She giggled and blew smoke in my face and flounced away, but I could tell by the way she looked back that she was amused. 'What a tease,' said Robbie as we watched her go.

'I guess so' I said, 'she's kind of well interesting though, don't you think?'.

'No I don't,' said Robbie firmly, 'she's just a show off'.

She was that all right, I thought but I knew it was a show I wanted to see. 'Well I think she's interesting'.

'Tarty more like,' he said.

'Anyway it's not important,' I said heading off one of Robbie's moral lectures. 'Let's start cooking the potatoes'.

'OK,' said Robbie and went and got the paper bag. 'We'll have to remember where we put them, my mother said we should let them cook for at least half an hour'.

'I'll be starving by then'.

'Well you'll just have to be patien,' Robbie took the potatoes out of the bag, there were two, a medium sized one for me and a really big one for Robbie. Robbie's mum had supplied them. Robbie took a stick and poked at the embers until a red hole appeared, 'there, that's just right', he took the potatoes, dropped them into the hole and raked the embers over again. He dug a stick into the ground. 'Here's the mark to show where the potatoes are'.

It was getting on for nine, all the little kids with their sparklers and their ooh and aah parents had gone, only the older kids remained. The fire was still blazing merrily added to by innumerable hands, scrap materials were easy to come by in our neighbourhood. I lit a banger and threw it in the fire but it didn't explode. It was my last one.

'Got any fireworks,' I asked Robbie.

'I've got a couple of rockets,' he said, 'that's all'.

'Let's light them then'.

'No,' said Robbie, 'I'm saving them for the end'. Keith came back with a handful of jumping jacks and a roman candle. 'Don't you have any fireworks that don't go bang?' said Robbie.

'Yeah,' said Keith reaching into his back pocket, 'I've got one here that goes sod off'. Keith and I laughed.

Robbie shrugged, ' I think it's time to get some more wood for the fire, just in case we run out'. He walked off purposefully across the waste ground, after a dozen or so strides he looked back, 'aren't you coming '? I shook my head. He turned and walked on.

I stood by the spot where the potatoes were cooking and stared into the red hot embers of the wood, as the wood burnt you could see the patterns of the grain etched out in duller lines of red, as the fire reached into the essence of the wood and erased the work of years in minutes.

Suddenly Tracy was there beside me, she opened her coat, 'It's nice to coom 'ome to a real fire' she said mimicking an advert on TV where everybody spoke like they were from up North. She breathed deeply and arched her back. I held my breath, that feeling again, only stronger. She looked up at me and wrinkled her nose, 'I've noticed you in school' she said, 'you don't run around like a headless chicken like the rest of them, you're kind of.....'.

'Cool' I offered.

'But not very modest I see.... He's a daft sod your mate Robbie innie? she continued, 'always po-facing on like someone's mum'.

'He takes life very seriously,' I said,

'more fool 'im, don't 'e know that kids just wanna have fun', She framed her face with her open hands, eyes and mouth wide open in an 'oh wow' expression like those girls do on the front of teenage mags, then she broke the image by crossing her eyes.

'I don't think he sees himself as a kid.'

'But he is 'inn'e, I mean he's not a middle aged dwarf or anything?

'Ask him,' I said.

'No thanks,' she closed her coat around her, 'not my scene at all. What about you,' she looked at me through those lashes, 'you serious?'

'nah,' I said, 'too boring'.

She looked up at me and smiled, standing there in her scuffed high heeled shoes and stockings, she looked so much like a woman that I felt afraid, inadequate, childish. I was suddenly struck for something to say. We both stared at the fire. I could make out whole worlds from the shapes inside the fire, Mountains, valleys, plains, glowing, inhospitable, hot dangerous landscapes. 'C'mon' she said suddenly, and grabbed my hand, 'where're we going?', she said nothing, we stumbled across the wasteland to the side of the bus garage where the high bulk of the wall turned the street light into deep shadow. There she kissed me suddenly before I could say a word. Her hand was in my hair and her leatherette sleeve was cold against my cheek, the feel and taste of her lips strange and alien. Then her body pressed against mine, it was body was full of soft, hard, mysterious places, I like this I thought, it makes sense. I pressed back, put my hands up her back inside her jacket and kneaded her tighter to me. It was real somehow, something felt real for the first time in my life. It didn't last long though. 'Let's go' said Tracy, disengaging herself as quickly as she had engaged 'I'm starving'. We wandered back to the fire, it was lower now, only a few boys remained to drift around its edge. I saw Keith throwing the last of his bangers at no one in particular and Robbie throwing more wood which he had got from somewhere on the fire in a determined attempt to keep it ablaze. Charlie and Tony yelled something unintelligible from the 5th floor of the flats and went in their respective doors.

'You got any money for chips' asked Tracy.

I confessed that I hadn't. 'You can have a baked potato though, it's cooking in the fire'.

'Ugh it'll be all black and burnt', Tracy wrinkled her nose.

'It'll be alright on the inside, you'll see - don't be such a wimp'.

'Alright' she said, though still wrinkling her nose at the thought.

I scrubbed out the mark Robbie had made with the stick and parted the embers with it.. Robbie was way over on the other side of the fire placing the gathered wood pieces in a careful pile, then I dug the hot potatoes out and lifted them with the stick into the paper bag. I gave the bag to Tracy with a conspiratorial wink. She winked back without knowing why. 'I'm off' I yelled to Robbie. He looked surprised but said nothing. Tracy and I walked across the road and took the lift to her floor. We ate the potatoes in silence on the landing outside her door. Now and then she leaned on me as we ate and I shoved her off playfully. We shared a sort of grown up secret about life. We didn't know what it was but we knew it existed and that would do for now.

She finished the potato , the big one, put the blackened skin into the bag and dropped it over the balcony. It hit the forecourt a second later with a wet thud. Then she kissed me and went indoors. I walked back along the balcony to the lift, stopped and looked out over Poplar toward the Lea Valley. It looked like all the other fires were out except ours, low but flaming to the last, it flickered on, lighting the circle of wasteland where the a few hardy boys remained. I could make out the shape of Keith, hands in pockets as he watched Robbie search vainly among the ashes for the lost potato.

HARRY'S BEAR

Winter finally came and put an end to our aimless forays between the gaunt pines. The air turned crisp and the crackling frost soon gave way to snow. Light at first, it gained in intensity as the bitter sun waned until the valley was full of deep lush flakes, obliterating without trace the meagre paths we had blazed through the forest wilderness. The woods became muffled, then silent and still, as if we were in the heart of some vast cocoon, enclosed from the loud, gaudy world by an aching whiteness.

They'd told us all about the cold, down at Ranger school. They'd told us how a simple error of judgement out on those unforgiving slopes could mean a quick, quiet, painless, frozen death. The craggy, broad-shouldered veterans of this cruel, ice world smiled with knowing glee at the perils we would face, two shit-faced, rookies from Cleveland? Why, the Park would suck us up and spit us out without even noticing.

Yes they told us all about the cold but they didn't tell us about the silence. About the way it crept about you and made you quiet, the way it edged its way into your bones more effectively than any winter wind, each day a little quieter, a little more introspective, a chance to think and think and go on thinking.

It upset Harry more somehow. Harry was my best friend. Harry had always been my best friend, I guess and Harry had always been real quiet anyway. Behind his precise, piercing eyes you knew there was a lot going on but he never let you in on it. Nor did it result in any sudden insights on the nature of things, no matter how long you waited. You'd think for someone who was quiet like that, being stuck in a quiet place would be ok. But no, Harry became increasingly restless from day to day, talking about what he would do when he got down from the mountain, where he would go, till all he seemed to be listening to was the siren song of the future. Now, the way I saw it, the future for us was six months off and to think about it was akin to thinking about Lake Michigan while being in the middle of the Sahara Desert.

I was going to have to keep an eye on Harry.

Things got worse one Saturday in November. It was the day before Misha's birthday. Harry never said a word about it but he seemed more hyper than usual, pacing across the confines of the room, fiddling endlessly with the radio dial until he got a faint and wavery sound of guitars which he assured me was WAXX Cleveland but could have been any old FM. The weakness of the signal made me feel suddenly remote, like I was down a deep well and I couldn't shout for help 'cause no-one would hear. I told Harry to stop fiddling with the dial but he didn't. So I went out to get some wood. Harry had left the axe outside and it took me 10 minutes to find it and dig it out by which time my hands were numb and I had to go back inside and hold them by the fire.

"Next time, bring the axe in Harry for Christ's sake." I say.

Harry says nothing and goes on fiddling with the radio.

Eventually I get the wood. It's quiet across the valley, silent and still, a big contrast from the manic energy that Harry is pushing round the cabin. Even the birds are gone from here, just trees and snow and rocks. The wind howls a little, high up in the crusted firs, light, like a sigh.

By the time I get back, Harry's finished with the radio and has started re-arranging the furniture, which shouldn't take long in a 12 by 10 room but looks like he's going to make it last. Moving a chair to one place then moving it another inch, standing back then moving it across the room and so on. I try once more to drag him back into the good old days, back where I want his head to be until this job is over. I launch into a tale about Mo Mancini and the time he went to Baton Rouge on the bus. I'd got to the part where Mo gets off in Ponchatoula by mistake, when Harry suddenly says.

"When I get back I'm going to buy a new jeep, one of those new Dodges with all the chrome and roll bars and a thing that goes over the spare tire. Then I'll drive clean over to Green Bay on one tank of petrol. Misha won't believe it when I come rolling past her porch."

Now, ever since I remember Harry's always had a thing about jeeps. His front yard back in Cleveland was always covered with some rusting specimen or part specimen of the Army's finest surplus and whenever you went to visit you invariably had to move a Willy's carburettor or a GM dynamo off the chair to sit down.

"Hell, Harry" I replied, trying to derail his train of thought "You've got a jeep, in fact you've got two".

"But not like this Joe," he said, his eyes were bright and feverish as he reached into his back pocket and held out a folded page from a glossy magazine, "not like this"

"Very nice," I said looking at the picture. It looked like any other expensive showy jeep to me, out of some magazine where everything costs more than you can earn in a month and looking at the picture is the nearest you ever get. "You got something to look forward to then".

"You bet", says Harry folding up the paper and stowing it carefully away in his wallet.

In the clear plastic pocket at the front of the wallet was a photo of Misha. It had been taken on the jetty at Egg Harbour last summer. She had on white loafers, shorts and a green t-shirt on which was written 'Mel's Snack & Go.' Her hair was back in a pony-tail and her legs were long and brown. "It's her birthday tomorrow you know," said Harry interpreting my gaze, "I'm going to radio down to Dawson Falls and get them to send a telegram. Won't that surprise her".

"I guess so," I said, "give her my regards".

Harry sent the telegram and seemed to calm down a bit, at least he stopped fiddling with the damn radio, though I caught him looking at the picture of the jeep about at least 20 times a day.

I realised now that we had made a mistake taking this job, at least both of us coming out here but after six months on welfare anything seems preferable to the slow certain erosion that doing nothing breeds.

Besides I wasn't thinking too straight back then.

By Christmas Harry has me worried. He's taken to saying nothing for hours, just sitting in the high-backed wooden chair and staring at me beneath squinting eyelids. He looks crazy as hell.

"Wind'll blow and your face will stay like that." I say, grinning, trying to lighten him up.

58

Harry just goes on staring, the corners of his mouth move upwards toward an almost grin then drop back into a thin line again.

The season of goodwill comes and goes without a sight of it anywhere in the cabin. Then on New Year's day Misha comes on the radio from Dawson Falls. She's not in Dawson Falls, it seems but she's managed to get some kind of phone link through to Ranger HQ.

"I sure miss you guys," she says. "Harry give my love to Mike."

"Don't worry," Harry says, "everything's fine."

One morning we find a bear has been through the garbage, only one, tracks coming down through the pines, the can lying on its side, dented with a huge blow. Two big black bear stools lie stark on the white carpet. I pick up the can and carry it off some way so it's no longer near the house. Suddenly Harry appears beside me with the gun.

"What the hell" I ask him.

"Let's get it," says Harry, "let's hunt bear".

"Harry, this shit is frozen solid, the bear could be all of ten miles away by now. Besides, look at the tracks," I put my foot in the nearest one there was room all round my shoe, "this is one big bear".

But Harry was already off down the mountain so I had no choice but to follow him. In the fresh whiteness of the previous day's snowfall it was easy to trace the bear's virgin steps. It moved straight, detouring only for difficult terrain and the occasional snuffle round the base of a big pine. I tried to remember what I had heard about bears. It was all bad, they were fast, they were strong they were dangerous.

After about an hour and just when I thought I'd got a chance to convince Harry to quit, we find another bear stool in the snow and this one is still steaming. Harry charged on down the slope. I let him go. I hung back, did he have a death wish or something? But what if Harry died up here on the mountain, wouldn't that solve everything? I saw myself for a moment standing on Misha's doorstep, shuffling the brim of my hat in my hands, saying "I tried to save him but he was too far ahead of me and I didn't have the gun" and she with tears streaming down her face, moving into my arms. I smelled her perfume, felt her skin just like that night, her fingers brushed my chest, I tasted her mouth again.

Suddenly there's a cracking of branches and I look round. Harry must be coming back up the slope.

But no -

The bear was twenty feet away and it was big. It looked at me without any expression. I had this sudden image of the movie King Kong like when he inspects the little people in his hand. I couldn't remember what you were supposed to do in this situation but figured it had something to do with standing your ground. I look at the bear and the bear looks at me. For a long moment nothing happens. Then I see Harry coming back up the slope and shout at him to kill it. The bear stirred like it knew what I was saying.

Harry stopped moving and raised the rifle. I did not want to take my eyes off the bear so I only got this glimpse of Harry taking aim. There was this sound like 'whump', something hit me in the chest and I sat down in the snow.

The bear turned and charged at Harry.

Before my head fell back I saw him shoot. Harry got the bear, he got the bear too.

TOMORROW MAY RAIN

I leave Rhys lying in his own puke because I am too out of it to do anything else. I have to focus hard to stop the room slipping away. I stand up - that's alright. I've just enough left of what they call sense to check that his airways are clear and he's breathing deeply. Then I split. The bartender's pissed off with me I can tell. 'He's just some guy I met in the Hofbraukeller', I lie through slurred lips and shrug. The shrug goes wrong. The shoulders go up and down too far and I feel myself falling backwards. A table stops my complete collapse. I take a stumbling sideways shift at the street, dreading the first breaths of air. All that good clean oxygen shaking hands with the alcohol like good old pals, sayin' 'We've got the fucker now mate, let's circulate'. I guess I've got about twenty minutes before I pass out. If I manage to go the right way I might just make the hotel. But my focus is shallow, squeezed close, just lights, pavement, walls. I try to remember the way we came but it's hopeless. It could be any street, any city. I think I've forgotten where we are, which country even. I sit down in a shop doorway with a heavy thud. Then the spinning begins in my head like I'm on a fairground ride going much too fast. I shake my head but that just makes it two rides, one going one way one the other. I try to get up again but my balance is all shot. What a state, I begin to laugh, what a state.

When I wake up it's still dark so I don't know how long I've been out. There's this girl standing over me, shaking me. 'Nick, wake up.' At first I don't recognise her, only hear this thick accented English and feel her hand on my sleeve. I sit up and leave my brain somewhere below me on the pavement. After a while it follows, sliding back into place with a sudden wave of nausea. I try to focus on the face as she tries to get me up. By the time she has succeeded so have I. It's the girl from the Polish band playing at the ZIM club, the ones we'd gone to watch the other night before our gig. We'd been introduced between sets. Greta or Gudrun she was, she puts my arm round her neck and I can smell her perfume. It's a nice smell, not hard and chemical like some. She smells of soft towels and warm rooms. 'Thanks Greta' I say., 'It's Gerda' she replies and we wander unsteadily off up the street.

The town is old, cold and silent, full of weary grey facades and little cobblestone streets that should look quaint but somehow only manage to be small. I try to recognise them. 'Might be this one' I say to Gerda. She turns to the left. 'Then again it might not' I add and we return to the street we were on. 'What's the hotel called' Gerda asks, but I have no idea. It's not that I've forgotten, it's that I never knew, never bothered to look but I know it's on a street full of shops selling pianos. I tell Gerda this but it doesn't help. I concentrate harder on the streets. It's not that they don't look familiar, it's more that I recognise them all, somehow, from some place or another. I begin to think that we may be really lost but then we turn into a square, full of ragged plane trees and grubby brooding statues of gaunt faced men. The hotel is just off the square, I know that but I still can't remember what the town is called. I ask Gerda. She tells me. It doesn't ring a bell.

I stop her by a shop window full of marzipan sweets and heart shaped bread. I lean so close my breath steams up the glass. I point out a row of figures walking past a marzipan house with pale white marzipan faces and bright coloured bodies. She pulls at me to come on but I hold her there and make her look. There's a fat man who's obviously the mayor and a band with a large marzipan drum. There are soldiers in neat rows, marzipan guns shouldered, marching in time. It's a triumph of good order. 'Look' I say 'There's a whole world just waiting to be eaten.' Then I draw a facsimile of the bread heart in my window breath and write Gerda in the middle. Gerda smiles and shakes her head. I'm feeling more in control of myself, like I've come up out of paralytic and back into drunk, walking down this dark street in bugger knows where, Eastern Europe, the World, with a blonde girl who smells nice. I feel ragingly happy and start to sing. After the first verse Gerda joins in and it occurs to me that this girl can really sing, not like those 'come see me wiggle my tits and ass' warblers that front up most circuit bands. You know, the ones that sound like they've got tissue paper stuck up their nostrils and are worried it'll come out during the performance. 'You're a good singer' I tell her, She smiles 'I'm the best, the bloody best, you know'. Then she laughs like there's some personal joke.

We reach the hotel and stand outside like lovers at the end of a date. I'm on a roll now, my night has been reborn. 'C'mon up for a drink' I say, 'it's too late to go home'. She looks at me and shakes her head, 'after all you've had I should think you'd want to sleep it off'. 'I'll sleep when I'm old', I tell her, 'in fact I may never get out of bed then'. She looks at me with her big dark eyes, 'People living like you do don't get old too often I think', she smiles ruefully not critical just weary. 'I know that' I say making her big eyed face back at her. She looks away then maybe a little irritated. 'I'm glowing like the metal on the edge of a knife, glowing like the metal on the edge of a knife' I sing over and over again like on the record. 'O.K. O.K.' she says, smiling in mock pain 'you're crazy, OK, you qualify right.' I think she's about to leave but then she turns and walks into the hotel. The good thing about these hotel rooms is that they're so cheap that the band members get one each. There's nothing worse than spending six months on the road with the belching and farting rhythm section who, no matter how disgusting you become, can always go one better. That said, it's not much of a room, with wallpaper the colour of stale bread and a big iron bedstead (somehow the word bed seems inappropriate) which creaks like an old park swing. Gerda takes off her coat and drops it on the only chair, she's still wearing her stage gear, the tight shiny black pants and loose mauve chiffon top.

'So where's this little bottle Nick ? I hope it's not Romanian, a truly shitty drink from a truly shitty country'. 'Nah don't you worry', I tell her, 'we insist that Lance ships out four cases of something suitably Scottish for each tour as part of the deal'. I reach beneath the mattress and pull out the bottle, then I wipe the smears off the two glasses on the bedside table and pour her half a glass, she says, 'Don't be stingy baby, - you know that movie?' I fill up the glass laughing.

Gerda sits down on her coat and props her legs up on the threadbare chair arm. Her silver lame stilettos are mended with masking tape underneath. She puts one hand behind her head and drinks with the other. 'Here's to Lance' she says, 'Lance is the fat man, yes?' 'Yes Lance is the fat manager all right. Here's to Lance's scotch' I say.

We raise out glasses and drink. My throat is sore after all that beer but the first swallow burns it numb and the second is just fine. It's still dark outside though you get that sensation that morning is creeping up somewhere in the texture of the darkness or the stillness in the air, like something old and animal in me knows the night will soon be gone.

Gerda waves her legs in the air humming to a tune that's in her head. I ask her what it is she's singing and she tells me that it's an old Polish folk tune that was maybe written by Chopin but it was hard to know as almost everything got attributed to Chopin in Poland. She tells me the song is about a young woman who'd got lost on a mountain while searching for her lover and had died there. The song says that if you went to the mountain and called out, you would hear her calling back to you hoping that it was her lover calling. 'Very sad,' I told her and asked what happened to the lover. Gerda took off her shoe and wiggled her toes, 'Oh, he got back safely, the men always do in such songs'. I said that I didn't know there were any mountains in Poland. 'There aren't' she replies, 'that's what makes it so sad'.

Gerda gets up and opens the window, the night air wafts in but it's no fresher, only damper. She leans out and looks up at the big church opposite. 'Look at that bastard thing will you, so big and smug and old. Do you know what it says to me Nick ?' 'You're going to tell me anyway I know,' I reply. 'It's saying I am important and you are not, so you must do as you are told, all fucking big buildings are saying this I think. God, this place is so much like home it makes me want to throw up. Cold places, clouds, fucking snow when it should be warm and everywhere history, old people, old buildings, staring, glaring. I see the look in their faces, arrogance, disdain. what for? for god's sake, what have they achieved other than to belong to some crappy little country that rips itself apart every thirty or forty years then puts another statue in the square.'

She turns back to me, her eyes a little wild, mascara smudged like she's been rubbing it. 'Where I come from everybody leaves or is wanting to, you know. Shit, I left home to get away from places like this and now look at me.' She shuts the window, shutting out the night. 'It's all going wrong Nick, It's all going wrong isn't it?'

'It went wrong a long time ago, I tell her, there's no other way it can go now.' I shake my head. I shake it too much and start to get dizzy again. I feel sorry for her in the same way I felt sorry for myself when I finally recognised the crock of shit that was my lot. My hands so full of nothing I could hardly carry it all. Gerda shakes her head too, shakes away what I have said. 'It should be like in the movies,' I laugh at that, 'Why not?' She points a finger at my disparagement. 'People know what they want life to be like 'cause they make movies about it, all the time'. 'What like Mary Poppins,' I ask her, She ignores me, lost in some private inner monologue. I wait for it to surface. She puts her arms round my neck, still holding the drink and I smell that soft smell again but now mingled with a malt edge. 'You know what. I love the movies,' she says, 'but I don't always watch the actors, oh no'. She waves a finger in front of my nose, 'I watch what's behind them. Big places, rich places, warm places and I think this is my place wherever it is.' 'It's nowhere, that's where it is,' I tell her. 'Then maybe that is my place, if you say so, nowhere'. She kisses me lightly, so lightly that at first I'm not sure she's done it. 'You ever played the Gulf, Nick? Nothing but shitty desert but boy is it hot and the money is great. Two years we were out there, two years of no Poland, no snow, no queuing for every stupid little thing. Then the Chinese bands came, working for bloody nothing as usual and they had all these little girls in lycra with no tits and tiny asses. The Arabs liked them 'cause they looked so much like boys, liked them even better than they liked blondes.' She finished her drink and held out the glass, I filled it.

So you must come from Liverpool, she grinned, all British bands are from Liverpool I think.' 'That's a load of bollocks,' I tell her, 'silly bloody European stereotyping'. 'Oh,' she pouts at me, 'where are you from then?' 'We'll.' I tell her, feeling a prat, 'Liverpool actually.' She laughs and taps her head which gets me laughing too. 'Will you go back to England, Nick?', she asks suddenly, 'will you go back forever one day?' It's a question everybody asks me sooner or later, like its important, like if they knew the answer they would have key piece to the jigsaw of my life or maybe they're just curious and I'm paranoid. It's one of those questions I stopped asking myself some years ago. 'Home is wherever I happen to be'. I tell her. 'Any bloody cities will do.

Kiev, Riga and Sofia, Tallin, Bratislava even bloody Minsk bring 'em all on "I'll never walk down Lime Street anymore" I croon, 'Though I suppose the song should probably now go I'll never walk through Lime Street pedestrianised shopping precinct anymore.' 'Don't you go home even to see your family?' she asks, surprised. I don't like these conversations, they always end up sensible and ordinary, so I stop it in its tracks. 'They're all dead,' I lie'. 'Oh' says Gerda 'I'm sorry'. 'Don't be,' I tell her, 'I'm not.'

Gerda leans forward and buries her face in my chest, She wasn't becoming drunk exactly but the scotch was bringing out something within her like chemicals develop an image on paper. She looks up at me with those dark eyes, now even darker. There's something about her that makes me want her and yet not want her, like if I screw her now, she'll merge with all those other near forgotten nights in towns like this where all I've got left is the trace of a smell or the fleeting memory of a touch.

I put my hand underneath her chin and I tilt her face up so that I can take a long look. I try to remember everything; the way her tousled fringe droops across her forehead, the colour of her eyes, the shape of her mouth. Even as I look I feel it slipping away, losing focus and I know she's going to elude me. She looks back at me just as hard and I realise that she's thinking the same.

'So, where do you go from here', she asks. 'Somewhere south', I say 'Bulgaria or Croatia'. 'Not many clubs down there', she assures me, 'It'll be all concrete gyms and assembly halls with tinny PA and endless calls for "All you need is love" and "Satisfaction".

'What about you?' I ask. 'North, worse luck,' she shakes her head, 'Moldovia and bloody Belaurus'. 'We were there last month' I tell her. Lucky if you get a bleedin PA at all - but it wasn't snowing there' 'It doesn't matter', she says flatly, places like that act like it's snowing all the time' she taps my brow, 'snowing in the head.'

Gerda takes another sip from her scotch then puts the glass down and begins to unbutton my shirt. I want to stop her but I don't. I want to tell her that I want to tell her something important but I don't know what it is but that the more that I talk the nearer I seem to get to it. Sometimes it seems so close, late at night, early in the morning, at times like these it seems so close but there's never enough time, the night never lasts long enough or the conversation ends or I become too drunk to know what anyone is saying anymore. She unbuttons my belt and thrusts her hands down inside my trousers with a little sigh and I know the time for conversation has passed. Soon we're naked and I'm laying her backward on the edge of the bed. She's very pale, pubic hair, armpit hair, all wispy and blond. She lifts her legs to facilitate my entry. No time for foreplay. The night is over and it's too late for whatever secret sweetness there might have been between us.

Gerda closes her eyes and drifts off into whatever movie is playing in her head leaving me alone in the cool, damp room. Over her shoulder I see that the sky is growing white behind the church. The spire is gnarled and twisted like an old root against the sky. The years it must have looked on at happy, lonely, ephemeral scenes like these.

I lean over and kiss Gerda again because I've never felt as alone as I do now, like the vast spaces of my life are all cold and open before me. I always knew I was going nowhere, I just thought it would take me longer to get there. She wraps her legs round me and smiles, safe for the moment in her dream.

Soon the sun is bright and high. I watch Gerda dress and feel a little better. She is a pretty girl, a nice girl, far too nice for me. I paint a little future for her which is rosy and quite absurd, far away from a skinny Liverpool Irish guitarist with a fractured history and a damaged liver.

She finishes dressing and turns to me. 'Will you come and see me at the club tonight?' Her smile is so honest and open that I just stare at it, caught for a moment in the simplicity of the thing. 'Of course,' I say. She kisses me and slips out the door. I watch her from the window though I don't let her see me watching, watch till she is a tiny figure at the end of the street. Just before she goes out of sight she turns and waves like she knew I would be looking all along.

It's then and only then that I remember that we're leaving today. I run after her in wheezy gasps, down the stairs and across the lobby, out into the bitter morning street. When I get to the corner all the roads are empty, just a couple of taxi drivers slumped asleep in their cars and a scruffy cream bus full of old women in black. I stare at them angrily, 'cause there's nothing else I can do, they stare angrily back. It's then that the tiredness sets in. I'm so tired than I can hardly stand, so tired that it's like the whole weight of the sky is just lying down on me. My mouth is full of bile and the first jabbing pains of dehydration are lancing up behind my eyelids. So I go back to the hotel and lie down on the bed and am still asleep when Lance brings the van along the street and toots the horn.

HOPING IT WAS A LIE

It was one of those early evening signings in a bookshop basement somewhere in the Charing Cross Rd, a basement full of a reverent, slightly creepy public who looked at him with a constant anticipation that made him nervous. Obligations to wisdom always made him nervous. It was all very well to have fabricated clever insights via the written word in the painstaking privacy of one's inner sanctum, quite another to be expected to ad-lib suddenly on the state of the nation, man's condition or the human heart. So he usually said little and nodded knowingly whenever possible, feeling slightly fraudulent, but justifiably so.

He smiled half-heartedly at a florid woman in a faded fawn two-piece and wrote 'To Marjorie - Best wishes to an avid Hunterite - Neville Hunter' as directed. Why was it always women who came to his readings? Didn't men read him at all? He made a mental note to ask his publisher next time he dropped in, perhaps they could do a survey or something. The thought of his writing only appealing to women depressed him.

'I so loved "The Peppermint Factor,' the next woman was saying, not content with just his signature for her £14.99, 'the characters were so believable, so like life', she mooned, caught for a moment in her reverie of how life was.

'Thank you,' replied Neville with a practised deprecation and looked at his watch. Thirty minutes of the signing remained, thirty minutes of the cow like obeisance of the Hunterites, all brusquely carried out under the watchful, uncommunicative eyes of Tolstoy, Faulkner and Joyce, each pinned to the wall in the region of their works and offering bargain deals on their oeuvre. Tolstoy seemed the angriest at his marketing, looking immensely gruff and disdainful from the depths of his bird's nest beard.

Neville sighed. He was fond of saying, to which ever friend or journalist he was talking to, that fame, however modest, was a by-product of success that he could do without. It wasn't true of course, without the fame he would have felt let down, undervalued, but at moments like this he was closest to sharing his public position. It was all very well being known and admired, but - well - he wanted to choose who he was adored by. He had his own idea of an ideal readership, a mental image of a particular group of people - young, intellectual, emotionally but not politically radical, innovates in living. They would read him and revere him for his profound yet enigmatic insights into the human condition. He wanted to be known as their mentor, not as the author of a series of mental wank books for the physically sterile and the emotionally abandoned.

'Please write with fondest regards to Heather,' said a thin faced woman with a chin length black bob that could have done with a wash, 'I've read all your books', she smiled inanely, 'they're ever so good.' 'Thank you' he handed her the book and quickly looked at the next person in the queue. 'Is this a form of sexual abuse?' he wondered. 'Author frotting, sliding slowly and imperceptibly up the side of a superior intellect, closing sweaty hands softly, first on sentences, then paragraphs, then whole lectures of the unsuspecting wordsmiths.' The next one came on. At least this one's pretty, he thought. He gave her his real smile. She smiled back and as she did so he had a fleeting image of her as a younger woman, on a sunburnt day on Hampstead Heath, wearing blue shorts and a white cotton Gypsy top, standing in the long grass meadow that runs up to Kenwood.
'Good God, it's you, Emily', He stared at her open mouthed.
'Hello Neville, I can't wait to read it,' she said holding out the book toward him with her long delicate fingers. '"The Suburban Sacrament",' sounds fascinating.'

One hour later, the signing over and the Hunterites dispatched on their early evening trains to all points safe and silent, Neville sat facing Emily over a bottle of Chateauneuf du Pape and a bowl of olives in the corner of a dark wine bar. The wine bar was a favourite among publishers and their clients as there was no muzak and people tended to talk quietly and reverently as if they were in a library. Mexican beers were not sold.
Neville picked up an olive and looked at it before popping it into his mouth. 'So', he began carefully, 'How are you Emily, how are things?'

'Well, as you can see, I'm no longer in the loony bin,' she said brightly.

Neville shifted uncomfortably at the words 'loony bin.'

'It's all right Neville, self-deprecation is a good sign in my case, not a pointer to a relapse - it's proof I'm 'facing up to reality', she made inverted commas in the air, 'I've been a rehabilitated citizen for five long years now - five years and no relapses.' She leaned back in her chair and smoothed her skirt as she did so.

There was a precision about the way she dressed now, Neville noted. Gone were the thrift shop earth mother threads, those old badges of caring and being 'at one' with things. There was something very business-like about her now in her smart blue suit. 'Five years and you didn't try to get in touch with me!', he reached for another olive as a prop, rolling it between thumb and forefinger, then piercing its oily bitterness with his nail.

'You were gone Neville, as far as I knew,' she said without rancour, 'besides the past was still a bad place for me then, full of dangers, not to be revisited.'

He took a swig from his glass, holding it close to gather the aroma of the wine, letting the fruit taste permeate his tongue. He remembered his visits to the squat red brick building on that god-forsaken Kent hill, up the long gravel drive the strange gaunt towers on the wings like something from Jane Eyre. Back then she had been a disheveled heap on the corner of the bed. She had said little and then mostly cursed. The day she screamed at him to go and leave her sight forever, he knew it wasn't her talking, but he'd had enough, he phoned a couple of times, no change and then he let it go.

He looked at her now. She had made it back somehow. It had taken her youth but she had won back all the fire and the beauty that had made her so special, he was impressed with her, though still a little fearful. 'So why have you come to see me now, after all this time'?

She laughed and took a sip of wine. 'It was purely by chance - honestly, I was passing, I saw your name on the card in the window, I thought why not?'

'Purely on impulse eh', he said, not fully convinced by the explanation, 'you always were one for acting on impulse.'

'One of my more endearing traits you always said', she fingered a strand of her long ash blonde hair. 'As you see I'm not as different as all that.' He lifted up his glass in the gesture of a toast and she did the same.

'So, how are you Neville? You seem to have come some way from your Earth News days.' 'Well, things have changed quite a bit for me as you can see', Neville motioned around him as if the wine bar somehow represented his life. 'The writing paid off after all. It took a long time but sales are very good now. I'm pretty comfortable and all that.' Why did he always feel feeble in the presence of this girl, this woman now, he corrected himself, her utter certainty was so irritating, and yet it had let her down badly, of course. He shouldn't forget that. Still here it was again, the slow, silky knowing smile, "the poor Neville, I pity you your lack of commitment" look. He swallowed his irritation and moved on. 'So - what about you? Where have you been for five years?' 'Oh here and there,' she shrugged, 'it was hard at first, mostly to get through the prejudice. Once a loony always a loony, you know, people worrying that you were going to start screaming and shouting at the first upset or fall down on the carpet and foam at the mouth at the slightest thing. But after a while when it doesn't happen, people forget. It wasn't until I began to travel that I realised that it's very much a British thing really, this fear of oddness, of broken protocols,' she sipped her wine in a thoughtful way, a way he remembered, as if there were always other ideas forming below those she could or chose to articulate. 'We're a bit naff like that as a race you know,' she said finally, 'closing the doors on each other's emotions, just in case. Anyway, now I live a normal life or at least as normal as one can get in the post-socialist, post-feminist, post-ecological, self-obsessive shopping culture that stakes claim to normality these days.

'We live in shallow times', observed Neville profoundly, 'it helps the insubstantial through their personal difficulties and leads them to new economic strengths.' He toasted his statement with mock solemnity then topped up her glass and refilled his empty one. 'So what do you do with your normal life.'

'I've a job with the Guatemalan Relief Organisation, just admin you know.'

'Ah Emily,' he nodded 'always the carer.'

'Don't do that,' she said, suddenly, angrily.

'Do what?' said Neville, meekly.

'Making it sound like some unattractive character trait, like loony left or politically correct,' she flicked her hair back out of reach, 'it's a clever trick, you know, making things that you find uncomfortable seem eccentric and odd but it's despicable and only shows people up for what they are.'

'Which is?' said Neville, immediately wishing that he hadn't.

'Those who want to make their lack of humanity seem dynamic, a pretend strength where there's only a fundamental human weakness.'

There was something about the look on her face when she was in full flow that he found enchanting. She paused, took a breath and smiled as if using some technique to adjust something within herself.

'Sorry if I upset you,' said Neville,

'Hardly' she answered quickly. 'It's just my point of view, that's all.'

'So will you go on working for these Guatemalan people?' Neville again looked to move the conversation on.

'For a while,' she replied, 'for as long as they exist probably, which may not be very long due to the lack of funding.'

'It doesn't pay very well then this job?'

'Of course not,' Emily smiled, 'they never do.'

'Shouldn't you be looking for something more lucrative at your age?'

'Of course I should,' she shook her head, 'if I was following the eco- pattern of our times, but I'm not, so I won't. While I was sick - in there - I thought a lot about myself, far more than you would in the normal day to day outside. I thought a lot about what had happened to me and why it had happened and what I wanted for myself, not about happiness but about being, doing things properly.'

'Being yourself – it's still the rage', said Neville, 'all the papers are full of it.'

'No,' said Emily, intensely, 'not deciding what you'd like to do and then justifying it through a lot of invented egoisms and imposing yourself and your newly-formed beliefs on the people around you. Just being part of what's there and knowing why.'

'I envy you, I never knew what I wanted until I was forty or at least I never believed that I could get what I wanted and by then it was too late or I didn't want it or something.' Neville finished off his self-pity routine with a flourish.

'It's not about getting what you want,' Emily was unimpressed, 'it's about wanting what you get or at least choosing the things you want from amongst the things you get.'

'Sounds utopian,' mused Neville.

'No, Utopian usually suggests the unobtainable, it's a label we give something when we've given up trying to get it, a sort of "nice idea but it wouldn't work" label, this is real, this happens. One of the things I've learned is that success, at least our society's version of it, means very little to the spirit, you've got to have some other meaning or you'll go mad.' She smiled at what she had just said and took another sip of wine.

He remembered her clearly then, the fiery, committed, dedicated, zealot Emily. Intense and fierce in life and in love, sudden in his life with her energy and dedication.

'So are you happy writing these books and being rich and famous,' she asked.

'After what you've just said I feel it would almost be impolite to say yes.'

'Say it if it's true', she said, 'feel free.'

Looking at this woman who had emerged from the broken shadow of a girl he had once loved, he felt the doubt stir within him. He knew he had been listening to the voice of his money for a long time now. Yes he had done well by what was it she called it? 'the eco-pattern of our times' but he wasn't convinced that he could have written any better with a little bit more honesty or a little bit more care. Did he find anything more than a womb like materialistic contentment with the house in Chelsea or the Devon farm? But then he knew giving them up wouldn't make him any happier, it wasn't straight forward like it seemed when Emily and the other Emilys he knew described it. There was a deep rooted cynicism about living that had dogged him from the beginning, whichever road he took he had a feeling he would end up in the same place. 'I'm as happy as I'm ever going to be,' he said finally.'

'What a depressing thought,' she replied.

'Yes it does sound it when I say it like that doesn't it?'

'Never mind Neville', she smiled, 'money helps after all, I never said it didn't. '

'So what will you do if this job folds?' Neville signalled the waiter for some more olives.

'I'll get another,' she replied, 'there are always jobs to be had in the caring professions. It's the big growth industry, provided you're not looking to get rich'.

'You still have them, do you?' said Neville, 'all those dreams about equality and peace and love and harmony?'

'Why not,' she shrugged, 'just because we couldn't make them stick didn't make them wrong, because despite everything we were right, of course we were. We weren't' foolish to want those things for the world - because the world wants them for itself, it's just going to take a lot longer than we thought.'

Looking at the light in her eyes he could almost feel the intensity of her belief. The old dried tendrils of his own beliefs stirred vainly in their sterile soil., he desperately needed some sort of belief to sustain that spark, a wellspring for his fiction, an antidote to the cynicism of the age. His age.

'Emily,' he said as if an idea had just struck him and had not been forming for a while, 'why don't you come and work with me.' She looked genuinely surprised, so he spoke quickly, 'as a sort of researcher and editor. I value your opinions, you know I always have. Your help will be invaluable and the salary - well just name your price really. I'll get the publishers to ok it. Think about it.'

Emily shook her head slowly and sadly, 'I don't have to, it's just a soft option, Neville and you must know by now that I don't take soft options. They're the same as giving up.'

'But, really Emily, I mean it you'd be most useful to me.'

'You make me sound like a clever gadget for saving time.' Emily picked up her bag, ready to go.

Neville rubbed his eyes in a gesture of hopelessness. There she was again making him the villain. 'I'm offering you a real opportunity Emily, realise that, and it's not out of pity.' He knew immediately that he had chosen the wrong word, out of all the options in the English language, he had chosen the worst possible, but it had, after all, been the one on his lips. As he carried on talking he watched her face close him out, her eyes grow narrow and silent. 'Surely you're not just going to get up and walk out that door and do your saintly, sackcloth thing and spite everything that might happen otherwise?'

'You can't grab it back Neville, the time, the hope, if it's gone, it's gone. I can't help you do that, only you can do that.' There were tears in her eyes and he realised dimly that she wasn't crying for herself but for him. She got up and put her hand on his shoulder. 'Don't get up, finish the bottle,' she said and was gone.

He stayed to finish the bottle and then ordered another. As he drank he felt the little lights going out in him one by one like a store closing up for the night, not an unpleasant feeling, but mournful and lonely, knowing that when the lights had all gone out you would still be there by yourself in the darkened store. What was it Emily had said about being yourself? He couldn't remember now. He raised his glass to the mirror on the far wall but the man in it barely acknowledged him.

MALVOLIO'S REVENGE

My name is Malvolio. This is my document, penned in the year of our Lord, fifteen hundred and twenty seven. This document for no man living but for posterity, that it alone may judge the actions of a man so wronged. When closeness to the hour hath faded and the heated bias and fashionable cant that little-doers stir have evaporated like a summer puddle, then perhaps my tale can be told. For my concern for justice doth outstrip the pettiness of this shallow and undeserving age. My suit needs wait for another more prudent time to be fully understood.

Now, I was once the object of much merriment hereabouts. Indeed much was made of the tale of my undoing. Sniggering jests did accompany me ere ever I'd walk abroad in these streets, i'faith for a small time my name did'st slip into colloquial speech. For to be 'Malvolioed' was to be well duped.

Thus it was, but time has rung some subtle changes o'er the scene. This gull's beak has proved exceeding sharp and the injustice that had lain in my soul for a bitter age is no more. Though there may be those who still see before them the self-same Malvolio, that same cross-gartered, strutting cockatrice whose very name brought bubbling to the lips a mirth of such relief, that it spluttered out from every corner of Illyria. No. I am no longer the same whipping post, the same Illyrian laughing stock of yore. I am as crowing a coxcomb as ever walked this land. Purity has aided me as ever - for this tale IS pure and more - it is a lilting ballad, a sweet quartet, an adiago of joy.

When hounded from the house of my Lady Olivia, under circumstances which I determine needs no retelling. My shame was so great that only my faith stood between me and that eternity which God, in his mercy, might have encouraged upon me. It was not fear that stood between me and that most profound of journeys, but my sense of Christian duty. For through the agony, I saw light. I realised that my humiliation, deep and hurtful though it was, was in fact merely the overture to my salvation. Suddenly I saw my divine master's purpose. This was

all no more than a test on my faith! My vain aspirations had been exploited and my perspicacity judged, I had looked for greatness to be given to me, tried too easily to mount the steps of wealth and power, steps that I should have known could only be covered by toil. Like Icarus. I had tumbled, my wings scorched, my fall swift - and yet I took heart in the knowledge that my trial would soon be over, I had survived calumny and now had only to endure the harsh but ephemeral edge of ridicule to be righteousness complete. Thus for a long time I contemplated no retaliatory acts on those whom I had so threatened, content as I was in my purged, my purified state. True, I saw it fit, despite several entreaties by my mistress, to quit her service. Not so much believing that my status with the servants of the household had been quite destroyed, (though this may indeed have been the case.) No, it was the mortification I felt when ere I set eyes on my Lady, when she, new and flushed from her bridal bed did rise, adoring and adored in that sublime ritual of unity which I myself would have gladly partook. This I could not countenance. E'en so, my departure I took in that same spirit of self-chastisement which gave form to the whole affair. These situations painful as they may have been were surmountable. If this had been all, then for sure, history's volition would have been appeased, but no, months passed, months in which I kept as low a countenance as the very stones on which a house is laid, invisible to all but a few - silent, almost furtive in my movements, spending much time in prayer and reflection.
Yet still the ridicule would not cease, the infantile sport which my tormentors had enjoyed somehow remained fresh and malicious gossips would whip it up anew each time it showed signs of slackening, not least those worthless villains who were the perpetrators of my downfall.

One day whilst walking in the street, unobtrusive, offering no man offence, that unseemly scullion Fabian on spying me did raise a crowd to taunt me and, of course the dog had such excellent first hand knowledge of my sad affair that his baiting was a great success.

The crowd followed me to my dwelling in spite of my protestations and remained outside my house for some minutes calling for me to appear 'yellow stockinged and cross-gartered' for their merriment. It was then I realised that this could go on and on - that there may well be no end to't. I felt sure my Heavenly Father did not intend me to spend my days like this. My lesson had been well learned and my humble piety restored me. I would not see my road to righteousness blocked by ones such as these.

Thus I did from that day begin to plan the way I might deal with this problem at the root, to fool my foolers, so that they, who told so well the tale of my shame, would so be gone. For missing this impetus, those of little wit or memory would lose my tale among the other histories of misfortune which each day brings in clusters to wanton ears.

My plans were in the end well laid. I took the law for mine own fledgling and it served me nobly, though I served it doubtfully. Anyway, tis done now. The crows will pick over what's left an only the end will remain. It was a time of headiness, made more sweet by that which had gone before. You might even say it was a modicum of greatness achieved. Most surely it was Malvolio's revenge.

I began with Fabian, he was, after all the proverbial straw to this suffering camel's back and certainly the most lightweight of my enemies. This truth notwithstanding, I did give special thought to find the punishment to fit the fellow. For e'en though there were enough knaves in one foul acre of this city, who at the bidding of a crown from my purse would slit his throat as he snored away through his oafish sleep, I would have none of it. No, his fate would fit him as perfectly as that which they had tailored for me, like a hand-stitched glove or a funeral shroud.

Fabian's habits were well known to me, for in my lady's interests I had oft times kept track of the whereabouts of her under-staff, lest they might bring the house of Olivia into disgrace or worse still, betray my lady in some false and greedy manner.

Thus it was that I was aware that Fabian had been in the habit of visiting, quite regularly, a loathsome barmaid creature, one Flavia D'Annunzio. Rumour had it that, in the words of wilful romantics, he was besotted with her. This Flavia, like many of her profession, warded off the hard times with the intermittent spreading of her corpulent thighs and partaking of certain emoluments resulting. Which as anyone knows is not uncommon in our land but nonetheless strictly against those ordinances that were struck in this fair city in Orsino's father's time. From this observance it was of little effort to arrange for Flavia's denouncement on such charge. An act which I surmised would rob the rogue Fabian of his beloved as he, in his way, had robbed me of mine. Fate, however, was kinder still - for it became known during the trial of Flavia, that Fabian, always one to squander that generous stipend that my Lady Olivia did advance him, had taken share in that gold which Flavia had acquired from hawking the fruit of her loins and thus found himself alongside his lady love once more, though in circumstances he can't have relished. Their banishment soon followed and their return to this land must remain unlikely for I have heard that life is much harder in our hinterlands and the span of man's days much reduced.

My revenge when it was first born was directed at the whole world or at least that part of it that washed these shores of Illyria. Yet it was not long before I had realised the identity of those who were the compilers of my plot, soon I had wheedled them out from the confusion in my mind and the woodwork of their deceit. I knew then, that those on whom the guilt of my ill-treatment rested were but five. Fabian, whose fate if not his complicity, I have already discussed. Then these four more; two great fools of the realm, knights Belch and Aguecheek, and the more subtle dentistry of servants; Maria Caponneta, now Lady Belch, and Giovanni De Fiasco commonly known as Feste, true fool and enemy of all our dreams.

Once I had dispatched Fabian, both the possibility and the enormity of my task assailed me. Such an undertaking was after all a commitment in time and money for which I scarce had the resource. Yet once the idea had been fixed in my mind, I could not relinquish my purpose. I must admit there were times when I sorely considered the abandonment of my quest. It was my own strength that kept me going, The courage of the simple man.

Though there's much done in the name of right that hides a vainer purpose and that which is pursued in the guise of interest can resemble quite closely the acts of false and all too human gods. I too may not be beyond a little vanity, as befits a man of my gifts. So be it. It is not of my making that man should so fear for his being as to create the universe from the spot where he is stood and yet to hide this obvious deceit even from his own mind.

Not wishing to o'er balance my little plot by reaching up too high into the challenge and convinced that my sleight of hand would improve with time and practice, t'was on the errant fool Aguecheek that I aimed my righteous vision. The loss of the Lady Olivia's hand had terminated the stay of the knight in Illyria for he, muttering sore at his loss, much abashed at the state of his finances and more than a little wary of the slight but vicious Sebastian would have no more to do with Sir Toby or his kin. So it was that to Ragusa I did journey. On the trail of the knight to see what havoc I could wreak. Some might see the knight as an innocent bystander, as one whose only crime against me was to stand by and watch the sport of his fellows. Not so, not so, our times are littered with the misdeeds of clever evil men who's acts could not have been achieved without the help of the innocent bystander, i'faith his culpability brands him, for his silence can only be taken as agreement as it has no other effect than to cement the deed.

So, on the trail of our feathery friend I did go.

Once arrived in Ragusa, it was of trifling effort to determine the whereabouts of the noble lord, for though Ragusa is a far larger province than our own, comprising some 3,000 leagues and some 50,000 souls, the knight Aguecheek was almost universally heard of there, for his insipid nature and his bumptious manner had marked him even among his native Ragusians, who are not renowned for their majesty and presence. I put up at an inn close by the cathedral that dominates the city of old Ragusa. My closeness to my God was comforting. It is no easy matter to explain one's intimation with such religious moments - there are those who's dialogue with God is so simple that it explains itself within the first word. Their ways are also perhaps those of the righteous - yet they are not my ways. I, who have given my life to a deeper explanation than that which most will employ, assure you that to walk with God in all matters is more than simply reassuring, it is to banish doubt to but a small thing, a thing that lingers more like a shadow than a truth and is thus so easily brushed from one's path at the moment of action. For three days I did nothing but contemplate my task, lying on my bed honing my purpose till t'was rapier sharp. Drawing my strength from the cathedral spire, as it towered above man's significance, reaching up like the index finger of a great hand, a signpost for the path to heaven.

When I did go abroad into the city it was not as you would see me now, for in such a place a man in Puritan dress would soon be the subject of comment and whilst it was of only slight chance that word of a Puritan abroad in Ragusa would alert my bumptious gamecock and put him on his guard. It seemed exceeding foolish to expose the sinews of my plot through such a careless oversight. For my purpose I had acquired clothes of frippery and fancy that are, (unfortunately), much like those of the current fashion. Though why such clothes, which are neither comfortable or practical, should achieve popularity is not of my whelkin.

When I did venture abroad my plan was fully cocked. I remembered how the knight had a penchant for duelling (or at least I should say that his misplaced zeal and his grandiose opinion of his moral character often led him in that direction) a direction from which by extremes of cowardice and luck he had always returned - to this fact that my thoughts did run. At the taverns I did make enquiries as to the caliber of the swordsmen of the town.

For I sought the worst swordsman in all Ragusa, a man reknowned for his failure to achieve success of any kind in combat. This proved both an easy and a difficult task. Easy, because as soon as my question was slid into the general conversation, the answer came back quick and certain. Difficult because that quick and certain answer was invariably that with no doubt the worst swordsman in all Ragusa was Sir Andrew Aguecheek.

In the end it was to Sir Andrew's manservant, one Giacomo Vecchio, that I was able to address my question. At first he answered much as the rest, but when pushed by my disbelief, I maintaining that, there must be one man in the land who Sir Andrew did not fear, he answered in the positive and a name was found. Vecchio told me of a most timid individual, one Sir Michele Sorcio, Duke of Formaggio and a distant cousin of Sir Andrew. Sir Michele it seemed had been much the butt of Sir Andrew's humour as a youth and because of his feeble acceptance of his cousin's malice had received much scorn from the knight. This he apparently bore without remonstrance and as a result Sir Andrew was much in contempt of him.

I determined to seek out this most paltry of noblemen. Vecchio told me that he could be found in Cavita, a small province to the west and there indeed I did find him, encountering him, inevitably, in an ale house. There were only two in that flea speck of a town and he was to be found in the first, prattling some ode about the Lord of Cavita's daughter, of whom he was much enamoured, yet his love was unrequited, the lady would not see him. I suspected that even if he was standing in front of her, the lady would not see him, for here indeed was my man. The sallowness of his complexion rendering his face more weasel like than that of his cousin. His clothes bore a similar mark of foppery and bad sense.

I made his acquaintance in the way that all travellers do when wishing to quickly overcome the suspicions of the natives. The purchase of imbibement is an act which, it seems, shows ones credentials as sound whether you be Duke or Brigand, devil or saint. The Duke's company thus won, we entered into an evening of conviviality. He told me tales of local indiscretions and I told him the tale of Cesario and the Lady Olivia, where most naturally the name of Sir Andrew was mentioned. At this mention he struck the table and uttered oaths as to the nature of the knight's birthright and many similar epithets. I inquired if he might not have some grievance with the knight and was received in the affirmative. Further asking why this grievance had not been taken up, the Duke shrank away muttered a little and then became silent. Responding to my sympathetic entreaties, however, he did admit that he had no stomach for the affray and could not raise his hand in anger, even in a point of honour. I told him I was sore to help him, him being such a fine fellow and a friend to boot and I pretended to give it some deep thought - twas then that I told him of my plan at the conclusion of which he roared with laughter and agreed his part in it forthwith. Thus the gin was cocked.

I returned to Ragusa ahead of the Duke, as there was still much to do. I had baited the trap but now I had to find the means to spring it.

There is, in Old Ragusa, as in all towns   on   this   earth, streets along which only foolish strangers travel. For strange though they may be, these streets are easily defined for those with the wit to observe them. These streets have fallen from God's hand (or have been cast down by him in disgust, as one might when one picks up a log in the forest and finds the underside crawling with insects.)

So, these streets lay where they had fallen, away from the shadow of the cathedral, in some deeper darkness of their own. Yet it was here that I went to find my needs; a small, insignificant but devilish villain whose swordsmanship was adequate to the task. It did not take long, thank the heavens, for me to encounter one whose build did suffice and his air of bleak courage and display of shadow fencing convinced me he was well able to fulfill my purpose. A small retainer was enough to whet his interest. When I outlined my plan he showed no surprise or distaste, concentrating as he was on the amount I had promised him at the completion of his work.

The Duke arrived the next evening looking very fine and playing his role with gusto. I had taken the precaution of finding out the whereabouts of Sir Andrew that day, for my broth was bubbling nicely and I did not want the heat removed. The Duke went straightway to the tavern where Sir Andrew was entertaining some 'friends', hearty sycophants all who watched his purse more carefully than he did. I followed at some distance, risking perhaps to expose my plot but keen to see it unwind. When I carefully entered the tavern, keeping my face in shadow, the scene had already begun to unfold. It had in essence been penned by me but the Duke embellished it admirably. I suspected that he had waited a long time for the opportunity I had presented to him and for once was giving purpose to his recourse. If Sir Andrew had been less of a fool, he would have sensed a new found confidence and aggression in the Duke's delivery and perhaps responded in a more cautious fashion. but like all those who only hear the sound of their own words, he let his past opinions of the Duke crowd out those that could have been formed anew in response to this revitalised display.

The dialogue from meeting to challenge was, in the end, as brief as one could have possibly hoped. Sir Andrew seeing the chance of a little sport at the expense of his cousin to set himself well with his friends, found himself outpaced by the Duke who, now relieved of the need to back up his words with courage, struck well and true with stinging epithets and similar badinage. Sir Andrew in his desperation to maintain face in these circumstances, was already on the edge of a challenge before the Duke delivered the coup de grace, that he had heard it said much on his travels that Sir Andrew had fought (and lost) a duel with a girl. Amidst the uproar that followed, Sir Andrew did strike the Duke on the face, thus rendering inevitable the challenge. T'was then at the immediacy of the Duke's call to arms that our frothy fellow began to sense that all was not as before and sought to back away. But t'was too late. His 'friends' had already begun to wager on the outcome and would hear no delay or dissemblance on the part of the Knight. He had once again risen to a lure placed there by one who held him in contempt, drawn there once more by his own folly - but this time happen there would be no escape.

The Duke, as rehearsed, strode out of the tavern into the night, shouting 'to the Square of San Giovanni with you, we'll see whose beard is false' and was gone. and gone he was, for once out of the tavern, out of sight for a second from the Knight and his crowd, the Duke hurried off at full speed, away from the Square of San Giovanni and his intended assignation and was soon to be settled safe and happy in his lodgings. At the same time, a short way along the street, a shadow detached itself from a doorway and made its way up the hill. Sir Andrew and his boisterous mob caught sight of this figure just before it turned the corner and followed. The figure looked much like the Duke in the identical apparel I had especially bought for him. In the moonlight of San Giovanni square, I gambled that the deception would not be noted. The excited crowd moved up the street bearing the now terrified Aguecheek before them. I followed at a slight distance, listening to the coarse shouts and entreaties of the drunken column, swaying as they began to climb, a triumphal procession on their way to disaster.

San Giovanni Square lay just beyond the Cathedral. it was really no more than the space left by the convergence of several dark narrow streets, but it had gained notoriety as a place where many secret duels were fought, as escape from the Captain's guard, should they choose to intervene, was easy through the labrynthine alleys of the old town.

The group arrived at the Square and I hid myself in a doorway at its edge with a good view of the proceedings. In the poor light the bogus Duke looked much like his absconded counterpart. Only a very close observation would have rendered the deception apparent for the impish fellow's hat threw most of his face into an even deeper shadow. My imp signalled that he was ready and the quivering Sir Andrew was thrust into the fray.

I had advised my imp to allow Aguecheek the upper hand in the early part of the combat. Not out of cruelty but to allay the suspicions of the onlookers as to the unequal nature of the contest. This proved no easy task, as Aguecheek showed no interest in closing with his opponent, content to make vague jabbing movements with his sword from several feet away. My imp was good for his price however and succeeded in closing with the knight from time to time and somehow making it look as if the knight had got the better of the exchange. This charade continued for some minutes, but as the knight showed signs of tiring and a drawn bout was not in my playscript, I gave a sign to my imp, who closed with the knight and appeared to slip. Aguecheek, sensing a victory, moved forward. It was possibly the first positive step of his life and it proved his last. for in a flash, almost with a sleight of hand, he was run through and died a few minutes later, the surprise so great that he said not another word. My imp left the scene immediately, before the sobering crowd took him to task for his deed. Pausing only to receive the promised purse from me, he faded once more into the mire from which I had summoned him, like a pike to a duckling he had struck and was gone. Moments later I too had silently faded into the darkness of the old town.

I felt no remorse at Sir Andrew's passing. For once again the duplicity of others had been his downfall. The moral of his earlier behaviour was there for him to see, but he had gone on his wasteful way and paid the price.

I travelled east in good spirits, but there was no complacency in my reflection on the excellent outcome of the venture. I knew that the hard part of my task lay before me. Still my success was fire to my growing determination and I thought much on my journey of Sir Toby Belch and his Lady Maria.

Since their marriage, I had heard all about the life to which their unison had led them. The irony of the liaison had not escaped me. Maria had struck her plan on the very back of my own aspirations, the outcome of which being, not only had she succeeded where I had failed, in her rise from servanthood to gentry, but the very condition of her rise had been my destruction.

The more I thought on this the more my taste for revenge was whetted, here truly, was the centre of my undoing, this callous, clever minx had sacrificed my name and reputation to her ends. A just punishment seemed impossible, then a chance encounter with a wayward servant gave me the opportunity I craved.

Rialto Ponte had been a footman in the employ of the Lady Olivia during my time there. Whilst he was of but scant use in this role, as I had oft to warn him, his fortunes under the vagaries of the new master proved even less auspicious and he had recently been dismissed by the very same. Thus when I met him he was full of vitriol toward those responsible for his situation. He greeted me as if I were his friend, (forgetting that I once shared the Lord Sebastian's views on his abilities) and entreated me to join him in a tankard of ale to hear his sad tale. Normally I would have declined such an odious offer but I was anxious for any news concerning Sir Toby's household, for I had become most restless in the pursuit of my task. Ponte spent much time in the relation of his own troubles, so much so that I almost yielded patience to his chatter. Attempts to divert his flow of woe were as much use as a firm resolve in an avalanche. I had begun to despair of obtaining even one detail and was about to leave when Ponte moved from his woes to his aspirations, citing Sir Toby's household as his hope for future employment. Once our interests converged then the opportunity to conduct a symphony of sentences was arrived at and one half hour more of the footman's rhetoric gave me my information and the gist of a plot.

Marriage had changed Sir Toby beyond recognition, I was told, the bleary, foul smelling braggart had been erased from view by the will of Maria. She by deft degrees of strength and cunning had moulded Olivia's kinsman to her own ideals. Sir Toby had at first resisted the portents of such a sweeping change in his ways. But having elements of both the coward and the dupe about him, he did soon succumb. Indeed, he began to   enjoy his life, for he discovered much unexpected pleasure in his new reformed state. His fortunes were repairing and he had begun to take an interest in his estate. Rumour had it   that he was much in love with his wife. However much I wanted these things to be true, for they gave good flight to my cunning, I chose to make further enquiries, for this transformation seemed so sudden as to be unreal. But the rumour was confirmed. In fact Sir Toby's reformation was much the talk of the city and it was a strange trick of fate that I, who had so desired news of the couple, should have had this choice snippet elude me for so long.

Now for the same reason that I had kept my eye on the wanderings of Fabian. I had also seen fit to keep study of the actions engendered in the pursuit of pleasure taken by my lady's waiting-gentlewoman. The accumulation of several years of such study had given me much knowledge of her.

Maria, was as you will have gathered, no simple servant, cowed to the ways of servitude and obeisance. She lived a full life both within and without my lady's house. There were several 'suitors' in Maria's life. Most of whom continued their liaisons up until the time of her marriage. E'en so it was fair to assume that such liaisons that remained had been brought to an abrupt halt. Maria being far too shrewd a politician to risk her newly elevated status in such a manner.

So if cucklodry did not exist, then I would have to invent it. Of all Maria's suitors, the one most ardent (and I believed the one most favoured by Maria herself) was one Ventata D'ell Arte, Captain in the service of the Duke Orsino. I made enquiries as to the Captain's whereabouts and learned that he was about to set sail on an expedition to the African continent. This was such excellent news that I felt my plot to be favoured. Even so, my plot hinged on two gambles, that Sir Toby knew not Ventata D'ell Arte, by appearance and that Sir Toby would not confront his wife with the information I was about to give him until he had proof of the situation. These were large gambles to be sure, but I had no other plan and I could not pursue this case forever.

So I wrote a short letter in a disguised hand and putting on my 'cavalier' apparel, engaged a messenger to take it to Sir Toby. The letter was straight and to the point. I wished it could have been in rhyme, but my wit does not extend to such craft. The letter said;

Sir Toby,

Your wife deceives you and it pains me to see you so misled. Act not on this simple statement but wait until the Sabbath when I will bring you proof of my words.

a friend

If my guess was correct Sir Toby would obey the letter, for I did not believe that the change in him had been so profound as to dispel the deep distrust in which he held mankind, a distrust engendered perhaps by the ease with which his own powers of duplicity waxed active.

Thus on the Sabbath I had the following letter delivered; Sir Toby,

I write to you as pledged, I can now tell you that the man your wife takes to her bed is one Ventata D'ell Arte, captain in the Duke's guard.

Your lady it seems has known this fellow for some time. The Captain has quarters in the old town. Beard the devil in his den and I'll warrant that he will confirm my claim as he is quite unashamed of the matter and boasts of his liaison with your lady in the taverns.

yours in sympathy
a friend

Ventata had, of course, set sail for Africa that very dawn. By the flexing of my already sorely taxed purse strings once more I gained access to Ventata's quarters accompanied by an actor, chosen for his similarity to Ventata, for if Sir Toby had seen Ventata it would have most likely have been through a drunken haze. Thus an approximation would do, though to ignore this detail might prove the scheme's undoing.

While waiting for Sir Toby to arrive, for I was sure he would come and come soon. The actor and I shared a jug of wine. He for courage and I to quiet my growing nervousness. We had just finished our second glass, when I espied Sir Toby in the courtyard outside. He was alone, a fact that greatly relaxed my thespian accomplice. I hid myself quickly in the next room, not a moment too soon for in the next second Sir Toby had burst through the door and stood red-faced and trembling in front of my false Ventata. All this I observed through a gap in the curtain. My Ventata was sitting where I had left him, but he now rose and spoke with much puzzlement and indignity. What pray is the meaning of this Sir?' 'You Sir', Sir Toby said, 'you are Ventata D'ell Arte ?'. The actor replied that he was. Sir Toby then went on to accuse him much along the lines of my letter. My Ventata, following the spirit of our carefully rehearsed scene, answered that he was indeed the lover of the Lady Maria and had been so long before Sir Toby had 'wormed his way into her affections'. Sir Toby spluttered at this, but continued 'I knew of your liaison with Maria before our marriage, do you tell me now that you still see her?'. 'But of course' my Ventata replied as if it were the most natural thing in the world, I must say the fellow was giving a most excellent performance, both relaxed and exceeding contemptuous. 'you don't think a simple thing like your ridiculous marriage could deflect the flight of our love'. Ridiculous, ridiculous, Sir Toby cried, seeming at loss for words. Ventata continued. "she laughs at you Sir Toby and I can see why. You present little of the picture by which she might mirror her grand desires. Could it be that you were fool enough to believe she loved you? Ha! what gulls are winged in Aphrodite's name, how far they fly from their nests! At this point Sir Toby endeavoured to draw sword. I had forseen this eventuality, however, and had chosen an actor who could fill the role of a captain of the guard in more than just appearance. My Ventata, moved quickly, firmly grasping Sir Toby's drawing hand and holding his sword in place. "No Sir Toby" he said "you do not wish to fight me I think. I am trained in all manner of combat and would give you no comfort at all in a bout. Leave well alone and go! Take what crumbs you have and be thankful. Tis more than you could have hoped for. Sir Toby seemed overcome by a form of apoplexy and did not move or speak for several minutes. Then as if by superhuman effort, he turned and stormed from the room. The laughter of my Ventata ringing in his ears.

What happened next was not of my observance but the details are now as well known by any man hereabouts. Sir Toby went directly from Ventata's quarters to his estate whereupon, meeting Maria on the balcony, he did run her through as she moved to greet him. No word passed between them. What thoughts Sir Toby held on that swift and fateful journey no man can know. Perhaps the discovery that the backwater wherin his soul had reposed was no more unnerved him and seeing the ragged waters of the world sway in on him once more could not compose himself to't.

Sir Toby was arrested within the hour and duly imprisoned for his wife's murder. The details of the meeting with the bogus' Ventata, which may have caused questions to be raised were never related. The trial became a formality, for Sir Toby was a broken man and showed no will to defend himself. He spoke rarely during the short proceedings and then mostly in oaths. On the morning of his execution, a wind blew in from Africa. a wind so warm and sweet that it spoke of life reborn. I had slept but little that night and as the day grew pale and the soft wind began to blow I walked to the balcony and watched the shadowy outlines of the town become clearer and the phosphorescent gleam beyond them become the sea.

That one such as Sir Toby should meet his end on a day so replete with the breath of new life, was an irony that had not escaped me - It seemed that the very elements conspired with me to turn the screws of my revenge.

I realised that of all my enemies, I despised Sir Toby the most for he had abused the privileges that life had given him and had abandoned honour and dignity for the pointless ribaldry which pleased no one including himself. A distant clock struck five. I heard in my mind the thud of the axe and I knew then, in advance of the news brought to me later in the day that Sir Toby was no more. I took to my bed and soon was fast asleep caressed by the balmy wind of that new day.

For a time I busied myself in mine own affairs. My fortunes much depleted-were in need of replenishment. Though I had saved piously well during the service of my Lady I had not been in any employ for six months past. The venture to Ragusa and various remuneration's to those who had helped me in my quest had added greatly to the drain on my coffers.

Once established in my new position I had little time to think on the past for the future had begun to shine and beckon.

One day returning to the dark seclusion of my chambers I sensed a presence. The darkness was not empty. I called out and a voice answered. That voice in the darkness I recognised well. Those mocking tones needed no face to give clarity to my memory. It was the voice of Feste the fool. 'How now, Master Malvolio, The voice said. "'tis a long time since we shared a darkened room together". I knew of what he spoke but ignored his taunt and asked him by what right he had entered my chambers thus. "Oh let's not talk of rights so early in our meeting", The fool replied, 'I'm sure we'll find that neither of us has much claim to such pearls.' I assured him I had no idea of what his babble signified and asked him to leave. My eyes had now adjusted to the dim light and I could make out his form on a chair beyond the bed.

He seemed to be smiling but the light was exceeding poor. "Come Monsieur Malvolio don't be modest." the voice continued, "the world should know of your inestimable cunning, item one Fabian, item one Knight of Ragusa, item one Lord of Illiyra and his esteemed lady." I had of course suspected all along why Feste was waiting for me in such a manner. It surprised me that he had managed to see my hand behind the woeful fate of his co-conspirators. But the word of a fool was not worth much and it was too soon to fear exposure. I decided to keep up the pretence. 'I know not what riddles you speak of, fool. Is it one of your jests? If so it is no funnier than your usual crop.' I replied.

'Now, Now, my somnolent hedge-creeper, there's no need to hide your light under a bushel, not with me.' The fool replied, 'Item one letter,' he waved a piece.of paper in the air and began to read, in what I can only assume was meant to be an imitation of my voice. 'Sir Toby, Your wife deceives you and it pains me to see you so misled....... I have both letters your Supreme Lightness, I found them whilst clearing out Sir Toby's chamber. They explained much that had troubled me. At first I thought he had simply been the victim of madness in the face of vicious gossip. But when I heard that Ventata D'ell Arte was in Africa and had departed thence on the very day that the second letter was sent, I smelt the merest hint of a plot. Sir Toby's manservant knew the messenger who brought the second note to Sir Toby and from him I gained a description of the sender. You relied too much on the ability of your puritan apparel to obscure the nature and mannerisms of its wearer, my meretricious Machiavelli, your ways are quite distinct with or without your vestments of 'piety'. Suddenly the strange fates of our other acquaintances seemed coincidental no longer and my enquiries proved that the circumstances of these happenings were not quite as first presented. What say you now Senor Malvolio, will you give me the lie still eh?.'

The clever rogue had divined well, but had naught but his deductions to support his claims. "An interesting theory fool" I said "but what of it?" The fool stood and waved the letters as he spoke. I wondered if I were strong enough to take them from him.

"By what right have you destroyed these people Herr Malvolio?, Is your heart so bitter and your ego so fragile that you need such a price for your self esteem?"

"These people were of no great loss to the world" I replied, "they spent their days in wastefulness and merriment. They defied God's great aim."

"You are an expert on God's great aim, then?" The fool retorted.

"I am one with his intentions" I replied.

"And what are his intentions pray?" the fool rejoined.

"That we should grow nearer him in every way" I added "through work, through self-betterment, through those who have these interests at heart holding sway over those who do not."

The Fool smiled at this "Then the world of joy and the world of duty cannot live together in your ideal, ist not so?"

"This is true,' I agreed "one or the other must perish, and I pray it is not mine, for if your world of devilment triumphs, Armageddon must follow swift."

"I see you are much enamoured with the thought of power," the Fool said rising from the seat "but beware, power alone is but a dry stick, which beats the wielder as well as that at which it strikes. Without merriment the world's colours blanch and you my black cat will blanch with them."

I laughed at this. "To linger in joy and merriment is to forget our divine mission,there will be time for such diversions when that goal has been reached."

"And when pray will that be?" The fool asked.

"When the almighty calls us to him." It seemed unlikely that the fool could argue with that which is ordained in even the most fundamental teachings, yet he continued in his course.

"Aha, I see your image of power is most convenient".

"God is all powerful and we are in his image". I said,

94

The fool smiled, the superior, condescending smile that I hated so "I suspect hubris here, my grim canary, you ascribe too much of your own desires to your unseen deity. The voice you hear in your head is not his but that of your own mad soul, your festering dreams of emulation. you are mad, as power is mad".

I was angry now, angry that the fool was somehow making fun of me.

"Power may be mad but joy is idle and idleness is useless" I said.

"Man can flourish without power but not without joy, " the Fool observed.

A very foolish statement as I pointed out. "Without power man is of no consequence."

But to this the fool returned. "Yet without joy his consequence is of no importance" the fool held up his hand as I attempted to reply once more. "You pride yourself on your respectability, Signori Malvolio, you pride yourself on your humility. Yet you are neither respectable or humble. You are cunning and conniving, you will twist any way to get your ends and then as if to slap the wounded truth once more you declare that your actions are righteous, beneficial even. You are a new breed. One that we simple purveyors of joy can only stare at and wonder, wonder what kind of- silence exists in those gaps between conscience and action, what giant leaps your thoughts perform to cross this chasm, what gyrations they must achieve to come up standing on the other side. Farewell my vainglorious mausoleum, if we never meet again t'will be untimely". He moved to go,

I called after him as I feared that he would take his evidence to the Duke, It was flimsy enough but the accusations could prove embarrassing to my situation. He turned in the doorway and said. "I have not yet decided your fate. If I thought I had enough to hang you, I would not hesitate to take my findings to the Duke, but for now such an act seems sadly premature, but mark you I have not done with this matter and remember I have the letters." With this he was gone.

I never saw him again, two nights later he was set upon and murdered at the gates of the Lady Olivia's house by a band of unknown ruffians. The letters were not found amongst his possessions.

Thus endeth the tale of Malvolio the humble servant. This paper now complete methink I will commit it to a still birth of ashes in my hearth. It is a little too salty a tale for one of my station. It would not do to have it fall into the wrong hands. For Malvolio the magistrate has many who wish him ill. No matter. I shall see them settled by and by.

Thank God for the righteous. For this earth would be in a sorry state else.

A CASUAL AFFAIR

When the evening comes and the sky darkens, the edges of the clouds turn bitter and blue. When the evening comes and the sky darkens, the day pales and falls. I watch as the light is lost. The slow careful process of night, each new colour just a tone darker than the one before, each a reworking of the old in the name of shadow. Yet when the final colour is laid, when night stands back from its meticulous canvas, the blackness is shot through with the lights of the city, the buildings mix in pale blue, ghostly yellows and greens ripple across the under-side of the clouds and the whole effect is quite undone. Yet still it is impossible to say which has the greater power to impress. The black which invades us when the careering globe turns its face from the sun or the host of defiant spidery lights blinking and winking their seditious glamour, triumphant yet somehow tawdry, in the great dark void.

This is a city like any other, fast to assimilate, slow to commune. A great pastiche heart of irreconcilable hopes and identical fears crushed into a few square miles of joy and suffering. This is a city like any other, full of people fast and slow and the fast try to drag the slow with them on their constant quest for greater speed, but the slow do not care. They know the fast do not matter. This is my city and I am surely one of the slow. I am free to walk its streets and smile its smiles. I am able to take my time. The city doesn't need me. It's a freedom of sorts.

For those who have the time to watch see many things, those who take the time to watch see much, but - and here's the sorrow, cannot put that which they see to any use - no that is not quite true, for those who see much know that there is much more to see, always more to see. always more to see than time to watch. However much time.

This is a city like any other full of streets that lead to other places. Places quite surprising, places full of noise, places full of almost quiet. I wait for them to lead me on. The shape of the evening is indistinct, ill-defined, a loose blur in my head. I wait for the moment to deliver it up. I have the time. I listen and hear again the high wail behind the blue light. Hear the invisible wires working nervously in the streets, working between the echoing weight and the sharp flat faces of the buildings. Between the invisible wires and the blue light there can be no calm.

I know the city is never calm.

Yes, I have the time, it is my secret gift to waste, the fat coins of minutes are heavy in my pockets, the bank roll of hours tight and new. At the end of the street my direction is unplanned. It is in itself my choice to make. The future can go either way, of course I know that spontaneity is a myth, but there's still that tingle of what might be.

I go left, the street is full of light and noise, a dozen little Babylons open to the pavement, each a perfect rendering of a promise, but no more. What else is new? The true debauchery of the original Babylon was that it did not fulfil its promise. For what is worse fake godliness or fake decadence? Surely those brave enough to submit to decadence should be given no less than the full measure of that to which they choose to succumb.

I am not without my love of sacrifice, not without my hope of secret joy. I am like a moth to these lights, ready for the burn. I am a child's grace bound down with the chains of age, cut with the whips of my needs, drawn by the power of perhaps.

After the first drink I breathe more easily, the alcohol fills up familiar parts of me, arrives in my veins to a friendly nod. Like an old friend arriving late to the party, shaking hands with all.

I am ready for the night.

I watch the people nearby, watch them talk and laugh, watch the way they smile, frown, smoke, drink. I to listen the things they say, their words echo without meaning in my head. I watch the long shining fingers of women, the blunt efficient fingers of men. The place is at once both bright and somber, a complex dissolve of browns and yellows, of happiness and sorrow, and fake happiness too which is a sorrow all of its own. I watch for women on their own, I watch for women still uneasy in this world of men relaxing, isolated by their vulnerability. I watch for one who is less uneasy, whose needs edge through, who waits fearfully for something to happen.

I begin the hunt, I stalk, I prepare the snare. My smile is perfect, studied. It holds a mirror to their look and offers back a familiar face, a safe face, a safe place.

A woman in the corner returns my stare, holds it as if to say 'There now, I've seen you - so what!'. A child's playground game of wills, a dare. I smile - she looks away. I know it will not be too long before she looks back.

I get up when I am ready. It does not matter what I say as long asI keep talking. It's in the pools of silence that doubts grow - for once forward momentum is stilled, reflection begins.

She watches me ready to deny, ready to take flight but I am already beyond those defences. As I talk I watch the 'no' fade and a softer acquiescence drift into her eyes.

When she smiles at me I'll take her hand or something similar. Something that reminds her of her dreams but light, light, no seriousness with which to scare. No cloying sense of need, just enough to keep her here while I talk about something - nothing, it doesn't matter. The sense of words is all we need - see my lip curling and my eyes dance. I watch her carefully for that mental nod the 'yes' that lets me in, my glance edges over the shape of her breasts, probes beneath the soft cloth. I'm still talking about anything, anything, my words are lost to me from the moment they are spoken, each one fashioned in cleverness, each one honed from a million thoughts from countless other nights spent out in the blue, blue light. Ah, the blue watches me always. Sometimes I walk for miles in blue streets. Sometimes I am sober and the streets echo with old history that I can make profound, sometimes I am drunk and the night rages dully in my head and the streets never map out, each one hidden behind its burning blue facade. She's still listening, I take her hand, she gives it in hope. Our wantings begin to merge. The bar becomes faded, slight and grey, dreamless men send out smokescreens to obscure the truth, mirrors get smeary and stale from looking. I finger the cold glass remembering past emotion. Once I did not hunt, did not move this way between the stones yet I have always known the secret waves that wash between these little islands of flesh and bone. I too am uneasy about caring, I do not know how much I care, I do not care how much I care. The analysis must wait, to point a finger at the moment is to fatally weaken it. The night turns in me again but I have nothing to fear. When I was a child, when night was forbidden and I condemned to sleep, still I'd softly crawl to the window and part the curtain, look out on the unmoving night. I could not know how well I would come to know that blue world, to part the curtain of my fascination and find its secrets in my veins, sly and silky, a grim joke shared.

She smells of fresh hopes, I offer her another glass, she accepts. I feel as I am part of many other nights - nights like this from the past. I am almost flippant as I talk now, I talk and joke and close and talk. The words may differ but the meaning does not. No matter how warm or funny or inventive I become it's an old, old tale that no returning smile can ever make new.

I want to give her more, can give her more if only I can get beyond this sense of waste.

I am suddenly tired and I kiss her hard, her mouth tastes of wine, her mouth tastes of something deeper. The bar fades to the edges of our night, its reality suspect, its purpose redundant. In the street I kiss her again. The edges of the buildings are blurred but the feel of the blue light remains, unseen wires jangle like restless birds in my head.

She doesn't live far - I'm glad.

Inside her house her living space speaks for her, denying the single dimension I want her to retain. I see the catalogue of her hopes and fears neatly laid out, ingenuously visible in every room. It will be harder for me now, I am getting too close to her life. I look up and see her again for the first time, her body still strung with the ends of kisses, she stands unsure in the crossfire of my gaze, coffee cup half raised. The difficult things get easier as the moment arrives, the difficult things get easier as the choices get fewer. I will do what I must and learn to love it. The moment squeezes us, we are closer and closer yet still apart. We peel away the part which is not us, looking for what we can.

When I realised that the burning did not last, that ecstasy like pain cannot be fully remembered, then I knew that love like all else was a shallow thing, transient and destined to fade. Great loves rang false. Obsessions were no more than clever illusions, mere tricks of the light. I who had such hopes for emotion, I who suspected that the heart might be big enough to hold all, I faced a greyer world. Bleak, barren, that which had once been exciting became melancholy, that which had offered fulfilment seemed futile. Should I create this love to watch it die, this bird, this child, this masterpiece of my heart.

To watch It die again and again.

No. There are enough deaths in life.

Yet still I am soured by my need to possess, still lured to dream false dreams and knowing them to be false then dream that I may dream them again. I will do what I must and try to love - her body warm and perfumy, pale skin orange in the half light. I cross her body in silence. I will do what is done and dream of wholeness. Soft, taut, turning, the flesh breaks free, she becomes a series of mouths each more voracious than the one before. She hurts me in her passion, hurts me as she hurts herself, wrapped in her dream of love in which I play no part. As my body, precise, pragmatic as ever seeks out its needs my mind escapes and goes tumbling across the night rooftops. Way above the lights, a childish figure hugging chimneys and sliding on the cold, old, shiny, slate; perilous between gutters, foolhardy on ridges, reverent at the highest chimney, dizzy with agility and purpose, dreaming of the distance and a chance to fly, knowing it's something to do with the sky.

When it's over, I know she is crying in the dark but I say nothing. I know she's not crying because of me, I have seen those tears often in one room or another, perhaps crying helps. I wait until her breathing becomes easy, relaxed. I wait until sleep creeps into her. Then I gather up my clothes and dress. I look at her face in its crumpled repose, the face of a child, far away from home. Still shining through the years but only just, as mournful as an old photograph. I walk out into the blue light that never dies. I walk in the cool false quiet of afterwards and await another day. I grow older but my world does not, it's just a casual affair.

SERGE DURING SPRINGTIME

Serge hated the spring, even though it meant that the cold days would soon be gone. For in those weeks the rain swept the city endlessly and he would be permanently damp and suffering from a cold. He would walk around in a sodden coat and jumper, through the colourless streets from muddy doorway to muddy doorway in a vain attempt to stay dry, then standing in the stuffy warmth of the Metro station with his cup and his sign, he would steam slightly the way racehorses did, his clothes sticking to his skin, clammy like slime. The smell of mildew in his nostrils, like he himself was decaying, rotting away.

In April the Seine flooded and covered up the spot beneath the Pont Alexandre III where he always slept. The loss of his regular spot was a double blow to Serge, not only was he forced to find somewhere else to sleep but so were dozens of others, for remaining places competition was fierce. The homeless community, so often supportive of each other became fractious, acrimonious, violent.

Over the next few nights Serge looked for other places away from the river. On the Rue Rambuteau at the back of the Forum Des Halles, the police sprayed him with hoses and pointed their guns at him pretending to shoot, laughing, saying, 'The season starts tomorrow, don't be here then'. At the back of the Lazare station he had found a fine dry spot, only to be kicked awake in the middle of the night by a large drunken man who had returned to claim his 'regular'. Serge decided to fight him for it but then others turned up and chased him off. He would not to go to the squares around La Chapelle as he had heard there were people there who injected you in the leg with heroin while you slept to get you hooked. After five tired nights Serge returned to the banks of the river. He walked from the Pont du Sully all the way to the Pont d'Alma, every embankment-side nook and cranny was full. Serge ambled wearily back to the Pont Alexandre III - if he couldn't sleep at least he would be in a place he knew. The parapets at this point were wide and flat with ornate Second Empire lamp standards sticking out at intervals, their bulbous bases full of curlicues and flourishes, big mythic fish and plants. It was precarious but comfortable looking, the open-mouthed, leaping fish offering protection against the wind. Serge climbed carefully onto the parapet over a sleeping man and settled himself in the niche, away to his left the glass dome of the Grand Palais glittered palely and downriver the twin towers of the Notre Dame were picked out in vivid white light, Serge felt very tired, the lights began to expand and contract as his head nodded from side to side.

He heard the car pull up but did not look, all sorts of people cruised these quais at night - not just the police; men looking for girls or boys on the cheap, gangs of self-righteous cowards looking for someone to beat up, dealers or just the curious on their way home to somewhere nice, watching with the same horrified fascination they did at the dead and the maimed. 'Not me', their eyes said, 'not ever'. Serge turned away from the sound of the engine. A door slammed, a woman's voice called, 'Hey you, - then louder, 'you, yes, you on the parapet'. Serge turned slowly, warily, to look. On the pavement stood a tall blonde woman in a black fur coat, her hands in the pockets, legs slightly apart, one shiny black stiletto turned outward, the coat hung open to reveal a tight glossy black dress of some kind of fabric Serge couldn't name that fitted like skin. She was slim and tanned and attractive. Serge sat up and ran his hand self-consciously through his matted hair. 'Yes, what do you want' he fixed his eyes on those long, long stockinged legs. 'You look so uncomfortable up there', she said softly, behind her a black Mercedes purred and glittered. As far as he could see there was no one else inside, no entourage waiting to beat him up. 'It's not so bad, you get used to it', Serge shrugged, 'But you must be so cold and wet', 'This is true,' Serge agreed. 'Come home with me and I'll give you a meal, a hot bath and a room for the night,' Her smile was open, warming. Serge looked at her in disbelief. 'Why?' he said simply. 'Why not.' she smiled wider showing a row of brilliant teeth, 'don't be so suspicious', Serge thought for a moment, what if she were a danger to him, he was so cold, wet and tired, what did it matter. He left the parapet and walked toward her smile.

In the car she told him her name was Sabine and how she had just come from a party in Passy which had been very boring. Serge only half listened, in the close confines of the car he had begun to smell himself again, fetid, stale. It threatened to overpower the delicate wafts of Chanel that came from Sabine. Next to her Serge felt less than human, ashamed and sorrowful for himself.

Her apartment was somewhere in the sixteenth arrondissment off the broad-tree lined Avenue Foch. Its high ceilings & windows were edged with deeply ornate carvings that belonged to a time even more unequal than the one they were living in now. The thought of people living like this less than a mile from where he himself spent his days made him angry, but what was the point? It wasn't something you could reach out and punch or throttle, this inequality, it was like smoke.

Two hours later Serge was sitting at the large polished dining table in a pale blue towelling robe. He had bathed and eaten and had his clothes bravely taken by Sabine to the washing machine. Serge was full and sad, his life should be like this, comfortable, safe. Sitting here warm and fed made the thought of going back to the streets like a pain. Seeing the tears in his eyes Sabine came over and put her arm round his shoulders. 'Don't be sad'. She kissed him on the lips, her hand brushed his leg and pushed open the gown. Then she stood him up gently. 'Go lie on the bed, I'll be there soon. Serge did as he was told. He lay on the bed staring at the sculptured ceiling, feeling vaguely excited. It had been a few months since he had been with a woman and then it hadn't been very pleasant; drunken, cold and damp, not joyous at all. Still, you took what you could on the street for there would very well be nothing tomorrow. Then she was beside him, her underwear like the rest of her was expensive, black and shiny. She moved quickly, deftly, straddling his body, 'Relax, baby, relax'. She touched his face with her hand, let her long hair stroke his chest. He closed his eyes for a moment, then opened them again, wanting to look at her, see her naked above him. Her hand moved suddenly and he saw the glint of something in it. He bucked with his knees and she lurched forward, the knife grazed his arm as she slammed

into the headboard with a gasp. He twisted sideways quickly to get away from her, from the next blow and went off the side off the bed. He fell to the floor, but the floor was no longer there. Instead he felt his body arch in space, his arms flailed for a hold, then his shoulder hit something soft. He opened his mouth to scream, it filled with water. Choking, he fought instinctively, as it pulled at him, pulled him down. 'I won't give up', he thought,
'I won't'.

Serge's head broke the surface about five yards out from the parapet wall. He took a deep breath of cold spring air, it was raining again. He swam slowly towards the steps beneath the Pont Alexandre III and cursed a world where even in his dreams he was punished.

INDEPENDENCE DAY

He awoke in the night heat. The windows were open but everything seemed closed and cloying. He shifted to a cooler spot in the bed but it was only a momentary respite. The blood was pounding in his ears like a giant surf. The green owl eyes of the LCD clock flickered to zero. 'It's Independence Day,' he thought, 'God bless America'. He lay for a while and waited for sleep to come, but it did not, he picked up on the electric rhythm of the cicadas in the lemon tree outside the window. It seemed as if they were the voice of the heat. Now and then the rise and fall of a siren told him that somewhere the city was still awake, somewhere other than his quiet neighbourhood streets, roaring with gaudy tabloid life.

Diane stirred in the bed beside him but if she were awake she did not let on. He got up quietly and went to the bathroom. On the way he checked the thermometer in the hall, past midnight and still over 80, tomorrow would be another 100 plus day and Diane would bitch at him because he hadn't gotten round to getting the air conditioning fixed. The bathroom was even more stifling, he breathed deeply, trying to get something that felt like air into his lungs. It seemed for a moment that he had failed and waited for the onset of asphyxiation with dull alarm, but he carried on living somehow and soon the panic stopped. He leaned limply against the wall and urinated into the sunrise peach bowl, watching the clear water turn a sickly orange. I shouldn't have had so many beers at Wes's, he thought, now I'm going to feel like shit all day.

Still the thought of not having to go to work cheered him a little. On the way back to bed he parted the curtain and looked out through the screen. The wire-meshed sky held all its usual bright stars. They never failed to amaze him, He loved to watch the cluster of moving pinpricks that denoted the passage of planes. He loved the thought of being on a plane looking out, the clouds, the ground far below, especially at night when the city was transformed into a delicate lacework of lights beneath him. He watched one pass over now. He envied them their journey. 'I'll speak to Diane about that trip to Europe again,' he thought and went back to bed.

When he next awoke, the sun was up, a bright strip of light glared at him like neon from beneath the blind. He heard the swurring sound of lawn sprinklers from the street outside and there were breakfast smells in the air. The bed beside him was empty. He leaned across and turned on the radio.

"Summer temperatures may be rising," said a voice, "but food temperatures are coming right down at Zetamart, At Zetamart we're actually lowering the cost of living, try our juicy New York prime cut steak, just 1 dollar 79 cents a pound or our family size bag of Doritos just....' He flipped the scan button. A similar sounding voice said "... before that you heard Nanci Griffith, Jimmy Buffett and K.T. Oslin and leading off was Willie Nelson. This is K-FROG bringing you the sound of country in L.A. with 10 straight back-to-back. Weather today will be sunny and warm. A high of 84 out there on the coast, 95 inland and out in the valleys it is expected to top a hundred for the 3rd successive day..." He switched off the voice, sat up and rubbed his nose. His mouth still tasted trashy from last night's Millers and his blood felt gritty and coarse in his veins. Same old 4th July he thought, only the hangovers get worse.

Every Independence Day they'd have a block party and each year it would be himself, Wes and Dan, cooking chicken and ribs through the dusk ready for the next day. While they prepared and cooked and stored the meat, they'd drink and talk and drink some more till they felt good among the food smells and the soft dusk of the yard and felt the camaraderie of old experience, of familiarities shared.

'The Dodgers have blown it this year, Mel'

'Sure, sure you've said that before.'

'What 12 and a half games back! You're out of there man!'

'They ain't started yet' Wes, watch 'em go after the all-star break.'

'Only place they'll go is down'.

Some years the Dodgers would be doing good and Wes and Dan would be quiet and it would be Mel that would open up, but mostly it was the old 12 and a half games back scenario.....

'Mel, you awake?' Diane shouted.

'Not especially,' he mumbled.

'You gotta go to the store,' she continued, 'you gotta go soon. '

'OK don't worry' he replied, letting his head fall back onto the pillow.

Diane appeared in the doorway, her hair was pulled back into a bun that accentuated the angular lines of her face. 'Mel, I need this stuff, if you're gonna get it, get it soon, otherwise let me know o.k.'

He got up and went to the bathroom. He avoided looking at his face in the mirror, concentrating on his chin as he shaved. He finished but didn't feel any more awake.

'Can I have breakfast first?' he said, going into the kitchen. The kitchen table was full of food; salad in earthenware bowls, dips in plastic cartons, sausages, big bags of potato chips. Diane flitted from one to the other like a slightly distressed bee. She threw him a look. He picked up his car keys from the side 'I'll get a couple of donuts from Winchells', he thought. As he drove along he began to feel a little better, the cooled air filling the can with a soft breathy hiss.

He drove up Santa Anita in happy isolation at an easy 35, the hazed over hills were no more than dark lines in a blue pastel landscape, it seemed like the whole city were adrift in a mysterious sea. There were construction gangs at work all along Roseville Boulevard, pulling down good old 50's houses to build two without gardens in their place. Wes called it the big squeeze. The whole city was like a building site these days. 'Waddya think of our city,' thought Mel, 'it'll be ok when its finished,' he answered and chuckled aloud at his own joke.

He stopped at the market first so he wouldn't forget the things he'd been sent for, he pushed the cart idly down the rows amongst the bright colours and familiar brand names, the food smells made him hungrier than ever. To the stuff from Diane's list he added, six Baby Ruths, a copy of the L.A. Times and a case of Miller. He rolled the cart out into the parking lot and stopped by the car, the heat was really building now and the parking lot felt as if it were under a grille. He had forgotten to put the sun shield on the windscreen and he had to run the air for a while before he could sit on the leatherette.

At Winchells he ordered a coffee and two apple & spice specials, It had been a while since he'd had donuts for breakfast. Diane thought it was gross 'you'll kill yourself,' she'd say. He thought about the possibility of dropping dead in the street, the embarrassment seemed more real than anything, but the odd donut wasn't going to count.
Back home it seemed there was even more food on the table than before.'Who's gonna eat all this,' he said. 'You never know,' said Diane, 'people get hungry. It took him a long while to load the stuff into the car. Diane wouldn't let Becky & Suzanne help because she was afraid they'd eat some, so they went back to watching T.V.

He was sweating profusely by the time he'd loaded the last coolbox. He smelled the stale alcohol from yesterday's beers on his skin. He pulled a beer from the top coolbox and took a swig, if he was going to smell of it he might as well drink it.

He got a garden chair from the back of the garage and sat down on it, then he got up again and took the L.A. Times from the car seat and sat back down again. The Dodgers had lost again and were now 13 and a half back. He didn't read the game report, Diane came out and stuffed a handful of washing into the machine, gave him one of her 'Thanks for helping, Mel,' looks and went back into the house.

He read though the funnies then went inside, "Anything I can do to help?" "It's too late now," Diane said, "It's all done". "You should've asked. "he said. 'Mel if you want to help, go look for something to do". He went into the lounge and watched T.V. with the kids.

After he had taken all the stuff and Diane and the kids over to Wes's, he brought the car home and then walked down the block. All along the street people were out on their front lawns, cooking, sitting, drinking, kids playing. Some houses displayed red, white & blue bunting and the stars and stripes hung waiting for a breeze. He waved at one or two people he knew, smiled at the rest. Some of them smiled back.

Down near Wes's house the street had been shut off, plastic milk crates barred the way of errant cars and a crayoned sign hung above them which said' Almeida Street Block Party 1990'.

A crowd was gathered on Wes's lawn, trestle tables spanned the drive and they had set up an impromptu stage made of old ply but with a real PA sat centre. Someone had strung a volleyball net across the street and a game was already in progress. He knew most of the people there, some of them he had known all his life.

Wes slapped him on the back and handed him a beer, Wes's wife Janine gave him a soft breathy kiss on his cheek. He noticed faintly that his kids were arguing already but they were off among the other kids and he didn't feel like it was his problem to sort it out. His hellos over, he wandered idly along the groaning food table picking up chips and nuts, here and there. Normally a party like this would make him feel excited and the excitement would make him loud, but today there was a hard knot of silence in him almost like a sulk, maybe it was indigestion or the heat.

He realised that Chuck was talking to him. ...So waddya think Mel should I get a Dodge or a Nissan". "Screw the money" said Mel "buy something American while you still can" and walked off leaving Chuck open-mouthed.

He joined in the volleyball game and gained some satisfaction from striking the ball hard and good a couple of times through the massed ranks of bronzed teenage bodies on the other side. 'You ain't there yet,' he thought. He was sweating hard by the time he'd finished though, the armpits of his shirt damp and blotched like a redneck.

He got another beer and some Chili and sat on the kerb underneath a tree. The heat was fierce. An egg catching game had been in progress earlier and Mel could see the remnants beginning to cook on the street. Janine came and sat down beside him and laid her hand lightly on his shoulder. "And how's old Mel today?" "Old," he said, "but still Mel, I guess". She ruffled the back of his hair knocking the baseball cap forward over his eyes. "Lighten up," she said and was gone.

He straightened his cap and watched her walk back across the lawn, Janine never seemed to change at all. She was still like the girl he'd known in High School. The day wore on, Mel talked to a few people, made jokes about the weather, about Quayle, about Japanese businessmen without laughing himself, made the odd sexual innuendo without insinuation. He began to feel something had gone from him but he didn't know what. What the hell was going on? He hadn't felt this old last year, what was this? He looked over at Diane, she was talking in her sharp solicitous way to the new couple from down the street, the Murrays. She made her points intensely as usual touching the husband on the arm briefly as they were made. Wes came purposefully across the lawn. 'C'mon everybody, it's show time.' People dutifully began to arrange their chairs in front of the stage, a few people from other parties down the street came over with chairs and set them down also. When the crowd was all gathered, Wes went to the mike, 'Ladies and gentlemen, welcome to the block party annual talent show and thanks for coming. Here's your MC for today's show Lester!'

Lester, Wes' 12 year old son bowed modestly at the ripple of applause. 'Thank you, thank you and for our first act we have Cindy, Jody and Becky dancing to Vogue'. The 11 year olds took the stage and began working their way through a carefully choreographed if slightly repetitive dance. If they lacked the polish of professionals they certainly weren't short on intensity. He watched his daughter as she wiggled her bottom at the rows of spectators. 'I'm going to have trouble with that girl,' he thought, 'sooner or later.'

The music ended abruptly and they straggled off throwing aggrieved looks at the D.J. They'll be need for therapy tonight he thought, "Mom he did it on PURPOSE!" 'Next,' said MC Lester also somewhat startled by the abrupt end, 'we have .... he scuffled for a moment for his cue cards. 'Caroline and Marina dancing to Straight Up.' The two teenage girls came out dressed in tiny skirts and high heels. These were kids from off the block. Kids pretend to be adults all the time but there comes a time when they begin to cross over for real. This was it for Caroline and Marina, in makeup and the tight clothes these weren't even the two kids who were playing volleyball a couple of hours ago, as Caroline winked suggestively at the crowd, Janine walked by with a plate of cake and Chuck yelled. 'Hey Janine, is that your girl?'

'I don't wanna look,' Janine replied with a wry smile and didn't. "California Girls" chuckled Mel and found himself humming the old song. He tried to remember the last time he'd been to the

112

beach, four years ago, five? 'Don't stare at their legs, for chrissake Mel!' Diane hissed as she hurried by with plates of chicken and salad, 'you're not at that tits and ass bar now.'

'Hell honey.' he said, embarrassed but she had already gone. He reached out for another beer and sat back down, more of a spectator than ever.

By the time the show was over the dusk had begun to gather. People began to drift away. Small children fell asleep in corners, shattered by the intensity of their day. Mel drifted between the remaining groups, feeling better now, feeling lighter somehow, more in control. On his way back from a trip to the bathroom he came across Marina in the kitchen sipping from a coke. 'Hi Marina,' he said, 'I loved your dance.'

'Why thank you.' she said and gave him a satisfied smile. 'Yeah,' he continued, 'it was real sexy.' She blushed deeply under her tan. 'It wasn't meant to be,' she said, 'it was just a dance.'

'Well anyway, it was swell.'

'Thank you again, I must go now.' she sidled out the door, Mel stood in the empty kitchen for a while, sipping beer and watching the blue, blue sky edge over with the dark. The party had dwindled now to the hard core of organisers and their brood. Part of Mel wanted to continue, to say 'Hey let's party, let's go downtown,' but the other part of him felt awfully tired.

He'd have another beer he thought and then see how he felt. Diane caught him down by the cool box.

'C'mon Mel, we should go.'

'Aw honey,' he said, 'its' only 8' o'clock.'

'And its work tomorrow' said Diane, 'these people have got to clean up this mess, have some consideration.'

He took the beer anyway and began to load the empty dishes into a box. Becky and Suzanne drifted by. 'Dad where's the car?'

'At home honey,' he replied.

'How we gonna get home then?'

'It's only a block.'

'I don't wanna walk' wheedled Suzanne.

'Dad -get the car.' said Becky flatly.

As he walked down the block he saw that almost all of the parties had finished now. The streamers and flags still hung there waiting for that breeze but the lights were on in the houses and people were watching T.V., they didn't see the first crackles of sliver light as the fireworks began over in the High School. Mel kept his eye on them as he walked slowly along, as they splayed up into the sky and mingled with the lights of the hills. The hills had always made him feel safe somehow, like he was perfectly in the palm of some hand. They did so again now and he walked on as happy as he had been all day. When he arrived back at Wes's with the car, Suzanne was crying with tiredness and Becky was slumped in a loud sulk on a lawn chair. 'Where have you been?' Diane asked,' Suzanne should be in bed,'

'It's too hot to rush, what's wrong with Becky?

'I told her she couldn't go on over to the High School to see the fireworks,' 'You can see them just as good from here honey.' said Mel, solicitously. Becky gave him a withering look and went back to sulking.

Mel stowed the things in the car and went to say goodbye to Wes & Janine. 'I think it gets better every year' said Wes 'Don't you'

'That's cause you get drunker every year.' said Janine laughing, Mel hugged them both and left.

The house shuttered all day was stifling, Mel opened as many doors and windows as he could but the sense of staleness remained. On T.V. they were showing the fireworks at the Rose Bowl, Mel wondered idly how much a thing like that cost, he'd heard somewhere that those big displays cost upward of $50,000 it seemed an awful lot of money for 20 minutes or so of oohs and aahs.

Diane finished stacking the dishwasher and said 'I'm going to bed Mel I'm pooped.' 'Ok honey,' he said, without looking round. 'I'll be there in a minute.' He lay back on the sofa and flickered through the channels with the remote. There wasn't much on. He watched a commercial for Jeeps and when the programme came back on he just left it there though he wasn't interested. For this moment at least the world wanted nothing from him. He closed his eyes to shut out the blue flickering light. In a few moments he was asleep, his snores mingled with the voice of the T.V. and the drone of the crickets. The blue light flickered on alone.

ANOTHER EVENING WITH SALLY NEARBY

' Sally why don't you just piss off and stop bothering me!'

He hadn't shouted exactly but his voice was loud and vehement enough to cause the couple at the next table to look around. She stood there fiddling with a wisp of hair, a slow flush spreading across her face. Her expression didn't change though and he knew that she was undeterred. Somehow his rejections only went to fuel the fire that she had built for him in the great big ventricles that throbbed away somewhere behind her bra.

He waited for her to speak, willed her to say something. Call him a bastard, spit in his eye, throw her Malibu and pineapple at him but even as he wished it he knew she wouldn't, that she would just stand there, the flush slowly fading from her pale cheeks, fiddling with her hair and shifting from foot to foot as if she needed to go to the toilet. She was so pathetic it made him want to shake her, to slap her until there was some hint of fire, of anger in those wan brown eyes, but he was afraid that if he did that he might beat her to a pulp and still not achieve the desired result.

She stared down into the pallid yellow liquid in her glass, suffering the exquisite pangs of unrequited love, reflecting, no doubt, that the joy of chastisement by the object of her adoration was far greater than any love that could be offered her by a lesser unchosen one. The complex pleasures of female suffering, he mused, instant sainthood for the price of a few good solid rejections and a couple of slaggings off in public - no doubt who the bad guy is in this movie.

He asked himself for the umpteenth time why he'd gone out with her in the first place. It hadn't seemed so odd at the time, he'd gone out with most of the girls in the office at one time or another with varying degrees of success. It was - well - it was just what you did, wasn't it? When you were young and unattached. OK she'd been different to most of the girls he'd been with, old-fashioned, kind of homely, she had intrigued him.

He thought that kind of girl had disappeared in the Sixties. You know waiting for you to open the door for her, always pulling her skirt down as if the whole world was just sitting there waiting for a flash of her knickers. Yes - it had been a challenge, no one else in the office had come even close. So maybe he'd tried harder than usual to break her down. Used more complex strategies to defuse her 'not there' and 'not now' responses. Crafty? Certainly, it was part of the fun wasn't it ? But this - surely he didn't deserve this.

He surveyed her now, looked at her carefully. She was a pretty girl really, slim and pretty and quite well presented. Not very educated, not very lively but nice in that ordinary sort of way. There must be someone in this city who was prepared to gaze cow like back at her and so create the great requited, the magic moment that she obviously craved. She stared on into her drink as if scared to look back at him, as if his gaze might burn her. He felt his anger ebb. She cut such a pathetic figure that it reached out and touched something in him - the boy who never pulled the legs off spiders. 'Oh for christ sake sit down'. She sat flinchingly as if she had been pushed, head bent forward, face invisible behind her fallen hair. He groaned inwardly. Why had he said that, now he'd be stuck with her for the rest of the evening.

'Sally, why don't you just go home?'
She shook her head and her hair flapped weakly. She had put the drink on the table and was staring at her hands, little unsophisticated hands with pudgy folds and blunt unpainted fingernails, palm up in a gesture of supplication like a child awaiting punishment, fearful but resigned to the inevitability of adult power.

He began to talk at her, hating silences of any kind between people as they reminded him of his teenage shyness, of those painful minutes, sometimes hours when the words crowded into his mouth but would not come, just buzzed round and round in his head unsaid, losing definition. 'Look we went out together but now we don't see - it just didn't work out, that's it, you can't make something happen if it's not meant to be'.

'But it is meant to be, you're just afraid of it' she said, drawn to respond at last. 'You know our feelings for each other are deep'.

He snorted in amazement. 'You're crazy, Sally, I'm sorry to say it but you are, completely bats.'

She looked up and smiled at him, it was a smile he had come to know well. It was a smile that came from far away in a place where the world was simple and everything was possible, a smile of great wisdom, of experience, of pity almost. Inevitably, it irritated the hell out of him, he hated the certainty people, people who looked at you with eyes that said "I know," when how could they possibly, how could anyone?

She hadn't been a virgin though - that had surprised him - given all the rigmarole he had had to go through, all the waylaying of folk taboos and moral dilemmas. He had felt relief at the time, relief because he had an old folk tale of his own that virgins were more "clingy." - Ha Ha.

Having slept with her he realised that he'd had some strange idea that it would liberate her from her puritanical past and that once so freed the chrysalis would open and a new, gregarious personality would emerge with a commensurate lust for life and love. It hadn't, she remained as insular in life and as listless in bed as she had ever been. Going to the pub or out for a meal with friends was an embarrassment, as ideas and laughter cascaded around her silent, unsmiling figure. In bed she was equally inert, suffering his exertions stoically. Thinking of England for England he called it.

So soon it had been time for "goodbye Sally". That was when the trouble had started. His farewell speech had been sorrowful but to the point, much rehearsed but still rather poetic he thought, remorseful without being apologetic. Once he had finished she had simply looked at him and said 'No'. 'What do you mean no?' he had asked puzzled. 'Were not splitting up and that's that. We were meant to be together'. 'Don't be ridiculous, were as about as compatible as a fish and a

118

bicycle' he replied realising he had mixed up a saying somewhere, a little unnerved by the look in her eye.

Over the next few weeks his life had become hell. First the phone calls, then the letters, long mournful letters in her precise tiny script, explaining why he was making a mistake. She would spring out on him in office corridors, in bars and restaurants, on doorsteps and station platforms. Never aggressive or even demanding but just - there. Promising new dates would slink away into the night after one look at Sally's suffering face. People in the office began to avoid him socially, knowing that sooner or later Sally would turn up with her special brand of awkward gloom to take the edge off the evening. The women especially, as if the power of her need had impressed them, began to blame him, to shun him.

Sally was moving beyond pathos into legend. She was the reason he was alone tonight - had chosen to be alone - now he might as well go home. He began to quickly drink his beer.
She was staring at him again, no ordinary stare, for it raised him to a level far beyond that which he could ever hope to aspire. What was the point of that?

'If you really loved me you'd leave me alone' He told her more out of desperation than hope.

She smiled, 'Once you realise how much you love me too then perhaps I will'. He pondered this, 'So if I say "Sally I really love you", you'll go away'. 'If you really mean it' she answered warily.

'Sally I really love you' he said, biting his lip. A big tear ran down Sally's cheek. Her face became angelic in its suffering it shone with a strange light, a transfiguration full of all the strength and beauty that sorrow can fashion. He felt himself drawn in suddenly. He forced himself not to touch her. 'Never mind, never mind' she said softly to herself, a little litany of comfort.

For a moment it seemed as if she had gone into some kind of trance, so still she became, a thing of alabaster or marble but for the bright glow that emanated from her and the water that gathered in the corner of each eye.

Suddenly as if something had been switched back on she looked at him, 'I'm going,' she said, 'I accept now that you'll never acknowledge the bond between us - but one day you'll realise that I was the one and you'll know that I knew and then you'll be sad too'.

As he unscrambled the logic of this he felt the old uncertainly stir within him - all his life he had fought against the knowledge that he wasn't sure about anything. Something you had to hide in a world where other people's certainties were constantly looking for a foothold in yours. He had vowed never give in to other people's certainties but it was a wall that was constantly breached. His facade too flimsy, too undermined from within.

'Wait Sally i'm going too', he said, finishing the last of his beer.

Outside she stood on the edge of the pavement waiting for a taxi. She did not look at him as if, the decision having been made, he was already out of her life. He felt lost and lonely all of a sudden, adrift in the dark spaces of the street, the city, of the vast invisible sky full of stars.

A black cab wheeled swiftly out of the traffic and came to a brisk halt at her feet. As she got in she turned to wave but he was already beside her. 'Let's share.' he said.

In the taxi she leant against him, her cheek on his shoulder and he smelt that curious almost odourless scent she gave off, milky, wholesome, untainted by living, by life. He could tell from the curve of her cheek that she was smiling. The thought made the hairs prickle on the back of his neck.

120

TILE

Sally said nothing as her mother drove, just watched the endless rows of shops and houses passing. The size of the city always scared her, a vast machine beyond her control, beyond her understanding; doing, being, great tendrils of happening snaking out ceaselessly, trying to cram it all into your head made you dizzy. They stopped with a jerk as a Volvo estate cut across the front of their Mondeo, instinctively snapping up the space her mother had ceded. Her mother always drove with a characteristic uncertainty that irritated Sally, always an apology somewhere not far from the surface, always undermining what she did, always effacing the effort, hiding the woman.

Sally saw that they were passing out of the city now. The houses were bigger, more resplendent. Pinched front gardens of slab concrete and stifled rose had given way to drives, lawns and conifers, they were nearly home. 'Home,' the word came up suddenly in her head, flat, short, deprived of all resonance but there nonetheless. 'It's changed a bit,' her mother was saying, 'you'll see, they've paved the high street and built a big new shopping mall, very grand, all glass and escalators, the smell of pot-pourri everywhere.' Her mother turned and grinned at her. Sally said nothing, staring out the window. Parts of her past, a store front, a corner, slid by like strange ghost ships, things familiar, yet things to which she did not belong. Still, she must have been here once for there was the Vijay corner shop, the Royal Bell pub and the Le Jardin restaurant. Not the stuff of imagination, surely? Then they turned into their road and the process was complete, as if like Alice she had walked through a magic door.

She shuddered and wiped her nose with the back of her hand. 'Are you catching cold dear?' Her mother said concernedly. Sally looked at her, surprised, 'oh no, it's... it's what happens'. 'Oh,' said her mother, embarrassed, 'I'm sorry'.

The house was as it always was, as it always had been, as it always would be. If it had forgotten Sally it didn't let on, just sat there acting as if she had never left it. Timeless in its half timbered, detached smugness, the obsessive precision of the front lawn, the bright cheery dahlias and lobelias, with only a straggly Yucca out of place amongst the horticultural elegance. She had planted that Yucca herself one spring in a strange fit of normality. Her mother had always hated it.

Sally got out of the car and without thinking looked in her pocket for her key, then remembered she didn't have it anymore. It had been lost or stolen somewhere months ago. She stopped in mid step and just stood there bemused while her mother flustered in her bag, hurriedly unlocked the door and pushed it wide. Sally went in, carefully, determined not to make any more assumptions. The memories opened up with each step, the past's gate was widening fearfully. Her mother waited for her to go on in, perhaps choose a room in which to sit; the front room maybe with its soft flowered sofas and shiny dark wood or the kitchen with its grand oak fascia and claustrophobically intricate little handles.

'Come in Sally, please come in,' something sorrowful in her mother's voice propelled her forward, she made for the kitchen, neutral ground. 'Would you like a cup of tea?' said her mother over her shoulder.

She didn't, but said she did to give her mother something to do. She sat down at the kitchen table and realised she was still carrying her bag. Packing her things that morning at the hospital she had noted the meagerness of her possessions, so few things. 'This is all my life is,' she thought, 'I can hold it in one hand, I could put it in my pocket.' She was like an animal that left no footprints, light as a feather over soft ground.

'Your Father's at the golf club' her mother was saying, 'he sends his love, he'll see you tonight'.

Sally was glad he wasn't here, did not want to see him yet, not sure if she wanted to see him at all. Sally sat and stared at the tea, slow bubbles escaped from the whirling centre, she put her spoon in it to stop it spinning but it would not stop just broke around the spoon and ran on, round and round the cup, she closed her eyes but the spinning was inside her head, she pushed the spoon down hard and the tea spilt.

'I'm sorry,' she said, staring at the hot brown liquid on the table-cloth, 'That's all right,' replied her mother, kitchen towel quickly on the scene, 'I'll get you another'.

'No,' Sally waved the cup away, ' I think I'd better lie down now.'

Her Room - she lay on the bed with the curtains closed, with the faint sounds of a suburban Sunday afternoon filtering through the window, the crunch of tyres on gravel drives, the buzz of lawnmowers, the high excited voices of children. Roddy had said that normality was just a device with which to enslave the mind, that it had no substance, that it was just a fragile façade but it seemed strong enough now, that mixture of gentility and optimism, of growing up quietly and well. She buried her face to the pillow, weak it may be but it was stronger than her, stronger than Roddy too, she guessed.

Her room - she looked around it - the Black Sabbath posters had been removed but the stuffed toys remained. Here and there expensive sports equipment lay abandoned, there was a photo on the dressing table, a girl stared back at her, a girl with long brown hair and big bright eyes, in her hand she held the riding hat, while her right arm hung round the neck of a pony, Topper was the pony's name she remembered but the girl was a stranger to her, too clean, too sunny, too bright by half. It had been a mistake to let them bring her here, a stupid, stupid mistake. She wasn't a child, she didn't need their help. But she was so weak now, so tired - she had to get better first, she had to endure this.

There were other voices in her head, low voices of resignation. 'Stop all this,' they said, 'stop it now before it all happens again.' She was so worn out even nothingness seemed difficult, complex, she must wait. No. She mustn't panic. Just hold on.

Finally she slept, curled into a foetal ball round a pale yellow pillow. As she slept the faces came, not clearly, no so she could call them by name but knew she knew them. What did they want

123

from her? Something, she could feel it, their wanting like a pressure around her, the very air turning hostile, dangerous but she didn't KNOW what they wanted. 'C'mon Sally,' they said, 'you can Sally,' but she really DIDN'T know what and she began to get scared. They came at her in slow silky waves caressing yet insistent. Then she was falling, falling beneath them, no chance to run, to escape, the voices were inside her now, clenched in her inner ear, their words licked at her, like a malevolent conscience, but it didn't matter, for she had fallen. There was nowhere to run to anyway. There was nothing else she could have done to stop them, nothing. It was a relief 'C'mon Sally, Sally you can.'

'Yes I can,' she said small and still.

'You see!' They all said, 'you see, that wasn't too difficult was it.'

'No., said Sally, 'no, not difficult, not difficult.' but when she woke up her face was wet and she had this horrible pain in her stomach. She went to the ensuite toilet and was sick, her own private toilet. 'What a lucky girl, she thought, no one's ass but mine.' She washed her face and looked in the mirror, a strange gaunt ghost stared back, she had once powdered her face to look that white, drawn in eye liner to look that black now she looked like it for real but behind the makeup she had been arrogant, cynical, assured the face that stared at her now was empty of these things. She smiled at the ghost, it made a horrid twitch of a grimace in return, she poked her tongue out at the ghost but she shouldn't have done that for she was immediately sick again. There's something especially horrible about being sick when there's nothing in your stomach, like wringing out a dish cloth to the last drop, her insides felt scraped and raw but the bad pain was gone. She went to her bedroom window and looked out. It was dark, no one moved in the dark night hours here amongst the soft beds and certainties, those cold blue moments passed unknown, while away across the rooftops that other world seethed and shivered and raged. If you don't reach the bottom then you're always standing on unsafe ground Roddy would say, she could see him in her mind's eye, leaning forward intently his hand roughly on the nape of her neck, his eyes bright forcing hers open, forcing hers to see.

She made herself lie down again but everything felt jumbled up, the moments were difficult to touch. In the hospital they told you about the pains and the shakes but they didn't tell you about the fear. How it sat in your body, ran like mad blood to sear your head and set your heart gasping and the loneliness they didn't tell you about that, the dark edge of nothingness that sits by your shoulder moving when you move, waiting when you wait. She sat up and switched on the light, in the light the fear was duller like she could touch it and stop it from moving around inside her. Her feet were cold, numb, she rubbed them until they began to tingle, pins and needles. She got up and hobbled round the bed trying to get the blood flowing. As a child she would go crying to her daddy and ask him to stop the horrible needles, 'I hate them, I hate them, daddy,' she would cry and he would laugh and sit her at the table and rub and rub until the pain was gone and her feet were warm and glowing.

The horrible needles.

The hospital used needles too. You couldn't escape that. If you wanted to get better or you wanted to get worse the process was the same.

When the pain in her feet finally stopped, she stood quite still in the middle of the room not knowing what to do. She wanted things to end, needed them to end but it didn't work like that and she hated that.

Life clawed at you, things cut and bruised you, spilt when you tried to carry them, broke when you tried to use them, disappeared when you wanted them and then there were the people, always wanting something from you not knowing exactly what but wanting it, desperately, just the same. Roddy had said that you couldn't avoid it, that there was no quiet place away from it all but that the secret was to let all roar right there in your head and not notice it, not even care - but she did care that was the problem, for a while Roddy's rhetoric had liberated her, she had escaped, fled from who she had been, the her they had wanted, needed her to be. Out there in those dark, damp streets she had gone looking for truths and had found them all. But the person who was Sally, the person who should have gone for ever, was she not back and being back was she not Sally once more? She sat down on the edge of the bed and for the first time in months, she cried. Tears ran everywhere on and on until at last she rolled over on her side and slept.

The next morning she awoke feeling dry and feverish, sticky with sweat, strange smells came to her nostrils, sickly smells as if her body was already decomposing in life. She took a cold shower forgetting to turn on the hot - forgetting that it would be hot, still she felt a little better. She stared at her naked body in the mirror, it was still a good body she thought despite all the things that had happened to it. Just looking you couldn't tell. She posed in front of the mirror, hand on hips, pelvis tilted forward but the flicker of bravado passed and she felt foolish. She dressed listlessly, the thought of the day, the hours ahead dismayed her. Suddenly she realised that she would be expected to eat a meal called breakfast - her mother would insist. Her stomach had already begun to knot at the prospect.

The smell of the kitchen hit her halfway down the stairs, that homogeneous wellbeing smell that emanated from all fully stocked kitchens, warm bread and coffee, bacon and hot fat, a happy complacency on which to begin a complacent day, she went into the kitchen her mother was sitting at the table with a cup of coffee reading the Daily Mail "Princess in new Row" said the headline, A bright clean table cloth had replaced the one she had soiled.

'Good Morning dear,' her Mother said gaily, standing up and beginning to bustle, 'how are you feeling today? Did you sleep well?'

'I feel a bit better,' Sally lied.

'That's good.' Her mother stood poised for action, ready to produce a range of breakfast options. 'What would you like to eat?'

'Just some cereal please.' To Sally that seemed the safest option. Her mother brought a cluster of boxes from the cupboard. 'I couldn't remember what you liked so I got a selection.'

Sally surveyed the boxes and chose from the most innocuous looking one, poured it out and added milk, the smell and the taste of it reminded her of baby food, slimy and inconsequential but at least she was able to keep it down.

'Your father sends his love dear, he had to go to a meeting in Manchester, he looked in on you last night but he didn't want to wake you.'

Sally was glad, it gave her another day to prepare to face him. At the hospital when he had come to see her, the sound of the sob in his voice made her want to cry. He was upset and nothing upset her father, she had reached him at last but in the wrong way.

Her mother moved cups from surface to surface, sliced bread and ran sink water, Sally knew she had something to say, would say it soon in an apologetic rush, she put down her spoon and waited.

'I've invited some of your friends round to see you,' she rattled the plates into the dishwasher.

For a moment Sally imagined the room filled with wild eyed dishevelled people then realised her mother didn't mean those friends.

'You need cheering up,' her mother was saying, 'you've been through a lot.'

'A lot' what a fabulously British piece of understatement that phrase was. 'So who are these people?' asked Sally.

'Melissa, Clare and Jenny, said her mother ignoring Sally's contemptuous 'these people.'

Sally groaned inwardly. Had they ever been friends? Did you ever really make friends when you were that young, that false. What possible good could it do her now to meet these people who belonged to an era of Bros concerts and Gymkhanas. It suddenly occurred to Sally that her mother hoped that Sally could become one of them again. That the my little pony girl would somehow re-emerge with bows in her hair, re-new her membership of the tennis club and find herself a nice little trainee stockbroker for a boyfriend.

Sally stared at her open mouthed. That was what they wanted from her, they wanted her back. She stood up suddenly and banged her knee on the table, clutching her knee she backed out of the room avoiding her mothers' solicitous arm.

'When are they coming?' she yelled as she hobbled up the stairs.

'This afternoon, her mother called after her, Sally are you all right?

Locked in the bathroom she began to feel calmer. Things resolved themselves in bathrooms and toilets. Silent enclosed little nausea rooms, full of cool tile and chrome and the sweet pervading smell of decay.

It had seemed easy at first, a game, an adventure, a relief. Sally had never felt freer than she did in those first few dizzying months, free from the no's and the don'ts, from the eyes of others, from the inhibitions of her creed. It had made her wild and careless and she loved herself for it. They had lived in a large tent under the viaduct near Waterloo Station. Roddy had found the place, the arch echoed constantly to the rumble of trains, high vaulted, black scarred stone that was always dark even on the brightest day. There had been five of them Roddy, Eric, Gene, Polish Jimmy and her. They lived off what the city didn't want or need, a meal here, a drink there. The drugs came later, the drugs were Roddy's idea. Even in the coldest wettest nights she had something that was hers, the cameradierie of people who knew what was real, tasting each moment, bitter and vivid, being alive without the baggage, the deforming, dulling trappings of the day to day.

Of course there were bad things, even before the drugs. Raids by policemen who couldn't believe you had nothing stolen in your possession. Attacks by drunks who resented everything and everyone and for whom they were easy targets.

She got wilder, sometimes because Roddy wanted it, sometimes because of the wildness that grew inside her, got out of control. Sometimes when she was bored she would go out and pick up men, bring them back to the tent and let them fuck her, for money or drugs or booze or just because she liked them. It's amazing how few men turn down a fuck on a plate like that, even though she was dirty and could have had all sorts of diseases. Just because she was pretty. That's all that mattered to them. That she was pretty and she would let them do it. Sometimes Roddy was there but he was never angry, never upset, he just used to light a cigarette and wander out to the river side. Later when they'd gone he'd ask her if she'd enjoyed it and usually she had, part of her had, because it was shocking, part of her because she liked the idea that men wanted her and part just because she liked to do it. Then one night she had slept with them all together, Roddy , Eric, Gene, Polish Jimmy in a tangle of groans, sweat in her eyes, their penises sticky in her hair and with each thrust, each bite, she had erased a piece of her past. Rub, rub, rub and when it was over they all went outside and she lay there slimy and wet. Then Roddy came back and turned her over and put his fingers in her anus and she had said, 'No, please,' but the words were small and tiny and unheard. Besides what good was no to her now. Then when he was inside her it didn't matter and she listened to the sound of the river lapping sucking on the wall and she watched herself disappear. Amidst the pain and the sweat and the strangeness of it all there came a sort of relief. That the person she had carried around with her all those years had departed and she was no-one at last.

She would never be her Mother now, her mother grown old and contented on the knowledge that such things did not happen. Ignorance had made her mother strong. Roddy had said that all you had to do to destroy these people was to take away their ignorance but that it was almost impossible to do as they clung to it more tightly than life itself. So her mother would not believe her, whatever she said. Sally realised bitterly that the truth, the truth she had spent her time and energy pursuing, had no power to hurt them, for the truth was an aberration easily side stepped, easily subverted or ignored. So there was no point in telling her mother anything, telling any of them anything. Their windows and their doors were shut up, cracks sealed tight against the sudden chinks of light, Full alert below lest the truth might sneak in in disguise.

No, a way forward was gone for her, extinguished.

She took her zipper bag from out of the wardrobe, Roddy's bag. In the corner where the edging was stitched she pulled the velcro carefully apart, the needle was still there undamaged. She took it out and felt in again, this time she came up with a little plastic bag, not much left, not much more than a day's ration, but now,

now that she was clean, it would be enough. She mixed the powder carefully at the sink and tied off a vein with her shoelace. She sat on the edge of the bath, needle poised on the edge of her skin. She wondered what it felt like to die, wondered how Roddy had felt that day in Baker Street station, lying in the dirty toilet, the last words he ever read obscene, his last smell shit. Roddy probably liked that. Eric said he was smiling when he found him, she believed him, believed that he wasn't just trying to be kind to stop her from crying.

That was when she started to get sick, from then. She had gone to the hospital to see his body, but his parents had got it, funny Roddy always told her his parents were dead. Yes that was when she had started to get sick.

She put her hand on the plunger, it was a good time to die, there was no reason not to. She thought of Auschwitz and Hiroshima; of old age and cancer; of aids; she thought of the unimportance of her existence amongst these huge vast planets of cold airless stone; of the endlessness of time; of loss, hopelessness and lost love. She began to sweat, to feel sick again.

What was she waiting for? What possible reason could she have to carry on?

But she didn't have it, what Roddy had. Somewhere deep and hidden inside her there was a streak of optimism, absurd, despicable, a wild hope that against all the odds things would turn out ok. And she thought she had reached the bottom! Shit! She wasn't even close. Life hadn't finished with her yet. It could not let her go because she could not let it go and she was lost and saved and lost again in one single act of belief. She let out a wail Oh! Oh! Oh!. Long and unearthly that echoed inside her, the noise breaking and turning inside her frail empty carcass. Oh! Oh! Oh!

When she realised that she really was not going to do it, she went to the mirror, wiped her eyes, made up her face and put on her tight black pants and satin top. It was a little crumpled but would have to do. Then she spent a long time on her hair. When she was finally satisfied with her appearance, she took up the syringe, put it in a plastic bag and smashed it.

Down in the hall the doorbell rang, Sally heard her mother open it and greet them, the sound of cultured cheery voices, happy and certain and full of life, those for whom everything was possible. One simply had to try. 'Sally,' her mother called up the stairs, 'they're here.'

Sally gritted her teeth and stepped through the doorway.

YOU CAN'T STOP ME FROM DREAMING

The sirens began as Fred Latham left Leicester Square underground, a few people ran past him to gain shelter but most, including Fred, continued on their way in the bright August sunshine. People browsed amongst the second hand bookshops along the Charing Cross Road and lounged outside the Porcupine pub with their drinks. The sirens had been sounding like this for weeks now but nobody had seen any planes, the early panic had given way to jokes and complacency. 'The jerries weren't coming.' 'They were scared of the good old RAF.' Fred wasn't so sure though, he'd seen German bombers the other week when he was down in Folkestone visiting his sister. They hadn't dropped anything but the sight of formations with the black crosses on their wings had given him a funny feeling. There had been a lot of talk about gas too and for a while everyone had carried the clunky metal tins slung from their shoulders and there were leaflets about listening for the ARP rattles and how to identify the smell of the different gases; mustard gas was like garlic or horseradish, chlorine like bleach, lewisite smelt of geraniums, phosgene of mown hay, hydrogen sulphide like rotten eggs and tear gas like biscuit. Fred's sense of smell wasn't all that so he thought he'd just wait for the rattle, though of course he'd left his mask at home again. Fred carried on up to Shaftesbury Avenue heading for Soho, up past the restaurants and shops with taped up or sandbag blocked windows, all with hastily scribbled 'We are open' signs waving forlornly in the soft summer breeze.

Old Compton Street was almost deserted though, before the war the area had always been seething, buzzing, any time of day; tourists, theatregoers, drunks and purveyors of the fleshpots thronging the street but since all the theatres had been closed down and the tourists scared off, the street had taken on an abandoned look.

On the corner of Greek Street, Fred bumped into Shirley, the new singer in the band , "lo, Fred where are you off to?" She had that bright feverish look of someone who was still out from the night before and swayed like a languorous reed on the edge of the pavement, her long dark hair slightly mussed. She reminded Fred a bit of Gene Tierney.

"I'm meeting Maxie for a quick drink in the Crown & Two Chairmen".

"That's what I need, love.' she said, 'a quick drink, mind if I join you?"

"I think we can stand it", said Fred, "got any cash?"

"I'm flush", she said, "got an advance from Jack"

"Lucky girl, that man's strictly C.O.D." She took his arm and they walked on in the sunshine.

The Crown was fairly full though it was still early, Maxie signaled to them from a booth and they wafted through the cigarette smoke haze to join him.

"Watcher, Shirley girl," said Maxie "you're lookin' a bit rough."

"Thanks Maxie, you know how to make a girl feel good".

"My pleasure, what would you like more of the same or something different"

"I'll have a G&T please," said Shirley, ignoring his remark. Maxie got them all drinks and they settled into the booth.

"So where you bin Shirley, up Mayfair way?" asked Maxie, his seedy smile on full.

"Maybe," she said, "Maybe I had a sleepless night because of the sirens"

"Weren't no sirens last night old girl, 'all quiet on the London front,' so to speak."

"OK smarty pants, believe what you like, people always think the worst of a girl anyway".

"'ang for sheep that's what I always say," Maxie nodded sympathetically, " 'ang for sheep cause the buggers'll 'ang you for the lambs anyway." Maxie leaned over and proffered her a cigarette. She let it dangle out of the side of her mouth like a Hollywood gangster's moll.

"Got any nylons, Maxie?" The cigarette bobbled between her full red lips.

"Never wear 'em girl," he said, "make me legs sweat".

"Well if all you can be is smart," she rose to go.

Maxie raised a hand "don't get all shirty, course I got nylons my sweetheart - this is Maxie, at you service" he bowed his head slightly.

"What about my stuff?" said Fred, "you got that?"

"In the back of the Austin round the corner - no sweat, pick it up on the way out." Maxie gave his high laugh and his sloppy sideways grin. Fred realised suddenly that he really disliked Maxie quite intensely. He went to get some more drinks. Despite this sudden realisation Fred stayed till closing time and he and Shirley ended up half cut at rehearsals.

It didn't make a lot of difference, though Fred was half a beat late on the coda to 'I wonder who's kissing her now' and he saw Jack shoot a look in his direction, but he didn't say anything afterwards, he couldn't really. Good clarinetists were thin on the ground outside the armed forces this year. "The show starts tonight at 10.00 as usual, be sharp," Was all he said. Fred thought he'd get a few hours kip.

He had this flat above a newsagents in Poland St, a five minute walk from the Cafe De Paris where he was playing. It was just a couple of grubby rooms but he loved the Soho life, the looseness of it all, the 'up all hours' feel of the streets.

It was now late afternoon and the market in Berwick Street was beginning to close up. He picked his way through the discarded crates and boxes, keeping an eye out for the unlikely event of spotting any abandoned fruit & veg.

Fred brought a loaf and a bottle of milk to supplement the stuff Maxie had gotten him. This stuff consisted of a pound of sausages, six carrots, two oranges and a jar of strawberry jam.

Fred carried it all up the dark stairs and put it in his kitchenette. Then he put an Al Bowlly record on the gramophone and lay down on his bed.

As the opening trumpets ushered in the crooner's voice, the dark began to creep into the room. Fred watched the cracks in the ceiling grow indistinct then disappear 'I'm waiting for a letter from you, I'm waiting for you to be true, I'm waiting it seems for one of my dreams to find you, till then what can I do'.... The next thing he knew the sirens were going and it was dark. He looked

134

at his watch but he could not focus properly on the luminous face. He fastened the blackout curtain and switched on the light.

9.00

Whew! He silently thanked the sirens for a timely alarm call, but his tea would have to wait. He had a quick wash and changed into his shiny lapelled jacket, a quick lick of Brylcreem and he was out the door.

The streets were very dark and empty though sounds filtered through the blackout screens. A pub piano tinkled away to gruff, unconcerned voices. Here and there groups of partygoers drifted between the clubs. Down along Brewer Street, the ladies of the oldest profession lounged in doorways, one or two called out to him - half-heartedly, as he was clearly a man in a hurry.

He made it through the stage door of the Cafe De Paris with 15 minutes to spare. He'd wanted to fit a new reed to his clarinet but that would have to wait. He slithered down the steep iron stairs to the dressing rooms, colliding with Sam Browne, who appeared from nowhere at the bottom. "Watch it Fred you'll ruin the suit" Sam brushed at the immaculate powder blue tuxedo. "New is it then - how many young girls clothing coupons did that set you back?' said Fred disappearing on the run before Sam could reply.

The cafe was heaving as usual. Fred took a peek through the curtain as he was getting into place on the bandstand. They'd recently added a few more tables to accommodate the demand, shrinking the dance floor area so that whenever the popular numbers were on, the floor became an indivisible sea of movement and timing and precision was necessary not only with one's partner but with those adjacent couples also.

Fred heard the hubbub reduce as the M.C. came on stage. "Ladies & Gentleman, for your dancing pleasure, The Jack Harris Big Band". The curtains rolled back and Jack strolled on to applause and signalled them into "Nevertheless".

Fred took a solo in E flat after 30 bars. The sound made the words in his head, 'Maybe I'll live a life of regret, maybe I'll give much more than I get but nevertheless I'm in love with you.' As he played he watched his notes reach the dancers, felt the bluesy sway deep and low on their hips. It gave him a thrill to affect them in this way. His solo ended and Pat took the mike. In that light, her blondeness dazzled him, in her shimmering white dress, a white gardenia in her hair, leaning back slightly to the sway of the trombone section "Maybe I'm right. Maybe I'm wrong, Maybe I'm weak, Maybe I'm strong....."

After the show he stopped Pat in the passage. I thought you were very good tonight" he said. Pat gave him her blonde look, "thanks Fred," she said, "you're a dear, I must rush, Sam's taking me to Magno's." Then she left having answered his unasked question.

Shaftesbury Avenue was more deserted than ever. Here and there the late night revelers smooched in darkened doorways, the odd taxi, their headlights reduced to a cross. Fred walked down to Piccadilly Circus, the night was still warm. He thought about Pat, about that time in the back of Jack's car, her perfume, the sheer feel of her nylon clad legs.... He had thought her his then for a vast optimistic heady moment, but he was wrong. Whilst he didn't like to admit it, Pat had considered him a luxury she couldn't afford - a man with no money. Fred stood alone in the stilled heart of a great city and was sad about himself.

His spirits were somewhat higher a week later when Pat asked him to a garden party. She had asked most of the band, but Fred saw it as an opportunity. Saturday September 7th, 23 Highgate Vale, starts at 2.00, bring your clarinet if you want" She smiled warmly at him, "yes do come," she said as if confirming something in herself. Fred said he would.

The next week finally passed. Fred got Maxie to get him some chocolate, Swiss stuff, that cost a lot, and he took his clarinet. 23 Highgate Vale was part of one of those 4-story, Victorian terraces, all the more imposing because they were butted onto the side of the hill and the gardens dropped a further level or two. From the cast iron patio one was treated to a panorama of London; the flats down in Camden where he'd lived as a kid and fainter in the hazy heat, the top of St. Paul's, St. Pancras station. The river itself was out of sight as the land dropped away somewhere beyond the station towards the river, beyond that however the distant unknown hills of South London were just visible. Fred had arrived about 3.00 when the party had just begun to get going. Pat looking resplendent in a strapless blue sun dress, introduced him to a couple of people, who were no more interested in him than he was in them.

Shirley came over, half cut already and kissed him on the ear. "Fred, Fred, what a glorious day," and indeed it was, as sunny and warm as you could wish. Fred looked across at the bright greens of the Heath and was reminded of a painting whose artist whose name he couldn't recall - but he remembered the title 'An English Autumn afternoon'.

"I hear they bombed up the river last night," said a man nearby, "Tilbury or Chatham or somewhere like that."

"That's all they'll do," said another, "oil and ports and the like, that's all they're after."

"Well I'm glad I don't live out that way," said a blonde woman.

"I'm glad about that with or without the bombs," the first man replied. They all laughed.

Fred had heard the bombs last night, faint but unmistakable, he had been visiting his friend Nigel who lived in Poplar. Again the uneasiness had spread through him, it was a strange sort of fear, like maybe he should run and hide but nobody else was, so it seemed silly. Shirley was back again grabbing his arm and spilling her gin. "Fred I'm going to sing will you play for me?" An impromptu bandstand had been rigged up in the middle of the lawn on which stood a lonely set of drums. One or two people had begun taking their instruments from their cases.

"Price of admission, is it?" grumbled Fred,

"C'mon don't be a spoil sport," urged Shirley, "you know I soar when you play," she leaned against him and he drew a resigned comfort from the proximity of her body. He got his clarinet and took the stage. Shirley smiled and fawned at the 'audience' as they assembled, "let's do Pennies from Heaven." They began. As he played Fred stared out over the city, vistas always had a profound effect on him, as if he were seeing and controlling the view. As he looked over to the East, a black cloud of smoke had risen from the flat lands in front of the green smudge that he knew to be Greenwich Park, a big fire Fred thought, some dock cargo, but then as he watched he saw another one appear some way off and then another. It was then he noticed the puffs of smoke in the sky, like a line of dull looking fireworks, he stopped playing. "They're bombing London," he shouted, "They're bombing the docks!" Attention was turned to the scene, some people drifted out on to the patio to watch, deprived of the violence of the sound of the bombs, it was like a generals eye view, like those paintings of distant battles where the features of the landscape are the most striking feature.

'Bastards,' one man muttered, slipping a prawn vol-au-vent into his mouth.

'Play on,' yelled a woman near the bandstand, 'don't let them beat us.' Fred resumed playing whilst thinking how stupid and pointless it all seemed, he remembered something about Nero fiddling while Rome burned.

The black clouds grew as the afternoon grew late after a while the hushed awe began to break down,

'Look there are some planes,' shouted one woman excitedly.

'What a fireworks show!' said another.

'That's not just the docks, they'll have got half the houses in Silvertown as well with that lot.' A man observed.

Fred thought of Nigel. A few people began to drift away, chastened, saddened or fearful at what they had seen but the party's the thing crowd remained and so did Fred. As the evening drew in you could see the lights of the fires which raged beneath the big smoky clouds. The mood at the party became more intense, the drunks got drunker, the maudlins weepier, the flirters flirtier. By the light of the fires of hell the band played on. Fred looked for Pat in the darkened garden and found her on the patio talking to Marcus Wisley a budget film maker. 'You'd be perfect for the part,' he was telling her, 'you're incredibly photogenic, you'd knock them dead.' Pat smiled deprecatingly, but her eyes glittered in the light from the burning docks. 'But I'm really a singer ...,' she began modestly.

'With those looks darling,' said Wisley with a mongoloid smirk, 'you can be what you want to be.' Fred left then, without a word, he knew he couldn't compete and he was through with standing by.

The whole Eastern sky was lit now like a vast sunset, what must have been whole streets looked like blown on embers of some gargantuan hearth and still the wheeling black birds tipped their cargo of death into the fire, devils dancing on the edge of hell's pit. He shuddered and turned away, his eyes would take no more, his brain had stopped processing the horror and he didn't want any more to do with those who remained on the terrace, spectators at Armageddon.

He was looking for his coat in the dark hall when he tripped over something, it was Shirley, she was crying in a soundless way and her mascara had spread across her cheeks. She gripped his sleeve as he sought to get away.

'They're killing all those people, they should make them stop.'

'Yes, it's a real war now, he said matter of factly, 'but there's nothing we can do it's up to the forces now.'

Still she would not let him go and he was forced to hold her as she shivered and cried.

"It's going to be like this, now, isn't it?' She sobbed, 'burning the cities, killing everyone beneath - killing us.'

'The RAF have been caught on the hop is all,' Fred assured her, though he had no idea if that was true, 'once they get up there, they'll blow them out of the sky – you'll see.' Though Fred himself didn't really see how that would be, had to admit that Shirley's hysterical assessment of the situation sounded likely.

While Fred wondered what to do with her, how to calm her down, all her could think about was Pat's eyes in the firelight. The sudden pang he felt forced him into action.

'C'mon Shirley love, let's go.' he helped her quivering girl to her feet and into her coat.

The streets of Highgate were ghostly and still. Down at the station there were no trains running and no cabs to be had but they managed to grab a lift with a jeweler who was heading for Holborn. 'It's terrible, terrible,' the jeweler muttered, 'these people are madmen, they're murdering babies again.' Fred could see his top lip glistening as he spoke, 'all they know is hate - it's true they killed my uncles and they were stamp collectors. He spoke as if this was the ultimate proof of German bestiality, which on reflection Fred thought perhaps it was. He dropped them off at the corner of Red Lion Street. Fred suddenly wondered if this had been a mistake as from this proximity the sound of the bombs were audible and the bombers could be heard passing directly overhead. Fred hoped they were empty. Shirley was a wreck and could barely stand. Fred shook her and she began to stumble along beside him.

'We're going to die!' she wailed.

'Not if you keep on walking,' Fred held her arm and propelled her forward.

They struggled up deserted Holborn and into an even emptier New Oxford Street. On the corner of Gower St an ARP warden stopped them saying "I'd get under cover if I were you it's all in the docks at the moment but you never know when they'll drop a load up here," this started Shirley whimpering again. "We'll get home," Fred told the man, "it's no distance now," the ARP man shrugged and wandered off. In Berwick Street Fred was amazed to see the Nellie Dean still open. He wasn't sure it was a good idea for Shirley to have another drink but he needed one. There were about a dozen people in the bar, they stared at them as they entered their faces were relaxed but unnaturally so.

'Hello Fred,' the barman was already pulling him a pint of mild, 'seen the fireworks?'

'Yes thank you,' said Fred, 'quite enough.' Nodding in the direction of Shirley. The barman looked at her and said no more and put a gin & tonic on the bar. Shirley drank it down in one shaking gulp, her hair and face were a mess. Fred handed her her bag from his coat pocket. 'Better fix yourself up love, no point in going round looking like the bride of Frankenstein.' She tried to smile and almost made it as she took the bag and slipped into the toilet.

'What's going on now Fred? Do you know?' Said one man. 'They're beating the shit out of the docks that's for sure. Charlie the warden said there's a thousand bombers with another thousand on the way.'

'The whole East End's gone, I heard.' said another.

'I'll thank you not to talk like that in front of Shirley.' Fred said. The man shrugged and turned back to his beer. Fred finished his drink and ordered another. Eventually Shirley came back, remade to her former sophistication, she flicked her hair and smiled queenly at the unseeing pub, only the slight unsteadiness of her gait betrayed her, she slipped onto the stool beside Fred and picked up her drink and as she did so she slipped her other arm round his.

She smiled brightly, 'Cheers.' she said.

'Cheers.; said Fred, their glasses clinked.

Above the low drone of conversation a harder drone could be heard, for as they drank the dark eagles of the Luftwaffe ploughed on over the blackened city, German eyes straining for a familiar landmark but there was only the glitter of the river in the moonlight to be seen, they banked and turned for home.

By 11 o clock they had gone and the city was quiet but for the distant ringing of bells; fire bells, ambulance bells, church bells and from the east the smell of burning. Shirley, who had been quiet for some time, turned to Fred. 'I don't want to go home tonight. I don't want to die alone. Can I stay with you?', she lit a cigarette and looked at him with smoke obscured eyes.

Fred really wanted to be alone, to lick his emotional wounds privately. 'It's not much of a place,' he said.

'I wouldn't ask normally, she interpreted his reluctance as chivalry, too beautiful to believe he didn't fancy her, 'I wouldn't want you to think that.'

Fred said he didn't think anything.

Berwick Street was empty in still warm August midnight. Normally there would have been the 'up all hours' revelers slipping in and out of the drinking clubs, a few women in doorways hoping for one more punter before a well-earned sleep, but tonight – nothing. It was if the normal life of the city had been cauterized, whether out of fear or respect or both people were staying indoors or in the shelters, huddled and hopeful in their make believe cocoons.

Fred gave up his bed and threw a pillow on his sagging couch. It wasn't at all comfortable but he knew that sleep was a long way off. When he turned around Shirley was already down to her underwear, smiling uncertainly at him. 'If you want to – you know –'

Fred went over and kissed the top of her head. 'It's been a tough day, Shirley love, we're both worn out. Let's see what tomorrow brings eh?'

Shirley's eyes were glistening as she nodded agreement. 'I am tired – so tired.'

She fell asleep as soon as her head hit the pillow Fred put the light out and loosened the blackout curtain, the treacherous moonlight flooded in and smoothed the contours of her face, pale in relief against the dark swirls of her hair, her youth suddenly apparent beneath the hard glamour. Fred touched her hair and she mumbled and tossed a little.

Outside in the silent, shocked city the all clear sounded.

A long high wail from the rooftops.

A long wail.

DOUG AT THE EDGE OF THE WEEKEND

Doug was first into the pub as usual. Jeanette, Charlie, Mark and the others were still hard at work, silly buggers. You wouldn't catch Doug staying a minute longer than he had to. He sat at the long mahogany bar and watched the bar staff work. He smiled at them from time to time as they caught his eye, wary of unnecessary conversations they stared back only fleetingly, suggesting that they had had enough insights into the human condition for one day. Doug watched on regardless, watching the pouring of long condensating glasses of lager, the backrush from the optics stirring bubbles in elegant amber liquids. Now and then he took a sip from his pint of Youngs and chewed on a nut from the bowl by his left hand. The paraphanalia of pubs had always fascinated Doug, the welcoming lights from the   shelves, the rows of bottles with obscure and exotic sounding labels, the smell of spilt beer. Doug realised that he felt more at home here than in the flat where he lived, but then the pale patchy walls of his lounge, the cold linoleum and the smell of burnt food   in his kitchen did not offer much in the way of competition. He let inertia pervade him, a sense of doing nothingness, being nothing that was almost sensual. The working day was drawing to a close for others now, every minute brought a fresh influx of tired faces through the door, some abject, grey, defeated but some still enervated from their days toil. Whatever the result of the day the sense of relief was palpable. Up and down Bishopsgate, in adjacent Leadenhall Street and on to Cheapside in the west the story was the same. The City week was ending, folding in on itself to reveal that truce laden no man's land between work and home. When the pub's flickered to bursting from the expiation of the day yet were closed shuttered and forgotten by eight.

By the time Charlie arrived he had to elbow his way through to the bar, Doug had a pint waiting for him.

"You took your time", said Doug, "

"Just got caught by Travers as I was leaving", Charlie took a deep draught of beer and then breathed out slowly, " - you know the old story I won't keep you if you're in a hurry, just keep a mental note to hold it against you some time in the future."

Doug snorted, "looking for promotion are we then Charlie boy?"

"I could do with the cash", said Charlie dismissively.

"You know what they say about the shit sandwich", grinned Doug, "well watch out here comes the shit baguette".

Charlie laughed "I won't get caught in all that company man, 24 hour on tap stuff, not me".

Doug snapped off an imaginary tape recorder, "that was Famous Last Words no 356, Charlie Watson recorded live at the Kings Head".

Charlie laughed uneasily "all right Doug go on and have your joke."

"Where's Jeanette and Mark", Doug enquired idly, "oh back there chatting about something, its murder trying to get them to pack up and come over, I gave up, they'll be here eventually no doubt." Charlie made a face.

"They'll have to watch it those two or people will talk". Doug winked and flicked a peanut into his mouth.

"Oh I don't reckon that would bother them at all - if you know what I mean", said Charlie pointedly.

Doug did, "do you think she fancies him then - Mr ambitious - the office boot cleaner".

"I reckon" said Charlie finishing his pint, "want another Youngs?"

"Is the pope catholic" said Doug, brandishing the empty glass. "I can't see why", Doug continued, "I've seen corpses with more life."

"But he's always the same isn't he", Charlie waved a tenner hopefully at a passing barmaid, "he doesn't blow hot or cold like you or I, women like that, I think, and besides he's going places in the company that boy".

"That's it then is it?" said Doug. "Beautiful birds like boring berks shock horror."

"Not all of them" said Charlie "but girls like her with the suits and the blouses,"

"- and the high heels and the long legs", added Doug, "don't forget them".

"Well - yes - those girls you do". Charlie finished. "You'd be better off with one of those blondies from the Word Processing unit".

"Thanks very much" said Doug pretending to stick two fingers down his throat.

No really some of them are all right and they like a laugh", said Charlie.

"They're all a bit stupid" Doug made a cross eyed face. "Sorry" said Charlie "but I didn't think this conversation was to do with the search for the Brain of Britain."

But Jeanette seems different, Doug mused, sucking up the dregs of his pint.

'Different from you Doug that's for sure.'

Doug gave him a shove. "Watch it you. You getting this round or what?

While Charlie was finally getting served Jeanette and Mark arrived. She had an infectious excitability, always chattering, grinning and shaking her head to shiver her swathe of dark curls, always moving close when explaining or listening leaving the breath of expensive perfume and a sense of warmth behind her. Tall almost gaunt, Mark was a study in immobility by comparison. It seemed that things flowed around him; fast, frenzied, frothy and meaningless while he moving on some more profound time plane observing like Buddha - but God he was boring. What could Jeanette possibly see in him. Doug looked at her now, the snub of her nose the long line of her neck her smile full and sudden, always a pleasant surprise even though it came often. Doug had watched Jeanette in his obscure way, watched her from the day she first walked in to the chicken run - the name Doug had given to the open plan office of Accounts Rendered.

He'd spend ages inventing pretexts so he could go over to her desk and tease her about something or another, act silly, tell a joke, anything to try and make her laugh.

He listened to her now talking about work, she never used to talk about work this much until recently, but then everyone talked about work more than they needed to these days. Charlie and Mark nodded knowingly, solicitously but Doug found it hard to concentrate, if there was one thing he knew for certain it was that

145

the job they all did was deadly boring and totally meaningless. If they did it twice as well or stopped doing it completely tomorrow nothing much would change, it was one of those self-perpetuating little admin departments that seemed to exist purely for those without the ability or the inclination for something more demanding more responsible to do. As far as Doug was concerned that was its charm. Now, suddenly they were being encouraged to make out that it too was significant, worth shedding blood over. People were falling for it too, to one degree or another, even Charlie who told himself he was above it all would soon be won over. Doug watched him now. "I'm drowning in the kind of paperwork you wouldn't believe, it's like a quicksand, the harder you struggle the higher it gets". He described the imaginary workstack with his free hand. Back when Doug began it was all different, nobody actually said outright that they were just there to bide their time and take the cash but it was a kind of tacit acknowledgement that this was so. The bosses never asked you awkward, unanswerable questions like, 'where do you see yourself in five years' time' and never questioned your commitment to the departmental cause because they knew without asking that you had none. "Manufacturing profits have risen by 26% this year though this only means a real profit of 2%, they say,' Mark intoned in the humourless voice of company speak. That's right, thought Doug, they've had the rest away. "Though it's disappointing in relation to previous years it's jolly good for the current economic climate". Mark went on, "Excuse me," Doug cut in, "I must have stumbled into a team briefing by mistake I thought I'd come to the after work drink, could you direct me to this please." Nobody laughed - there was a time when there was mileage to be made from deprecating toil but this too it seemed had passed away in the new seriousness. "MY liquid assets have depleted disastrously,' Doug continued, holding up his empty pint, "any chance of a loan." They laughed this time and Mark went off to buy a round. Doug smiled at Jeanette as Mark disappeared up the bar to try and get served. "He's a walking balance sheet isn't he, they should send him out instead of the report and accounts." "He knows his job." said Jeanette curtly, she gave Doug a warning look which he didn't see intent as he was on fashioning his next amusement . "I can imagine him turning up at breakfast between the cereal and the toast. 'Manufacturing profits have risen by 26% this year though this only means a real profit of 2%'" Doug mimicked nasally, "Any chance of a cup of coffee miss, only I've got 24 more houses in the street to do before 10 o'clock." Charlie laughed. Jeanette did not, "You think your smart don't you? Just goofing around the office and wasting everybody's time. It's only people like Mark that keep people from you from being found out." "Woah, Woah," Doug made the time out sight, "Peace, Peace have I touched a little nerve here or what." "I'm sorry Doug," she said, the smile dragging the composure back, "I don't like to see people like Mark ridiculed just because he's so serious and such an easy target." "Ok. Doug raised his hands in a gesture of supplication, "I've got the message."By the time Mark returned with the drinks, the fragile camaraderie that passes for office friendship had been restored and the battalions of dead from the army of Doug's heart had been buried quietly without ceremony in unmarked graves and Doug was doing a trick with some matches.

Some of Doug's cronies from salaries turned up soon after and the non-serious took centre stage and held it for the rest of the evening. Doug worked hard to be the funniest of a very funny group and probably succeeded. Mark and Jeanette remained to one side of the group, not out of it but not really with it either.

The closing bell sounded and last orders were rushed in regardless and the bleary eyed and the self-righteous both got ready to depart. Outside the streets looked wet and cold and abandoned.

Doug slapped his cronies on the back and did high fives with them in the street outside. Mark and Jeanette stood and watched them for a moment then walked off toward the station, "Hang on, Hang on," said Doug trotting after them, "I'm going to the station too."

They crossed Bishopsgate and passed under the bright glass arch of the new station.

Doug said goodbye at the top of the escalator and watched them go, their togetherness apparent, cheerily unsecret.

Something in Dougs chest felt stifled for a moment, 'silly bugger' he told himself and shuffled off, slightly unsteady now to get his train.

The train left its labyrinth of tunnels and ran up and out onto the man made embankment of garages and lock ups. Doug looked out at the places passing, places as familiar as his own face, places he saw twice a day five days a week, places he had never been.

The city was full of lights now, every one stark and intense, every one sharp and burning in the black night air. Doug was reminded of the candles that burned in the naves of vast dark, empty churches. His mother had always told him that each one represented a human hope. He wished them all a good nights burning, then went through the motion of licking his thumb and placing it on the top of an imaginary candle. This done he closed his eyes for the rest of his journey.

SOME OTHER DAY

I first met the poetess Robyn Adams in 1968. It was at one of those Wednesday night readings at the Three Horseshoes in Hampstead. I would attend these readings on a fairly regular basis, impressed by the sense of literary eclecticism rather than the poetry itself, for the readings were liberally peppered with those poets who were soon to become famous in a way that poets never really had among the wider public, cresting a wave of popularity that the literary arts had scarcely enjoyed before and certainly haven't since.

They're all forgotten now of course.

In those days I must confess I found most literature a bit of an affectation and drew my ideas on the artistic from personality. Personality was after all a tangible form, something with an emotional and erotic charge of which art, I felt, was purely a symptom. This tactile viewpoint of things explains quite easily why I was so drawn to Robyn Adams. I can't remember what she read that night or even whether it was any good - but I do remember the way she read, the big passionate eyes, the crisp mouth that reeled off syllables like sharp 'so there' missiles, certain and final. She gave the impression of being what we used to call 'sorted' and in an environment where the increasingly flaky was becoming increasingly fashionable, it was a relief to encounter such forthrightness. I remember I spoke to her briefly after the reading. She was at the bar with Brian Patten and one of the Chelmsford poets.

I didn't bother with the 'I really liked your work stuff.' Compliments were considered puerile and insincere back then. I waded straight in with 'you seem to prefer the sound of the words to the meaning of them'. The crisp mouth formed an almost smile. 'The sound is the meaning, I don't have to prefer it'. Talking to writers always put you at a disadvantage, for they knew everything about their work and you were left to interpret and fumble. I persevered. 'Then do you find you have to sacrifice a certain structure in your work to fulfil your commitment to the sound of it.' 'There is no structure to sacrifice or hadn't you noticed?' She laughed, Patten and the Chelmsford poet laughed too. She had long dark wavy hair which she held in a clasp at the nape of her neck - Pre-Raphaelite hair my friend Nick used to call it. I remember fighting off a strong desire to kiss it, so strong in fact that I was forced to excuse myself and scuttle off to a far corner of the bar before I did just that and put the Three Horseshoes out of bounds to myself, on the grounds of embarrassment, forever.

The texture of things have always been important for me, not just skin and hair, but wood and cloth are capable of arousing deep resonances, emotions, memories - stipplings and grains, veins and stems, the stuff of the construction of things, the being of things, bursting with the vigour of being. Robyn Adams may have been an unknown factor covered up with the cleverness of education and the techniques of society but her hair spoke of her, the true her. It was someone I wanted to know.

Not being obsessive in the pursuit of my desires, I did not follow her home, nor did I follow her to Norwich, Cambridge, Bristol or Liverpool which is where she went next, according to Poetry Review, but I did keep an eye open for her next London reading. It happened three months later, I went along feeling a little foolish with myself but I wanted to see her again, if only to see if she caused the same reaction. This time the venue was unfashionable West Kensington, edged in somewhere between a plethora of tube lines and the vehicle choked Cromwell Rd. I sat at the back and waded, unlistening, through a gaggle of lesser poets. From what I did gather it was the usual mix of English oblique gentility and American noun worship. Robyn came on near the end, she wore her hair loose this time, a wavy glissando, a shiny cascade, a deep dark storm. From time to time she would brush it back from her face as she read or hold it thoughtfully while rendering key passages. It was as abundant and resilient as her words. I was enthralled.

This time I did better in conversation. After the reading she was sitting at the bar alone. She looked tired, vulnerable. I offered to buy her a drink, she said 'Scotch' without looking round to see who was offering it.

'It must get tiring,' I said, 'reading poetry in places like this night after night.'

'Not so much tiring, more hallucinatory.' She stared deeper into the tumbler, as if there might be an answer there, 'the words lose their meaning, you reach out into these rooms of expectant faces and the poems end up by being about what they want and not what you said.'

'But surely that's not necessarily a bad thing?' I offered, remembering all the discourse about readerly and writerly texts from Uni.

'Not bad no but.. frustrating,' she took a swig from the scotch, 'there's something about the insularity of the whole thing that's beginning to haunt me. It feeds off itself, it justifies itself to itself'.

I felt that that was much of the pleasure of art and culture, but I guessed that such an opinion would be judged facetious in her current frame of mind, so I said nothing. This was apparently the right thing to do. Robyn looked at me then, for the first time, an appraising look, 'Sorry, you've caught me on a down night', she poured the remainder of her scotch into the one I had bought her and lifted it. 'Here's to the three muses, may they protect us always from the pain of truth, by the way,' she added, 'what did you say your name was?'

In that way I sort of became Robyn's friend. I didn't get to go home with her or sleep with her or anything a la sixties, but she gave me her phone number. I think I was put on some kind of reserve friend list. That was ok. I liked her but I didn't need her constantly, it was a bit like that then - you tended to be intimate with a lot of people without really being close to them and close to a lot of people without being intimate with them. It was a good set up in a way. You got rid of a lot of sexual hunger and got the opportunity to concentrate on other things.

Robyn and I would meet for the occasional drink or meal and I'd go to see her read whenever she was in London. I had been right about her, she was straightforward in an admirable way, maybe you didn't always like what Robyn had to tell you but you knew there weren't any hidden reasons for her saying it. The only time Robyn became difficult was when she was going through one of her 'contempt for humanity' phases as she called them. Then everything 'stank like someone had pissed on it' and nothing but nothing was worth doing. If you tried to cheer her up it just made her angry. 'It's the happy at all costs brigade that allowed the world to become such a mess in the first place!' she'd shout. You just had to wait it out. I didn't like to see her like that but I couldn't argue with her logic. On certain days and looked at in certain ways, the whole thing was indeed pointless and deeply depressing and it was true that just because you had built a flower garden over a cesspit, it didn't mean that the cesspit had gone and what was more honest here - the flowers or the shit. The trouble was that her diatribes against humanity always ended up directed back against herself and I'd be forced to sit and watch her taking the pain of the blows she aimed.

At the beginning of 1970 Robyn got an offer to tour the West Coast Universities. In the wake of the beat poets, all modern poetry was being considered radical and lucrative. American tours were suddenly opening up for people who until then had been unable even to pay the rent on their bedsits regularly.

'I'm not sure I want to go,' Robyn told me, as she showed me the letter from her agent.' I'm not sure I want to be liked unreservedly, the way the Americans like people.'

'That's not a good enough reason and you know it but I'll give you one if you like.'

'What's that?'

'I'll miss you,' I said.

Robyn went

Robyn was due back in September but she was a hit in the US and although she would never say so in her letters, which contained cruel observations about the American way of life, I think she liked being there. An East Coast tour followed and then the Midwest. Eight months became a year and then two. Robyn became a distant voice, faint and intermittent, the tracing of lines on thin blue vellum, a warm voice on a hissing transatlantic connection. I got on with living or rather living got on with me, which is after all what really happens.

152

Living in England, which was always a grubby, mean sort of affair, was about to enter a down phase. It's always difficult to establish when the 60's bubble was finally seen to have burst. I guess it happened at different times for different people. For me, it occurred about the time I realised that nothing had changed and nothing would change. That I would grow old and die outside of any of the promised nirvanas that had once seemed so close, so inevitable and I would remain mired and muddled in the cruel grey expropriated world of dishonest toil. The establishment, which had gone to ground in all the 'new world' euphoria, had quietly re-emerged and begun to reclaim that which had been lost to them - their ground - they insisted, their way - the only way - and because we had come in soft, we went out soft, we let it go so easily - but it was still hard to see it go. It may have been as late as 1972 for me - though the signals were there much earlier than that. Most of the people I knew became drunks rather than have to measure up to the demands of the new reality. That or they moved to the West Country – where most of them became drunks anyway.

I became a drunk because letting go seemed preferable to holding on tight to something I didn't want. The world I had wanted, I had believed in was gone, rejected as utopian, ridden over by the loud voice of money. As the 60's culture evaporated so did my allegiance to the society that remained. Life, it seemed, was just a high jump contest, clearing the bar successfully only encouraged them to raise the bar higher and higher and urge, jump again, jump again and you knew that however well you did that one day you would knock the bar off and then they would lose interest in you turning away with a slightly disappointed but secretly smug 'I knew it' on their lips. So as 72 became 73, I drifted away from reality -working by the hour in a succession of no-count jobs which I did badly or not at all, a fact which nobody seemed to care about, lost as these jobs were in the secret corners of the big machine.

The trouble with this nether land was that it didn't protect you from the pain of living, only from the disgrace of participation, it was as if my life had ended but it wasn't over – nor, after all, was I ready for it to be over, if only on the grounds of curiosity.

But I got lower month after month. I guess I was entering my final make or break phase with it all when Robyn Adams turned up again.

It was a Wednesday as I recall, around lunchtime. I should have been off somewhere stacking shelves but I was still in bed nursing the remains of a hangover and looking forward to the next. The bell rang and I considered not answering it. In the end I decided it would be a good way to get me out of bed and do some writing. I had begun to write you see. Looking perhaps to write the life I could not live - not poetry though - for poetry was far too realist for my needs. So I opened the door and there was Robyn Adams. She looked different, older, though not physically; it was as if something in her persona had shifted.

'Hi,' she said, 'can I come in? You look a mess, by the way.'

'I am a mess,' I said, 'I've been a mess for a while.'

She dropped her shoulder bag on the floor, moved some dirty clothes from the sofa and sat down. 'Well I'm a mess too, honey, perhaps that's all life makes of you. '

Somewhere America had ceased to be the country it had been, she said, as we ate a belated breakfast in the café across from the tube station. Somewhere, someplace, she had woken up to the awful truth about the direction in which the planet was headed and whereas for me it had been a long slow process, for her it had come suddenly and the sense of shock was still with her.

It had happened one night in a commune out in the Salton Sea. A 'brotherhood' from out of the San Gabriel wilderness had breezed in, shook everyone's hands, speaking of brotherhood and sisterhood and passing round the home grown marijuana. Then during the night they had systematically looted the commune shacks of anything of value and disappeared into the desert.

'Freedom from oppression has morphed into freedom from responsibility.' She shook her head ruefully, 'The chancers still run the game – at every level. "I don't believe in material things" has become "I believe in my right to take your stuff, because having stuff is uncool." The giving has stopped – the taking has begun.'

'Welcome to my world,' I placed my hand on hers to still its restlessness.

I was happy to see her again and for a while I became focused. Life was there, after all, waiting to be lived whether we lived it or not. I hooked in to a little optimism, but at times it was little more than bravado. Made closer by our shared sense of disillusion, we saw a lot more of each other over the next few months. We tried, I think, to bring back the euphoria and optimism that we had both felt back in '68, but somewhere the heart had gone out of it and with it our belief that it could be really recovered. We lived the days as best we could, pubs, clubs, art, culture, but the excitement that came with the total newness and the sense of change was gone, there was no change after all, we saw that now, just authority in its many different hats, lurking behind whatever you tried to do.

It was harder to make a living doing poetry now, the student circuit was almost dead as the incumbents of the universities preferred to spend their time studying, poring over investment portfolios or showing each other their bottoms in the student bar, No one wanted culture any more, least ways any kind of culture that spoke of revolution or communal love – or even human kindness. Freedom was out and inner space was in, the I in all its forms, me, my, mine.

Robyn got a job teaching English to 12 year olds, she had been a teacher before the poetry - I hadn't known that but then I knew little about her as I had never asked and she had never told - but the teaching was a mistake, the poverty of the future was too much in evidence – the way in which the focus was on producing cogs to fit into the big machine – not living, breathing, loving, caring, responsible citizens - she gave it up and became a temp like me.

The big advantage of temping was transience. You weren't asked to belong, commit, understand, bicker, gossip or take sides. You weren't expected to forge a career or adopt corporate values, you weren't expected to have a vision or a mission or be ridiculously over qualified for your role. All you were expected to do was turn up and work, if you did the job well it was an unexpected bonus that made them happy. It was what work should be, without all the baggage but also, of course, without the security or the future. Not feeling the need for either of those, that suited me fine,

Robyn had this little one bedroomed flat just off the Old Street roundabout. In the ground floor of an old five-storey Victorian block of flats. The sound of the traffic choked City Road was always faintly in the background. Sometimes we would be temping at the same place, then we would lunch together in some small Italian restaurant, if not, about once a fortnight I would drop round to see her.

Robyn's moods were becoming more marked, the periods between crazy happiness and bile inducing despair were shorter. Sometimes my 'English dry humour,' – 'gallows humour' my father would call it – could snap her out of it but sometimes even taking the piss out of the absurdity of everything provided no antidote to - what I can only describe as – her belief that she had failed to live up to her image of herself – at least the one she hoped to be – and that she was totally to blame.

'You know that homily about "you can be whatever you want to be if you try hard enough" – it's bullshit.' I'd say.

'Maybe, but achieving to the Americans is like Catholicism is to the Irish. It's in the veins – rationalising it doesn't solve anything.'

I stuck to my task of bringing her out of the dark valleys of her mind. But her downs were easier to manage than her ups, which left her dizzy with possibility and hope. Perhaps I should have encouraged her at those times. But …

Hope.

I have an issue with hope. Nothing has ever pained me more or made me feel more ridiculous than hope. The 'what was I thinking of?' 'What did I expect?' moments when reality had punctured my illusion of hope. The most destructive thing in the world, I decided – hope – nothing in our understanding of our history, our anthropology gives us any glimmer of hope and yet it's there, in everything we do; we hope to succeed, we hope to win, we hope to live. Why? Oh it's a grandeur of sorts – or a sweet foolishness at least - but where does it come from, this capacity for optimism? And why, once we've spotted it, analysed it, dismissed it, laughed at it, does it continue to fuck with us?

I felt Robyn's desperation keenly, yet had no answers, for there were no answers save forbearance. For Brits like me forbearance was in the DNA, for Americans like her, weaned on winning and triumph, the landscape looked bleak.

There was still a poetry scene in London but it had refocused on the wheres rather than the whys of things, as if in defiance to that trend Robyn's poetry had become more why ridden than ever. She still read often and occasionally got paid for it - though less often. I could feel the rooms of listeners growing uneasy before the directness of her gaze, the purity of her attack - no longer willing like their predecessors to allow her words to pierce them, slyly defensive, internally secret, they closed to her, preferring to hear the poems of other losses, other failings. Their little bundle of pity tinged with contempt was not for their own doorstep.

She started a small writing class that dutifully met once a week in the concrete bleakness of City University, bored middle aged women with romantic souls, bright eyed undergrads with fame on their mind and bitter men who hoped to flay the traitorous world with their coruscating epithets. I couldn't decide which group depressed me more, for surely, I too, looked to flay the world before my eyes.

Drifting has its own beauty, its own comforts. There's guilt that you are letting yourself down, there's what others think of you – the look in their eyes ranges from disgust to anger, depending on their inner politics. But you get over that, beyond that, used to that. When nothing matters – then none of that matters and you reach a state of grace. The toys are out of the pram for good, the nose cut off in spite will not grow back.

Whether you are in the eye of the storm or the lee of the bay, all is calm.

Robyn was learning this but the lesson was hard for her, letting go of aspiration was hard and it was tearing something inside her. She knew she was to blame, the universe was meant to be hers, if it wasn't then it must be her fault.

I could calm her but not for long, the little machine that wound her up would start again. Sometimes her anguish was so great I had to restrain her from doing herself harm. During one such session, having pinned her down on the sofa, she stopped struggling, smiled up at me and said, 'We should fuck. It might be good.'

It was probably not a good idea at that point, but I had waited so long, wanted so long for the moment to arrive, I was in no shape to play the strong hero.

And it was good. Good enough for us to do it again – and again. I guess we became lovers for all the wrong reasons, more by instinct than desire, more by need than by allure, but the nights I spent swathed in her hair rekindled the spark in me - the future - that bitter Shangri-la of all human hope began to twitch again, its shape indistinct, but undeniably out there once more.

It was 1974, the Vietnam War was entering its final bloody phase and London was full of Americans whose draft numbers had come up, one such evadee was Randy Buchanan, a tall, muscly, blond, confident, quietly spoken, self-effacing musician. He and Robyn went way back, they said, and I waited to see what trick life was playing with me. What damage Randy would inflict on my fragile hold on Robyn?

For a month they were inseparable, whenever I met them, which I did from time to time as a kind of 'remember me?' exercise rather than a desire to see them together, they would still be rambling on about old times in Saint Paul, Minnesota, a lot of which seemed to relate to falling over in the snow or some such, there being a lot of snow in Minnesota apparently.

Then one day I bumped into Randy in a pub in Charlotte Street. 'How's Robyn?' I asked him, casually, once I'd got my beer.

'Wouldn't know man, haven't seen her in a while.' He replied, he seemed neither sad nor glad about this.

'Oh?' I said, quizzically, inviting him to go on. For a moment he seemed about to change the subject, but then he turned and directed his matter of fact mid-western stare at me.

'Robyn – Robyn, what's that English phrase?' He searched his thoughts for a moment, 'she 'does my head in. I had thought, maybe, now she was older, things might have changed - and some things have' – but not the necessary things.' He drifted away for a moment, thoughts held in some past moment, no doubt lyrical but now laced with the bitter dregs of truth, 'She is so able, yet so perverse. It's like she sees things of value and recoils, hates herself for doing so, then does it again.'

I presumed the thing of value he was talking about was their relationship.

'Do you love her? He asked me suddenly, bringing the full power of his blond, sunburnt, gaze upon me.

Startled, I answered truthfully, 'I – I suppose so - yes.'

'Go see her then man, She needs someone who loves her.'

'Don't you love her? I asked, confused.

'Sure, but she knows that – now she knows that it's over for me.'

'But surely –' I continued, pleased but sorry for him.

He held up a hand that said don't ask. 'Love her but don't tell her – don't make my mistake.'

'But she might change her mind.' I heard myself say, the selfish gene, kicking me as I did so.

'No, man – it's done. I'm off to Sweden in the morning. I hear they have a healthy draft dodger entourage there – and a lot of snow. Yeah, it's done man – go see her but take care. She's a runner pal, believe me.'

Returning home to my flat that day, I took stock of myself for the first time in years. Two rooms, a kitchenette and bathroom, tiny and old, rented for a pittance, but uncared for and decrepit, A life adrift - the watercourse way of zen, I had once told myself - once kidded myself. "The rocks will not harm you if you do not fight the journey." I knew it was bollocks of course but it had a comforting feel to it.

Only those who have everything and those who have nothing have a chance to be free. The rest of us have to duck and dive and dodge and weave and eat the shit sandwich and take the slings and arrows of outrageous society.

I took a deep breath, I couldn't just let my life drift on - nothing just didn't seem as attractive as it once did. I went to the call box on the corner and phoned up my temp agency.

'Hi Sally, it's me, I'm thinking of going permanent, perhaps I could drop by tomorrow lunchtime see what's going.'

After a moment's shocked silence, Sally said. 'Never thought I'd see this day, come on down, we'll see what we can do.'

When I got there, she said 'You're in luck, remember Ray Smith who you worked for over in the Department of Trade last month?'

I did, one of the few managers who treated his staff like people.

'Well he needs a full time clerical assistant and he said if we could find someone half as bright and half as efficient as you he'd be happy.'

'Link us up,' I told her. If I was efficient, then what did that make the rest of them? I thought. So, under Ray's gentle understanding and astute tutelage I re-entered the world of the living. I was preparing for normality, though I wasn't completely sure it was a good idea..

A couple of days after I started work I dropped by Robyn's place, not sure what I'd find or how I'd be welcomed. I knew as soon as she opened the door that she was in a manic phase. Her eyes glittered with humour and intelligence but it was a wired glitter, there was no warmth there. She was working on a new set of poems, she said, something quite different, something that reflected the post utopian angst, she gathered up a fistful of handwritten sheets and began to read. They were clever, they were heartfelt, but oh so bitter. The sorted Robyn was moving to a sharpness, an edge. The wry was becoming a snarl.

'Wow,' I said, and it was a wow, but it was a wow tinged with concern. The poems were pictures of scars and the lacerating edges of the words made you want to step back.

'I'm moving on.' She smiled. I suddenly felt cold.

She didn't actually GO anywhere though, at least not geographically and our on/off, off/on relationship resumed much as before. We still enjoyed each other's company and each other's bodies but the intimacy was tempered by Robyn's wary distance, as if, after Randy she was on the lookout for emotional traps.

Robyn was invited to have her poems in an anthology of 20th century American women poets, on the same pages as Anne Sexton and Sylvia Plath. I think she was pleased but her only comment was, 'Just me and Adrienne Rich left alive, Death is a high price to pay for immortality.'

The Seventies ticked away, Robyn reached 35 a month before me. I went round to celebrate her birthday and found her surrounded by manuscripts, typed and handwritten. 'Half my allotted span – time to take stock, apparently. So I went to the store cupboard and came up with this.' She gestured to the piles.

'Quite a body of work,' I offered, sensing deprecation was at work.

'Body is a word – corpse might be better.' She got out a black bin liner and began to shovel the manuscripts inside.

'You're not going to throw them away?' I was suddenly worried that I might be witnessing an act of artistic self-flagellation. Her puzzled look reassured me.

'I never throw any work away. I was taught that,' she carried on piling the papers in, 'but I certainly don't want them around my feet – there's no comfort to be found in them.'

Maybe it's not comfort we should seek, I wanted to say, maybe we should just forget all the trying to be – and just be. I sensed, however, that there was a combative air in the room and that anything I said would be disclaimed and denied. So I just smiled and held out the bottle of cheap champagne I brought. 'Happy Birthday.' Was all I could say. Robyn pulled a face but got glasses from the kitchen.

There is always a point in any sort of relationship where you question the path you are on, however smooth or bumpy. The 'do I go forward or do I walk away' moment. I played both scenarios out in my head to see where they left me emotionally. It was closer than I thought but the go-forwards were more needy. In Robyn I saw something I wanted and she was the only thing in the world that I could say that about. Randy Buchanan's words still echoed in my head. 'She's a runner pal, believe me.' So I needed to approach my desire obliquely.

'We should go on holiday,' I told her, offhandedly, one day. 'Weather's warming up, city's starting to stink, we should take off for a few days.'

'I don't have money for leisure,' she shrugged, 'I spend all my spare cash on scotch and typewriter ribbons.'

'On me, I ventured.

She looked at me, trying to gauge my seriousness, 'But don't you spend all your spare cash on scotch and typewriter ribbons too?'

'I've been cutting back, surprising how the change mounts up.'

'So – if I agree,' she held up her hand, 'which I'm not doing yet, where would we go?'

'I know a guy that will let us stay in his holiday place in Merlimont-sur-mer, dirt cheap.'

'France, is that?'

'It is, just across the channel, not exactly the Riviera, but good food and wine, patios and beaches, shopping for groceries in the local market, eating snails -.

'I'll pass on the snails,' she said.

'But you'll come?'

'OK, as long as it really isn't costing you a fortune.'

'Self catering, two as cheaply as one and all that.'

'OK,' she digested the idea, 'thank you.'

She showed no apprehension at the idea of sharing my company exclusively for that many days. So far so good.

As it turned out the holiday was perfect, the weather was great. Merlimont was straight out of fifties French seaside towns scrapbook, quaint and a little down at heel, the whole town purpose built for leisure. The little house, two up two down, was in the street behind the seafront, close enough to smell the ozone from the sea and the french fries from the café on the corner. The bars played Johnny Halliday and Dalida, Joe Dassin and Sylvie Vartan, music that perfectly understood the French summer..

We drank Bordeaux wine and ate a lot of local seafood. Cooking more often than eating out, sitting at a salt scoured table in the scrubby miniscule garden area in warm candlelight, happy as moths in the glow, listening to the distant sound of the restless sea. We went to the cinema one evening, a film called 'À nous les petites Anglaises', about young people at the beach, the cinema had sand on the carpet and smelt of damp from a damaged roof, Robyn thought it was perfectly cute and we sat there eating sugared pistachios, not understanding one word of the film, but absorbed in the action and glorying in the foreignness of it all. Robyn was halfway towards a decent tan, she was relaxed, at peace with herself and sexy as hell. On the last night, I cooked a steak dinner, opened a bottle of good red wine and afterwards we took a final stroll along the seafront.

I took a deep breath. 'That all went very well don't you think?'

'A lovely holiday,' She took my arm and snuggled up, perhaps it was only to ward off the breeze off the channel, but I took heart.

'We should be together,'

'We are together.' I couldn't tell from her tone if she was puzzled or evasive – too late now.

'I mean on a proper basis. I think we could. We laugh together, we cry together, we fuck together, we share a toothbrush occasionally -sounds like a relationship to me – besides think of what you could do with the rent money. We could even get married.'

Robyn laughed, 'You.' she said searching my face for my intent, 'what are you reaching for, what are you hoping to do?'

'I don't know, exactly.' I told her, 'but I know it involves you.' She looked at me for a long time, I had clearly caught her off guard. Finally, she said. 'You know I don't deserve you, I treat you like shit and you just grin.'

'Your idea of shit is my idea of not tough.' I assured her.

She kissed me fiercely, suddenly, looking to devour or obliterate – I couldn't tell. I held her head, my hands in her hair, her hair wrapped around me in the breeze, covered our furious kiss from view. Then she smiled, a smile of the old Robyn, that American woman's smile, it had authority and sexiness in one go. 'OK. I guess it makes sense.' I was about to suggest that it wasn't the most positive response to my gallant proposal when she kissed me again, long and hard, beneath the flickering lamplight outside the Café Squale. It was one of those moments that just stays with you forever.

So the modest wedding was set, the paperwork put in order and the sandwiches made. A dozen people would descend on Islington Registry office on a Saturday; A handful of mutual friends; my mother, my sister and her husband, a couple of Robyn's poet friends, her publisher, her agent. It was summer and it was raining. The wedding time approached with no sign of Robyn, the wedding time passed, by a little, then a lot. We waited in the pouring rain for something to happen, looking down the bleak empty street, the brown facades of the houses closed against the weather. This is not a day for new beginnings, they said, this is a day for remembrance and regret. The street remained empty. Robyn did not come.

When I got home soaked and sobered, having apologized to all concerned and absorbed their pitying looks and stock consolations, I found the note on the mat 'Sorry I couldn't come or I would have ended up marrying you and what would have been the point of that. R x.'
The moment that I felt I could have argued that question was somehow gone, I had kept a little argument locked inside my head but somehow I had lost it. It was out there in those wet brown streets, out there it still meant something but it couldn't be used anymore. I called Robyn's number but there was no answer. She was on a plane by then, I found out later, heading back to the vast impersonal land of the huddled masses, of course it had failed her once before but it was indeed vast. Perhaps it harboured a place where one could be unknown and unknowing.

Robyn Adams died in 1981. She parked her Toyota on the Oakland Bridge and stepped off in to the waters of San Francisco Bay a long way below. Some papers said it was the Golden Gate Bridge but I've seen the photos and it was definitely the Oakland, people are always making that mistake.

It was funny, although I hadn't seen her for several years, her loss was still numbing, suddenly finding a hole in my life I could now never fill. Robyn had seemed, had been, such an immense presence. I had always thought it would be me that died young, too good for this world (ha, ha) and gone before my time and all that. But I'll grow old like the rest, I know that now, and I guess living on in any terms has something to be said for it, after all, but it still feels like a compromise.

CHANSONS DU NORD

Fabienne was a cafe singer from the Rue Gay-Lussac. She lived in two rooms above a chocolate shop at the point where the street flattened out and ran into the square with the Lartigue fountain. Paul met her in his early days in Paris when everything he saw still glittered with a magical chic, arriving in a fierce hot summer when the cafes had burst into the streets from behind their transient glass walls and the baking hot Metro smelled of vanilla and aniseed, he was struck by an overwhelming sense of life being lived and on a scale he had not envisaged. Here the monochrome Godardian landscapes of his formative years, those nights spent in strange London cinemas in thrall to the Nouvelle Vague, flowered in technicolour around him. Here was the life of the city, here in its active heart, he could taste, almost touch the roots of that intellectual world for which he hungered, light years away from the smug posturing of his English peers, who lived behind opaque glass and white net, where opinions were things best kept to oneself and love, sex, God, humanity or death were not acceptable subjects for after dinner conversation.

For two weeks he did nothing but walk in the streets and look. He sipped coffee, wine or beer when he was not thirsty, just so he could sit and be part of the atmosphere of the cafes and bars, or at least pretend. He brought books in yellow covers with the pages uncut. Balzac and Flaubert and Zola, with many words he did not yet understand but he was full of anticipation. His landlady, Madame Forestier, called him Monsieur Vatkin losing the 'S'. She warned him that the girls who walked the streets around the Gare St. Lazare were mostly boys and that he should not buy his meat at the Boucherie Monceau on the corner as he was a cheat. She brought him fruit almost every day from her brother, Marcel. 'It's his job,' she would say, 'you eat,' as if he were in some way undernourished. That he understood little of what went on around him was really part of the charm, but he felt everything here more keenly and he was desperate to belong.

Fabienne was in Paul's philosophy class though she would not, she assured him, be taking the exam. 'I wish to know, to

166

understand, not to prove it'. They were taking coffee on the Boulevard St. Michel while around them a lunchtime Parisien crowd talked excitedly, gesturing with forks and glasses, Waiters whizzed by with trays full

of bottles and steaming plates at alarming speed. Fabienne lit a cigarette and blew an insouciant stream of smoke at the ceiling. She had dark bobbed hair and large animate eyes that were constantly alert, constantly observing, it made her seem more than unusually alive. She had opinions on most things and was dismissive of those who did not or preferred not to air them, to him, fresh from an arid self-absorbed Wimbledon she was the most exciting woman he had ever met. Her English was much better than Paul's French and though he had asked that they talk French as much as possible she soon tired of his ability to express complexities via the language. "Nous parlons Anglais" she would say "ou je vais m'ennuyer".

They would lunch every Friday in the Cafe Maubert after classes. Paul was building up to asking her out in that formal British way he couldn't shake and it was harder than usual for him. He was so in awe of her.

'Thinking is a most important thing', she was telling him, 'It is the best thing,' she waved and blew a kiss at a man who had just come in, 'that's Jerome, he is a writer in Cafe Theatre, he is very clever, his plays have much passion,' she spoke the word passion slowly as if loathe to give it up.

Paul made a face. 'You were talking about thought.'

'Yes - it is after all, is it not, thought that has given us the best of what we have, not action', action just brings us trouble'.

'But surely without action thought has no meaning,' Paul countered, irritated by the insular nature of this idea.

'This is not so necessary, I think, to show what we have thought all the time, this is what men do, they see, they must touch, they lose, they must sulk. Thought is a pure plane where everything is possible, I love it'. Paul felt the focus of the argument shifting, falling away from him, danced away from him by the elusive thought processes of Fabienne. 'But surely' Paul, signalled for another coffee and though doubting the wisdom of being so dogged, continued, 'if the products of thought cannot be turned into reality then they cannot be of any real benefit to humanity?'

'It's not important,' she waved her hand in a dismissive way as if throwing something out, you should not think it so, it will make you dull.'

The thought of appearing dull in the eyes of Fabienne ended his resistance.

Though he would never admit it to Fabienne, Paul disliked philosophy or at least the dry stuff they taught in the seminars. If it had not been for Fabienne he would have cut them early on.

'I'd like to hear you sing,' he said, one day as they were leaving the café.

'I think you would not,' she laughed, 'they only pay me because I am pretty for them and look good, I have weak voice.'

'Still I'd' like to hear you.' Paul persisted.

She turned and looked at him, a trace of annoyance in her face, the full lips set in a line. 'I dislike this positioning or whatever, you do. If you wish to sleep with me please say so and we will do so and you can stop being nice to me and can then decide whether you like me or not'.

Paul was stuck for words.

'You come over tonight,' she said, '21 Rue Gay Lussac 8.00 then after you can decide whether you wish to hear me sing or not'.

He watched her go, she walked quickly but it remained sensuously slow in the memory. He wondered about reality.

He was waiting dutifully outside no. 26 at 8.00 on the dot, he was about to begin the climb to the 4th floor when he saw her coming down the street.

'You are on time,' there was a tinge of surprise in her voice, 'what an interesting thing. Do you like my street?' she added.

She was wearing black tights and a loose silk top, the bareness of her shoulders emphasised the length and line of her neck. Paul felt his mouth go dry at the thought of what was to come.

'It is an important street in the history of Paris you know,' she was saying, 'in '68 many battles were fought here between the police and the students and here, right here –' she stood on a spot at the edge of the pavement teetering on her heels. For a moment Paul was afraid that she would fall into the traffic.'- or somewhere nearby, anyway, was where they shot Raoul Rigault, the Communard, they were going to arrest his neighbour for no reason than he knew Rigault. Rigault came along and saw the commotion and said "It is me you look for, leave this man alone" and they pointed a pistol at him and told him to say "Long live Versailles", he shouted "Long live Revolution" and they shot him there on the spot. Robspierre was right,' she spat into the street, suddenly angry, 'you must show the rich no mercy, for they will have no mercy for you. So next time you must make sure they do not come back.'

'That's a very strange idea,' said Paul, alarmed by the violent intensity of her feeling. 'It's true though, it was win or die for these people and they knew it. This I admire, it is a shame they lost.' she kicked at a small stone and it skittered through the passing cars, 'but then you can be sure the world would be no better than it is today – still history might be less dull. We must fuck now,' she said suddenly, taking him by the hand, 'or i will be late.'

There had been a couple of girls before Fabienne, but they had been furtive - almost shameful occasions, full of anxiety and moral uncertainty, committed in the near dark in front rooms in silence lest the sleeping, trusting parents wake. The only post coital emotions they offered him were remorse and fear. With Fabienne it became a celebration, a fanfare to youth and vigour, a complexity of tastes and smells, a heightening of the sense of touch, a sudden vivid unison – all wrapped around with the tangible aroma of chocolate and vanilla that emanated from the shop below.

Afterwards, as he lay dazed, rather than exhausted in her arms, she told him 'You can go now if you wish, it's ok.'

He was hurt, 'I'm not like that - here just for that.'

'Yes, you are, You are here just for that, because I asked you here for that. I tell you to come, you came,' she giggled, 'that's a British double entendre I think.'

Paul blustered, 'but it wasn't like that, I mean –'

'It's no problem, not for me. I wanted you, you wanted me –
that's good, Now you come hear me sing, if you want to hear me
sing, otherwise you go home o.k.
'OK.' he said, 'i come hear you sing.'

She was right when she said she didn't sing too well, it was
one of those breathy, girly voices that the French have always
seemed to like(or at least are happy to tolerate when the singer is
gamine) which was odd given the full expressive and resonant
voices of their truly greats.
There was quality in what she did though, but it was as
much visual as musical. Dressed all in black, with black eye
shadow and a gash of red lipstick across her lips, the paleness of
her face was accentuated which in turn accentuated the fullness
of her features, she stood motionless except for the occasional
raising or lowering of her arms. Her songs were bleak and
simple; lost loves and faithless men, soldiers tormented by
memories of war, loneliness, despair.

The Bar itself was called the Bar Vitrine and it was situated
in one of the scruffier streets around the Place de la Republique.
It was long and thin with tables crammed into every conceivable
space. That night the air was vibrant with the energy and ideas of
a crowd, though not all young, each exuding that frission, that
bubbling excitement that came from taking much enjoyment from
their lives. After her set Fabienne came to his table, soon they
were joined by Jerome, the man she had greeted in the Café
Maubert, he was tousle haired with deep black, unfathomable
eyes rather like Fabienne's. She kissed him on both cheeks,
'Salut,' Jerome offered Paul a thick tanned fist. Paul shook it
gingerly.
They were soon joined by another two men who turned out
to be Henri and Lucien, dancers, fresh from their stint at the
Folies Bergere, glitter shone in their eyes and hair.
'I thought the Folies Bergere was all women.' Paul said,
becoming childishly irked at being slowly marginalised from
Fabienne's attention.

Henri looked at him with a resigned smile, as if this was a question he was all too used to, 'They need the men to carry them.' They all laughed at this except Paul.

The conversation flowed between art, philosophical ideas, politics at a speed that Paul's French could not fully follow; there was a discussion about the end of the Vietnam war – clearly no one at the table liked the Americans, The role that someone called Guy Debord may have had in the demise of something called, Situationist International. Whether Michel Sardou's songs were meaningful, that Truffaut's film about Adele Hugo was dull and he should stick to Parisien trifles,

Fabienne saw that Paul was lost to the conversation and feeling the outsider in the gathering was beginning to sulk undemonstratively in that curious way the English have of not really wanting to be any trouble, even when demanding attention. 'C'est trop rapide pour Paul. We speak English.' Paul felt a little embarrassed by this, especially in the way they all had no trouble at all switching to English.

The discussion moved on to Giscard D'Etaing, 'the pocket De Gaulle', as they called him.

'68 is finally over,' Jerome shook his head in disgust, 'the public didn't grow up.'

'Yes, they did, they grew up bourgeois.' Henri gave the insouciant 'what can you do' gesture.

'- and closed the door on a beautiful future.' Jerome continued, half sorrow half anger.

Fabienne would have none of it, 'Once that door is opened it can never be closed. We saw what was behind it, many did. That memory will remain and the spirit will return.'

'But when?' Jerome took a long draught of wine, as if to kill the taste in his mouth.

'Not for years. You must have patience.' Fabienne's tone suggested that they had had this conversation many times before and her patience with it was at an end.

'I can't wait for years, doing what I do, living in the old way, waiting for the better world.'

'I don't see there is a choice, Jerome,' Lucien reprised his resigned smile, 'change happens, but not in the way we had dreamed.'

'Not at all as far as I am concerned.'

'We must keep telling the story, Jerome.'

'-and if no one listens?'

'Then keep telling it until it is the only story. It is a true story, after all, we dilute it at our peril.'

'It is our tradition,' Henri put in, 'you must believe in this otherwise there is only deception and smallness.'

Jerome was adamant, 'The idea of right and left is an out of date equation – there's no tradition left to mourn.'

'You can't put it like that,' Lucien was getting angry with Jerome, 'It's a betrayal.'

'I agree,' Jerome poured another glass of wine from the carafe and filled Paul's empty glass at the same time, 'but it is I who am betrayed, as these ideals crumble, I try to recover myself and in this very movement I am lost – so.' He shrugged in a way that said "end this conversation." They did but an awkward silence descended instead.

Paul had been too young when the freedoms demanded by the youth culture had become political, he had been 14 in 1968, he had followed the protests with great interest but was in no position to join in, that said, the ideals that had been currency then had seemed self-evident and the fact that the world had not changed hugely for the better was a sobering one. Paul looked into the faces of the men round the table and he realised that they had seen this utopia first hand, had been there to walk round it, touch it and because of this they were lost, perhaps irrevocably so. Should they, as Jerome insisted, walk away? Could they even do so with the embers of that promised world still burning in their eyes?

Only Fabienne seemed immune to the bitterness, for her it seemed that life was still there to be taken and she would, in her way, of that he had no doubt.

Paul hadn't expected to be going home with Fabienne but it hadn't occurred to him that she might be going home with someone else. When she rose to leave, Jerome pointedly rose too. Paul shot Fabienne a disappointed look of which she took no notice.

After their departure, Henri and Lucien stayed on for about half an hour, then left, thanking Paul for his company and his English perspective, whatever that had been.

Paul stayed on, Henri had bought another bottle of Gros Rouge but had hardly drunk any. Paul decided to finish it whilst ruminating on the bittersweet nature of things, maudlin and warmed by turns as the moods rushed through him and the wine did its work.

Paul not a lightweight drinker, his early student years had confirmed that but that was beer – the vinegary red wine was another matter and in the small dark hours of the night he found he was very drunk indeed.

By the time he found his way back to the Place Republique his sight had narrowed and his step unsteady. He felt ragingly cheerful though, as if some secret of life had been revealed to him, though what it might have been he couldn't imagine.

He managed to identify the Rue de Turbigo and began his journey homewards.

The city was eerily quiet, though the streetlights still floodlit the scene, everything was still and empty, as if he had blundered onto a stage where the play had finished and the audience gone home. Paul stumbled along until he came to a broad avenue he knew to be the Boulevard Sebastopol, he knew he could follow that, cross the river and be home, but he was running on instinct now, he focused as best he could and weaved on.

As he crossed the Rue de Rivioli at Chatalet, he came upon the figure of a man lying on the pavement. The man was clutching his chest and Paul thought he might have been stabbed, bending down as best he could, he moved the man's hands – no wound, no blood. The man began snoring loudly. Paul stood up and as he did so he noticed another figure then another all along the pavement and he realised that these were homeless men lying on the metro gratings for the warmth they exuded. Paul began laughing to himself as he made his way towards the Pont au Change.

What happened after that he had no memory of once he awoke, fully clothed, in his bed. A feeling of nausea hit him as he tried to move so he stopped trying.

Eventually the pain in his head, the dryness of his mouth and the need to urinate forced him to take on the dizziness. Four glasses of water and a shower later he could almost face the day, waving away his landlady's attempts at getting him to eat but glad for her coffee, he made his way to the lecture hall and sat slumped at the back, early but needing to avoid the spinning that occurred whenever he passed through bustling spaces.

Fabienne came in looking fresh and alert, 'You look like shit,' she told him.

'I feel like shit,' he assured her.

'Good night?' she grinned.

'Thought I might ask you the same thing,' Paul immediately wished he hadn't.

Fabienne frowned, 'You are jealous, of course, I should have known, little boys like to own.'

Paul was in no state to argue. 'Give me a chance, Fabienne, I only grew up yesterday, I'm still getting used to adulthood.'

Paul could see that this reply amused her. She took his head in both hands and whispered in his ear, 'We fucked Paul, we can fuck again if you want but not if you want me to be your girlfriend. I'm not that woman.' Then she went and sat near the front of the hall.

Paul remained where he was with his nausea and his disappointment. He knew he had a lot to learn about life, love and the changing ways of women. He knew he wasn't a misogynist – he admired women and never blamed them for the emotional chaos they left him in – it was, after all, his chaos, not theirs. Nonetheless he found it hard to shake the idea of relationships, of being with one person and sharing and growing. Pleasure was all very well but – still - if this was the world now, perhaps he could find an equilibrium.

For the next few days Paul wrapped himself in his dreams of love and angst, he read Rimbaud and Apollinaire, Prevert with his sense of loss like a ghost in every poem, Baudelaire's paeans to the body of Jeanne Duval. To say Paul suffered exquisitely would not be quite correct but indulgently certainly. He was at an age when he felt emotional about the world and was already sensing that life would not deal him the full deck he craved, later he would learn to take things less personally, but for now...

On the Saturday Fabienne took him up to the Butte Chaumont, the rocky park that sprang from the slums of Belleville. There in the long grass beside the lake she let him caress her small breasts beneath her blue linen smock and on a quiet bench among the winding paths, lift the smock and kiss them, she toyed with his hair as he did so, in a strange way he liked that best. Afterward they went to the nearby Pere Lachaise cemetery and looked at all the most famous graves; Wilde, Piaf, Morrison, Victor Noir with his much rubbed groin 'for luck'. Paul sought out de Balzac, Proust, De Musset and Moliere, Fabienne, Colette, Modigliani, Apollinaire and the 'Mur de Federes' where the 1870 communards had been massacred. 'That's us,' she said, 'Only they don't use bullets anymore, they just take our dignity.'

Back in her apartment she made ferocious love to him with tears in her eyes. Paul, enervated and terrified by turns, concentrated in performing for her until she was ready. When she finally came she collapsed on him panting, then smiling at him, breathed, 'Tu es gentil.'

For a few weeks they saw each other regularly, always at Fabienne's choosing, Paul was still uneasy about 'living in the moment', it sounded modern and sensible in context of the new faster society that was forming around him, but it still felt too light, too empty to sustain a life. He would roll with it for now, if he wanted Fabienne he had no choice.

They would watch films in the tiny cinemas on the Grand Boulevards, cinemas that when you entered you felt you were walking back into the 1930s, art deco cornices and brown wood walls, complete with usherette/bonbon sellers with pillbox hats and frou-frou skirts. On Sundays they would go to the flea market below the Periphique at Saint Ouen, where Fabienne would buy retro clothing and Paul old novels and posters. Fabienne would pose in her new acquisitions on the metro going home, like Anna Karina in Pierrot le Fou.

Towards the end of October the weather turned, rain set in and brought gloom to the grey slate rooves and a slick, greasy shine to the wide boulevards. They bought hot dogs from the stand outside the Sacre-Coeur, the baguettes toasted on long metal spikes, the dubious flavour of the sausage smeared over with ketchup and yellow mustard. Sitting in the garden at the entrance to the funicular, Fabienne contemplated the low, grimy clouds that reached across Paris and talked about going South for the winter.

'Like a bird,' Paul amused, despite the alarm he felt.

'Don't joke,' Fabienne returned, 'I hate the winter.'

'Comes every year.'

'And so does my hate.'

'Where will you go?' Paul was imagining she went through this passage of discontent every year, but then she said, 'Jerome is going, he's had enough of Paris too he's got himself a place in Bandol. I'll go with him.'

'What about your studies?' Paul suddenly found he was staring into the abyss.

'They mean nothing, I told you that, I was just bored during the day.'

'So you'll waste all that work.'

'It wasn't a waste, I met you.'

Paul ignored this, 'What will you live on?'

'A guy came into the Bar Vitrine a while back, he runs a club in Cannes and he offered me a 6 month contract – a perfect antidote to horrible winter, don't you think?'

'Do you trust him?'

'I don't have to trust him, i have a contract.'

'You know what I mean.'

'Oh that, so what, what's so terrible about that?'

Paul felt anger rising but held it in, Fabienne's insouciance was her own defence mechanism, he knew that, to attack it only inflamed it. She would go, he would lose her – the little piece of her that he had – that toe hold on that mountainside in a high endless wind.

'When are you going?' He said, trying to keep emotion from his voice.

'My train's next Friday.'

176

Paul looked down into the dregs of his empty coffee cup then back to Fabienne.

'Us' was all he could say.Fabienne put her hands over his in a conciliatory gesture, 'There is no us, only you and me. You once called our relationship Idyllic, the meaning of this word I have discovered is for a happy situation that is unsustainable, so you were right – though I don't think you meant to be. It is unfortunate that as humans we are unable to contemplate the idyllic for very long before it ceases to become idyllic. It is too bitter to be an irony, too tragic. What manifest lives of peace might we lead if

we could take our pleasures as we find them - but no - there is a qualification - always. Paul could see that Fabienne took comfort in this thought. Why not? It excused her completely.'

'I don't agree, we could grow together, understand each other better.'

'Do you want to understand me Paul, or do you want to put me in a cage where I will be safe for you? I can assure you my plumage will fade in such a situation far quicker than it will fade anyway.'

'I love you.'

'Of course you do, I would be upset if you didn't, but your love doesn't change anything. You say I'm leaving you, but in six months' time your year will be over and then you will be leaving me.'

'I could stay.'

'Don't be stupid.'

'or you could come to England.'

'Even worse.'

Paul knew she was forcing him to realise the underbelly of fraud that ran through his emotions. He didn't like it. He wanted to get up and go, wind his way down the Square Willet to the metro and try not to cry but the thought of no seeing her again froze him. They sat in silence for a while till it became uncomfortable.

'Can I see you once more before you go?' he asked.

'Meet me Wednesday at the Café du Nord, Two o'clock.' Then she rose and left. Paul let her go, her tone had been final. His legs felt suddenly weak. The clouds pushed lower over

Montmartre – the heavens were collapsing in a riot of black and grey.

Paul met Fabienne in the café by the Saint Martin canal. It was a strangely mild day for late October, an irony not lost on Paul and it was warm enough to sit outside on the terrasse beside one of the iron footbridges.

'This canal was once an artery of Paris, now it is just for the ducks and the tourists.' Fabienne wore a long coat with a fur hood, for her the day was clearly not mild.

'Will you come back to Paris – when the winter is over?'

'Who knows, Paris is becoming ugly, a little fantasy for the almost rich. The poor people are being driven out of the centre and they take with them the true flavour of the city. It will look pretty, cleaner, sanitized but its soul will have fled – I'm not sure I can belong there in that Paris.'

'So I won't see you again?'

'No, you will have new adventures and new girls. Please tell me you will have new girls. Don't pine over the me you thought you knew.'

'Perhaps, but I'll never forget you.'

'I should hope not,'

Paul had told himself that he would not go to see her off but as the day came he found himself full of self-sorrow standing on the platform of the Gare de Lyon beside her. He looked at her, hoping it would not be the last time, but knowing somehow that it would certainly be; her black hair growing longer now, her neck long, her lips wide, her eyes full and enchanting - was that a little water he saw in them? - Perhaps not, it was after all a very windy day.

'I do not like to say goodbye,' she told him, 'it is cruel, it is too sad - but life is this, so I go.' she kissed him briefly on the mouth and drifted swiftly into a gap in the busy throng that swarmed the platform. He stared at the gap incredulously looking for some final glimpse of her or a part of her amongst the welter of heads and shoulders, but there was none.

SANDERS OF THE RIVER LEA

It happened the summer it never rained.

A lot of things happened that summer, but some you remember better than others. My old man had a theory that that summer was to blame for everything, but then the old man spent his life finding culprits everywhere.

It's the 'eat,' he said rolling a thin emaciated cigarette, 'we'll all go loopy if it carries on, like in Sanders of the river,' he tapped the forlorn cigarette on his tobacco tin, losing some of the meagre contents.

'That was the drums,' I said, 'the drums that sent them loopy.'

'The drums meant 'eat,' he asserted leaning back, his thumbs tucked in his braces, 'they were whatsit-bolic.'

'Symbolic.'

'Yeah, that's it symbolic, the drums were symbolic of the 'eat that drove em all crazy.'

'It only sent the white blokes loopy,' I said, 'it was only the white blokes.'

He went quiet then but I knew it would only be a matter of time before he found something else to say on the subject so I went out into the yard. It was small our yard, really small, really just something to keep the backs of the houses from touching, just a bricked round concrete square with a little bit of earth in the corner. That was the old lady's vegetable patch which looked even more glum than usual. I'd helped her dig it for victory back in 1942.

'Good job they weren't relying on us,' I said, when the first year yielded three small carrots and six potatoes. 'It's not the food,' she'd told me, 'it's patriotism.'

Well the cat dug up the carrots when it tried to bury its crap so I started calling it the Nazi. My mate Joe said it should be hung and would have done it too except that he knew what my old lady would do to him if she found out, so he laid off but I could tell he was tempted. Anyway, as you know, the war ended but the vegetables somehow survived, never getting any better never getting any worse. but it looked like this summer would do it.

Can't say I'd miss it, she only keeps it out of habit, I'm sure and it's not doing her back any good all that bending.

The sun was very hot and the yard trapped it and made it hotter, it bounced around the concrete and evaporated the air. I wondered if it would be cooler by the river. It was but a short scamper along the back wall that ran between the houses, taking care to avoid the rusty wire netting at the backs of the rabbit hutches and pigeon runs, then across the grass strewn rubble that had once been no 23, over the road and up the wood yard gates. The gates were high but full of foot and handholds. I dropped to the wood yard floor and climbed the slope of timbers that rose almost to the jetty side and looked out over the River Lea. The Lea is a hidden River it curves for six miles like this behind high walls and warehouse gates, threading through gasworks and refineries past rusting barges and peeling factories, spawning cranes and dock basins all decrepit, all in some stage of decay.

A secret river, dirty and dark.

I sat on top of the rough pine boards, the smell of resin was strong but there was at least a faint breeze, just enough to make it bearable. It was Sunday and school began again tomorrow another pointless week ahead where the teachers told you what they did in the war and why we should be grateful that they did it and why we should be exasperated that we hadn't been there. I stared down at the water a silver flecked film drifted across the muddy soup. At the edges, the low tide had exposed the cloying quicksand mud and the rotting timbers of the wharf, I shivered. It was horrible down there, if you fell in and swallowed any of it then you were dead he'd heard unless they pumped your stomach within an hour or so, that's if you didn't get stuck in the mud beneath the water. People had fallen in there and never been seen again his old man had told him, he could believe it. They found Leroy though, though in his way he also disappeared for ever, it's all how you look at things.

In the beginning there were the four of us; me, Joe, Powellsy and Sullivan, we'd sort of grown up together during the war and we thought we were pretty tough, we all lived in Ettrick

Street down by the docks. Now Ettrick Street had its own wartime kudos being the first street left standing between there and the East India Dock wall come VE day. Where once we had looked out on the houses of Aberfeldy, Bonner, Culloden and Dee streets (alphabetic and scotch see) there was nothing - just us and half a mile of rubble. We were the great survivors and we swaggered through the debris. The ruins that determined our status became our playground. The fragile shells of burnt out houses became castles, pirate ships, beachheads and then once a concerned, harassed council had bulldozed them flat, we uncovered the cellars and coal bunkers and they became blockhouses, caves, dungeons. We fought in the debris together and apart, makeshift guns carved from the side of orange crates, Indian trails already forged in the new grown foliage. As time went by we grew another layer, Frostie, Bal, Dave and 'Jo-ugly' Johanssen. Jo-ugly was asthmatic and often got sick while we played. This made us laugh cause we were tough and we laughed at everything.

Then there was Leroy.

Leroy was the only black person we had ever seen. He didn't seem to belong anywhere. He didn't go to our school and he didn't live down our street, he just wandered up one day while we were playing on the debris and joined in the game. We were a bit taken aback by this cheek perhaps that's why we let him join - if he'd just asked we'd have said no for sure. We never invited Leroy to play ever but if he turned up and joined in we continued to let him though we never talked to him much and he didn't' talk to us either.

As the summer got hotter and longer arguments would break out sooner go on longer, boredom would come quicker, sometimes we'd just sit in the street and stare. Nobody knew quite what to do and to make it worse our parents became morose too, so there was no escape from the bad moods. I began to wonder if it would ever rain again. My old man was in his element with predictions of doom and disaster, he was at his happiest when the order of things was threatened and he could pontificate on the possible consequences but that's the irritating thing about pessimists, they are always proved right , sooner or later.

We were playing cricket outside the bus garage, chalk stumps on the brick wall, freak bounces off the cobblestones were no excuse, balls hit over the wall into the factory yard were 6 and out even if you climbed the fence and got the ball back. Leroy had arrived late and demanded an innings. Joe made him wait until last. Leroy fumed at the ineptitude of our bowling clattering the metal doors of the bus garage with the flat of his hand every time the tennis ball missed the chalk. Joe shot him one of his looks from time to time, the sort of looks he had given our cat, Finally Leroy's turn came and we all resigned ourselves to a long innings. The best we could hope for was that he got carried away and clouted it over the factory yard. We didn't understand what made Leroy so good at cricket, what made his motions so fluid and deceptive but we all knew it annoyed us a lot. I was bowling, I remember thinking, I might as well try a cobblestone bouncer, try for some wicked deflection to bowl it straight would be tantamount to slinging it straight down the road myself. I took a wide line to the left, the ball bounced about two feet to the side of Leroy and took the hoped for but undreamed of edge and arced behind Leroy brushing swiftly but discernibly along the chalk bails. 'Out!' yelled Joe triumphantly, 'out first ball.' 'You fuck,' said Leroy, 'no way.' 'Out no trouble,' said Joe, 'bye bye Leroy.' Leroy stood and stared at us, his nostrils flared, the gaggle of white boys closed in. 'C'mon Leroy, you're out.' said Bill, 'Out! Out! Out!' yelled Frostie. 'Out! Out! Out!' they began to chant. It was my turn to bat next, I walked up and held my hand out for the bat. Leroy held it to his body unwilling to cede but unsure what to do next. 'Give it to him Nigger.' said Joe fiercely, the bat swung suddenly and caught me just below my left ear. Stars were followed quickly by cobble stones. As I lay there in the dust I heard the scuffle break out behind me, Leroy was surrounded by a thrashing, enraged mob, he lashed out with the bat but for the second time that day only hit thin air. Joe moved underneath the lunge and smashed him back against the wall, just as he was about to disappear beneath the mob he pushed himself clear with the strength of the terrified and ran. They gave chase but of course had no hope of catching him. Joe was back in a few minutes,

'You all right?' he said.

182

'Yeah I think so.' I rubbed the side of my head gingerly, no blood, just a swelling.

'I almost got him – I'll get him the next time.'

'Let it go,' I said, 'he's just a loopy kid.'

'No way. I'm not'aving snot noses like him bashing my mates.'

The others trailed back, 'what a bastard, said 'Powsy', Sullivan shook his head angrily. 'He's dangerous using cricket bats, he's a coward.

'We'll make him pay you see,' said Joe.

'I'm not playing with 'im again said Frosty that'll show 'im.' 'I'll get 'im,' said Joe. They stood around for a while uttering threats and reliving the incident and each ones part in it 'i got im a good one in the ribs,' 'caught im wiv me bat,' 'kicked 'is arse.' the truth of which debatable from the outset grew taller and taller with each new telling. Then we picked up the bat and ball and went home. It was time for tea.

July ran into August and the endless schooless days began, we wandered the back streets of Poplar, up and down the piles of rubble in and out of the ruined houses looking for adventure, treasure, danger. We risked life and limb amongst the shifting, groaning 2nd floor timbers of the shattered terraces on Dock road, kicked up the dust from the fallen plaster, lurked by the river's edge to watch the barges cleave the silt brown water and send it curving towards us till it hit the concrete wall with a flat wet slap. Our unity began to buckle as the days passed. In the middle of August, Frosty announced that he was moving to Ilford with his mum and dad. Two days later he was gone leaving us his collection of old pram wheels and a bemused smile. The weather threatened rain but delivered none - just humidity and hope. I closed my eyes and waited for autumn to come in the same way that you wait to get old.

We were in the derelict water tank outside the school running up and down the diagonal concrete sides, Powsy has a skate on which we sat upon and slid grittily painfully to the bottom. getting both feet on a single skate was a problem but the sense of movement was worth it.

Then I saw Leroy - a faint figure on the debris above the water tank. I hoped the others would not see him but Sullivan yelled, 'Leroy; up on the tip.' In an instant there were four of them running up the side of the tank. Leroy saw them at last and ran. I ran too confused and running into the street all noise and clatter between the slow moving trolley buses. Leroy would have got away again but for a bit of bad luck, round the corner into Leven road leading the pack by a healthy 80 yards he ran smack into Bill, and Jo-ugly's brother David. There was nowhere to go but over the wood yard gate, so over he went but then the really was nowhere else to go. I reached the top of the gate just in time for a last glimpse of Leroy scared but defiant atop the timber planks, a club of wood in his hand, all instinct and nerves ready to fight or run, ready to survive. I don't know who threw the rock but my money was on Joe. Leroy saw it coming and ducked but the movement loosened the top plank.He wavered for a moment then disappeared soundlessly over the edge. The river was running full, out to the mouldy Thames, we rushed to the edge but there was no sign, not even bubbles. The man in the bus station called the police. We sat and watched the boats search. The police talked to us all - we all said it was an accident. There was nothing else to say really.

They found him after four days out near Tilbury - if he hadn't got caught on one of the ocean going barges he'd gone all the way out to sea they said, The gang broke up after that. It would have done in a few months anyway, once we'd left school. I see one or two of them around but we just nod I can't say we are really friends any more.

Oh yes I did rain.
Last day of September 1947
Too late for Leroy though.
Too late for us all really.

THERESE

Hope is not a thing to give a body lightly. It is more dangerous than any weapon man has ever made. It makes the down-trodden surly, the gentle vicious, the placid angry. For hope always carries such intimations of sweetness, such visions of happiness that the simple touch of it upon our hearts will reawaken the torment we had forced ourselves to forget. For once hope has arrived, once the damned little ferret is out of the bag, he'll not go back in. Now, either we'll succeed or we'll spend our remaining days in rancour and despair, wishing only for death.

Those who hate us for the fear we have created, this new fear, this fear which has been hiding in their worst nightmares for so long will of course take care to judge us badly. Perhaps on another day, at another time, I might agree, for our actions must resemble the frothy ravings of madmen and madwomen but they have not seen, not felt what we have felt and cannot tell the truth of what we are and how we became so.

In truth I am myself on occasion tired with these days of blood, of the baying constancy of the faithful, as they cheer each death to the echo. No I am not blind to it. I see the faces of the innocent and the brave fall beneath the same blade, the same gore spattered edge that dispatches those greedy fools.
Justice would be welcome but justice is too difficult for the poor to achieve, too difficult to understand and justice takes too long. Revenge will have to do.

Defarge is a good man but a man who needs constantly watching. He knows what his duty is but like all men will drift from his purpose if there's good tobacco, good wine or good conversation to be had, but no worry, I'll not let him forget - for I don't forget - not for a moment.

These days the streets around the shop are never quiet. St. Antoine throbs with the dizzy passion of freedom. Long-term prisoners are said to grow quite faint when brought into the

185

sound and light of the world outside their cells. Imagine then these poor souls whose prison has been their lives and the lives of all those gone before them. Imagine how the colour must blind. How the aroma must overwhelm.

It's good for business, that's for sure. The shop has never been busier. Thirsty work revolution, it's not just the gullet that's in need of succor, the head dries out from all the thoughts that assail it, the spirit flags at the thought of all still to be done.

At least the waiting is finally over. It was the waiting that took its toll. Each day smiling to the spies and rogues, watching their clammy coins clatter on the counter. Smiling, smiling, letting the forward one's hands linger at my waist, like some slutty barmaid might. Smiling and pouring. No dissent here kind gentlemen, it's just a wine shop see. We are business people too. Devout supporters of the King. God bless him. All the while waiting, their names knitted into the roll. The roll of dishonor, the roll of death.
Waiting.

Defarge wants to help Manette. Like a good faithful dog he binds to his master though there are to be no masters anymore. His mind is sharp, his spirit strong but his soul hasn't understood. If it's left to people like him we will fail. This is no time for sentiment. No time to cling to things once held dear. No time for mercy.
D'Evremonde's nephew is at the Conciergerie at last! No way back from there. I am overcome with the sudden desire to dance.
When I was younger I'd love to dance, with my thin waist and my gypsy hair I'd make the men dream. Wild hair, wild steps. I'd dance barefoot at the summer fairs, twined up with flowers, flowing like wine. Sweet days. They seem like some far dream, too happy to be true; sunlit meadows, long, empty beaches where love would surely find me - given time.
My sister Rosa loved to dance too. I taught her all the steps I knew and as she grew so her beauty grew until she was as beautiful as any princess. More beautiful, for her humble state

186

tempered a kindness and modesty that the pasty faced fine ladies from the chateaux could not manage for all their breeding.

Too beautiful for life or so they said, those who would have resignation as our only comfort, the priests and prefects, defenders of a violated faith.

They saw the D'Evremonde as stones, as gods. Immutable. That which must be endured, like heat and cold, hunger and thirst. I saw only men, vain, weak, feeble, protected by a single idea, a clever trick of the mind. My family destroyed to feed their boredom, squashed as one might a bug that wanders idly past your foot. I learned that much from them. You never let the bug go. That is the secret of power. You don't have to raise your foo, but you do. Always.

They left the bodies in a ditch, Rosa, my brother Mathieu. Like dogs knocked off the highway by a careless carriage. Mathieu, a terrible wound in his chest, the blood fled from his face, clotted sticky in his savaged gut. Rosa unmarked as if asleep, a little bruise upon her cheek, a little marsh grass in her hair.

Asleep.

All the goodness she had to give snuffed out because it had dared to shine in a place where such a light was not expected. That light was not theirs to take but they took it anyway, because they could, because there was no-one who could stop them.

Well, now they are well stopped and my only regret is that I cannot bring them back to life so that I might kill them again, over and over. For to die once is no fair recompense for all they have done - to us all, to our past, to our future.

So I'll finish with Lucie Manette and her little D'Evremonde brat. Then their line will cease at long last, as it must if the hopes for our future are ever to be realised. Vengeance has its own rules, its own hunger. I'll not come up short in my purpose. The pistol is heavy at my breast like a little one squirming for a teat, the dagger at my thigh, steel to my design.

Before d'Evremonde bows to Madame Guillotine, he'll see his daughter's pretty blonde curls one last time, cut from her head beneath the chin. Then I'll watch in his eyes the despair I know so well. How deep. How deep that hurt can pierce, beyond the pains that wrack the flesh, beyond the death that awaits us all. Then his sorrow, like mine, will be complete.

Tell the wind and fire where to stop.
But don't tell me.
Don't tell me.

A SMALL VALLEY IN THE FOREST

Bert Morris stepped slowly down off the coach and surveyed the little square. Right away he recognised the baker's and the bar. A further glance and there too were the town hall and the chemist's. It was all eerily similar, so unlike his own home town which had been by-passed and Arndaled and Tesco-ed out of all recognition, here was Lavallois-sur-Foret almost as he had left it fifty years before. As he shuffled round to the back of the coach with the rest of his comrades to get his case, the band struck up and made him jump. 'Bloody trumpets,' he muttered under his breath. The driver handed him the suitcase but it was immediately taken out of his hand by a smiling young woman in a green dress.

'Here miss, that's my bag,' Bert protested.

She carried on smiling. 'I am Nicole, I am to help you while you are here'.

Bert put his hand on the bag. 'I don't need a woman to carry me bag, I ain't got to dribblin and droolin yet'.

'But it must be so heavy,' the woman continued in good English.

'I carry me own bag,' said Bert 'always have and the day I can't,' he paused contemplating the unlikelihood 'well I won't bloody go anywhere'.

The woman shook her head unoffended. 'Ok Monsieur Morris, if that is your wish'.

Bert was startled that she knew his name then remembered the badge they'd made him put on on the coach. 'It'll help you get settled that much quicker', the man with the clipboard had told him when Bert had complained that it made him feel like a bloody evacuee. He'd meant to take it off but had forgotten.

'You will be staying with me', the woman was saying, 'you and a Mr. L. Williams'. She looked back into the milling crowd of old soldiers. 'Which one is he, do you know ?'.

'He's the Welsh one' replied Bert, 'spot him a mile off, the one with sheep's wool caught in his fly'. Bert spluttered a raucous, coughing laugh. The woman looked at him uncomprehendingly. 'Welsh see?' said Bert, spluttering again. The woman clearly remained unenlightened. After some searching through the drifting and milling soldiers in the square (by then another three coaches had arrived and disgorged their loads of bereted, bemedalled old men) they found Taffy Williams. Bert was pleased to see that time had been no kinder to Taffy than it had to him. Bespectacled toothless old fool, Bert chuckled. Age had bowed the dashing young Welsh Tank Driver who had shagged his way across half of France before the clap had laid him low on the edge of the Ardennes forest. 'I'll bet he can't even unbutton his trousers now', Bert thought, 'daft old sod'. Taffy came up and held out his hand which Bert shook diffidently. 'Lo Bert you're still a miserable old git I bet', Taffy said, by way of greeting. 'I'll bet you've not stopped moaning these last 50 years. Glad I wasn't there old lad, I would've fucking shot you'. Taffy chuckled. Bert scowled at him. The woman put their cases in the boot of her car and invited them to get in. 'We got ourselves a looker, eh boy', Taffy whispered to Bert. Bert looked at the woman again. She was a redhead, with deep green eyes almost the colour of her dress, slim and nearly as tall as Bert in her heels. Bert grunted and made a face.

Taffy got in the front. Bert saw him looking at her legs as she drove. 'Old bastard,' he chuckled, 'he'll never give up'.

'You been back here since '44 then' Taffy was asking him. 'No' Bert told him 'I never saw the point'.

'I was here in 69' Taffy waved out the window at a couple of old men sitting on a bench, 'Johnson that was and Hewson'. Bert didn't remember them, 'Yes, I was here for the 25th and again in 84 for the 40th, but this is the big one, eh boy, half a bloody century, don't seem possible.'

'Seems like longer', Bert muttered, 'seems like for bleedin ever'.

'So why you here now then', Taffy asked him 'if you don't like it so much'.

'I wouldn't have come this time', Bert grunted, 'didn't want to at all, but my daughter bought me the trip, thought it would be a nice surprise, daft cow. Still I wasn't going to let her waste all that money'.

'Well it's good to see some of those old faces again, even yours', Taffy continued, 'Jesus, so long ago now. Doesn't it bring a lump to your throat ?'
'It does' Bert retorted 'it's called phlegm'.

They drove for a few minutes in silence then, past rows of tiny artisan houses, now mostly derelict, that led to the edge of the town. To break the uneasiness that had crept into the silence, the woman introduced herself again. 'I am Nicole Haudepin' she said, in her almost accent free English, 'I will be your host and guide for the three days you are here. There will be much happening during this time and a chance to visit old places and meet old friends. Tonight you are our guests for dinner and in the town tomorrow there will be a celebration lunch at the Hotel de Ville. Some of the people who were in the FFI at the time will be there to meet with you and remember'. 'Oh' Bert was suddenly paying attention, 'who exactly ?' 'Oh, lets see', Nicole wrinkled her brow, 'Armand Metier and Louis Delbrand, Helene Lascelles and of course my grandmother Lucie Marielle. Do you know any of them?' she asked.
Bert looked out the window. They were driving up the Caen road along the edge of the Bois d'Lavaillois, A group of picnickers had set up their tables in the clearing where Bert, Captain Loring and Louis Delbrand had once machine gunned a Wermacht major and his driver to death. Bert still remembered the look on the driver's face, his eyes writhing in his head like two frightened animals trying to escape from a cage. 'Yes I know them all', he told her, 'Lucie, so she's your granma eh', he mused, 'yes I can see it now, you've got her eyes and that smile'. 'Lucie,' said Taffy suddenly 'wasn't that - ow'. Bert had slumped forward suddenly and elbowed Taffy in the back of the neck. 'Oh sorry mate, lost me balance' Bert apologised. Taffy, old soldier that he was, got the message.
The Marielle farm looked so much the same that it made the hair prickle on the back of Bert's neck. 'Lucie is here?', he asked quietly. 'Oh no', Nicole informed him, 'she lives in Rouen now, has done for many years but she'll be here tomorrow.' Nicole showed Taffy and Bert to their rooms. Bert's room had been grand'mere Marielle's. The room was much less gloomy

than he remembered, possibly because the thick yellow-brown wallpaper had been replaced with whitewash but he recognised the bed, a huge heavy dark wood affair that had belonged to Lucie's parents. Bert went to the window and looked out, the June day was drawing to a close, the sun had fallen behind the high woods and they looked like they were cut from black paper, a child's idea of woods, full of gloom and witches and goblins and dark, dark secrets.

The dinner table was full of food and surrounded by beaming Frenchmen who didn't understand a word of English. Bert found his French which he hadn't used for fifty years coming back slowly, Words for butter and sausage, polite little civilities, apres-vous, ca va, stuff like that. He still couldn't understand half what they said though and he knew that Taffy didn't either. but he worked out that the swarthy man at the head of the table was Nicole's husband Lionel and the other three were Lionel's two younger brothers and Nicole's brother Luc. All of whom worked the farm. Lots of nodding and smiling and raising of glasses went on and Bert was feeling quite tiddly before they'd even got to the main course. 'Did you know my grandmother well' Nicole asked Bert. Taffy spluttered in his soup. 'We worked together' Bert explained ignoring him. 'I was here ahead of his lot,' he gestured at Taffy who was mopping his chin, 'parachuted in. By the time they got here it was mostly over'.
'Oh you were with the special force', Nicole nodded, 'how interesting. Grandmother has spoken of them. 'Cormorant and Puffin,' she paused thinking '-- Shearwater and Gannet'.
'Ay, you was well named boy,' said Taffy – 'Gannet'.
'You are -- were Gannet, how interesting. Then you must know this farm well, she beamed, 'how perfect for you to stay here now'.
'Yes' said Bert scowling at Taffy over his last remark. 'I spent quite a bit of time here, back then'. He wondered how much she knew, how much Lucie had told her, wondered what had happened since. 'So do you still own all the land around here that you did then.' he asked. 'It was quite a lot then I remember, quite a spread.

192

'No', Nicole pouted apologetically 'some of it we sold off for houses when the town expanded back in the 70's.'

'Not up on the forest edge, was it?' Bert's knuckles were white where they gripped the edge of the table.

'No, no, Nicole assured him, alarmed by his concern, 'that's not good land for houses, no the bit down by the river'.

'You know' said Taffy 'I never had you down as a conservationist Bert'.

'Comes to us all in time'. Bert nodded, sitting back down> 'We all gets mellow'.

Taffy nodded in agreement and raised his glass solemnly, 'too true'. He peered at Bert through his bifocals. 'You all right, Bert you're sweating a bit'.

'It's the soup' said Bert 'too bloody hot'.

After the meal Bert went for a walk in the farmyard. He'd eaten and drunk far too much and he knew he would pay for it with a restless night but he'd enjoyed himself nonetheless, though he wouldn't be admitting it. The moon was full and the cobbled courtyard was bathed in a bright blue light that reminded him of another June. Where in the deep shadows by the barn he had first kissed Lucie Marielle. The taste of her lips came back to him quite suddenly, vividly, and he turned half expecting her to be there, giggling and shush-ing him, placing her finger on his lips, leading him further into the shadows.

'Sod it', said Bert to the French night sky, 'bloody sod it'.

The band, for the French never seemed to do anything vaguely official without a band, sat at one end of the Salle de Fete in their smart red and blue uniforms and welcomed them in with fat, warm, slightly discordant renditions of 'Colonel Bogey,' 'The white cliffs of Dover' and inexplicably 'Congratulations'.

They stood and looked at each other, the old soldiers, stood and looked at what time had made of them all. Hands were shaken and backs slapped as they bustled from one half reminiscence to another. Very little was asked about the intervening years about work or families, homes or gardens. The war had been the moment of supreme significance in their life though of course they had not known that then.

Bert stood in a group that contained Taffy, Johnson and Hewson, someone had given him a glass of red wine and he was nodding at whatever it was that Johnson was saying but his mind was elsewhere and he was wishing he hadn't come, not just to the do but to France. The little knot of fear and shame was working away inside him, like a tumour that had been dormant for years, suddenly once more malignant.

The French contingent arrived about 1.00. Bert recognised Lucie at once, she was as lovely and elegant as ever but now without colour - her red hair, stark white and her rosy cheeks pale. He wished that he had been there to see the young girl grow to fullness. He felt a tear prickling away behind his lid. He snorted it away and strode forward. She spoke before he could reach her, something in her voice made him falter.

'Albert, it is you yes, now you come back eh'. Her mouth was smiling but her eyes were not.

Bert shrugged his shoulders like an errant schoolboy four feet away 'Life' was all he could say,

'Yes I know about life, Albert. It is you that I do not know'. Bert made a face and shifted his feet. 'Things happen', he looked for more words, 'things you can't imagine, that change things'. 'Like English girls no doubt.' Lucie kissed the cheeks of a couple of men in greeting but kept her eyes on Bert.

'If you wish' Bert held out his hand and led her to a seat. She let him without further comment, her hand was bony and thin but the skin still felt smooth.

Colonel Waterson as tall and as straight as ever was at their table, he stood up and held out a large leathery hand. 'Hello Morris good turn-out what, glad you could come'. He bowed to Lucie. 'I like to keep a handle on the chaps, how they're doing and all that'. The Colonel spoke as if they were still all under his care, a battalion of men to be organised and looked after for life. 'Smithson's dead, you know, cancer and Welch died way back in 74 -- a car crash and Captain Loring and Major Peters, all gone now.' He spoke with an air of bewilderment as if with the end of war the toll of lives should somehow have ceased. Lucie smiled at him kindly 'It is the same with us M'sur,

194

Rene Duchamp and Phillipe Suboise are no more and Pascal Roget he lives in America now so he might as well be dead'. The Colonel chuckled, Lucie smiled again.

'What about that chap Jean Foucart?' the Colonel enquired. 'He was very big with your lot wasn't he? What happened to him?'

Armand Metier, who was sitting nearby, shrugged 'He disappears at the end of the war, about the time you moved on towards Belgium, in fact. Some say the Boches got him, some say the Americans took him and set him up in some CIA thing. Louis Delbrand swears he saw him in Algeria in '62".

'Oh that would be just like Foucart', the Colonel agreed. 'I never knew a man with such a love of secrets. What about that, Morris, just disappeared! Did you ever see him, Morris, after that?'

'I think they're about to serve the food' Bert replied 'and the mayor's going to speak'.

The mayor spoke of sacrifice and honour and debt and courage at some length. Bert didn't mind though as it gave him a chance to look at Lucie without the necessity of having to talk to her to try to explain. For what could he say, the only satisfactory explanation would be the truth and that would be worse. The afternoon wore on, meagre bellies filled , the more delicate digestions took water with the wine where once the carafes would have flowed.

Taffy made a toast to the 46th Tank 'To the scourge of Europe - all the way to Berlin'

'But not for you old boy eh' said Johnson sitting next to him, 'more like all the way to the clinic.'

'I got there in the end, didn't I?' said Taffy colouring, 'we all did even old Bert.' Taffy waved his glass in Bert's direction., 'Old Bert, who shouldn't have been there in the first place, keen bugger.' Bert made a sign for Taffy to shut up but he didn't notice. 'Yeh could've stayed here, old Bert, taken it easy in the land of the good old vine', Taffy took another sip, 'but not old Bert - all the way to Berlin. Mad bugger, could've been killed a hundred times'.

'Sit down you old drunk', Bert yelled, 'and keep your opinions to yourself '.

Lucie was looking at Bert now 'You chose to go ? You wanted to leave? I thought you had to'.

'Course I had to,' Bert waved an dismissive hand in the direction of Taffy 'pay no mind to that old fool his brain's gone'. Lucie looked unconvinced. 'All I know is that one minute it was I'll be here all summer, next you were off up north with the tanks. Was it me you were running from? You can tell me now surely' Bert looked at her. Inside the old woman he saw the young girl waiting for a reply. He looked away, 'In a way yes, I thought you wanted Jean, that once the war was over things would be different. I thought that's how it was'. Lucie gave a snort 'Jean wanted me, there's a difference. I saw through him even then, even though I didn't know what I know now.' Bert looked at her, 'know now? What's that?' Lucie leaned near whispering 'Very few people in the town know this and the mayor doesn't want it spread. The honour of the town is important to him.' Bert shivered and waited, waited as he had always waited. 'Jean was a traitor, He was working for the Germans,' Bert thought he'd misheard her, she whispered so softly. 'What? What's that?' he said. She repeated the word "Traitor". Bert looked incredulously at her, then gave a wild bitter chuckle. 'The bugger, Mr FFI himself, Mr. "I am the spirit of France" a traitor'. Lucie shushed him and continued in her low tone, 'Papers were found in Berlin after the war, many years after the war. He'd been in the pay of the Boches all along. That's why the St Lo raid went wrong and they were waiting for the two American airmen at Cabourg. So it's no surprise that he disappeared about the time that the Germans did. One thing I'll never understand though'. 'Oh', Bert looked worried again 'what's that?' Lucie took a sip of wine and looked back at Bert. 'He knew about the plan to blow up the supply train from Rouen, why didn't he tell them? It was a crucial to their defence of the valley. He had the power have us all destroyed', Lucie shuddered, 'why didn't he use it?' 'Perhaps he didn't have time' said Bert, coming back from far away, ' things were happening pretty quickly then'. 'Perhaps,' said Lucie, 'anyway we'll never know'. 'No' said Bert 'we never will not now'. 'So you see there was no Jean in my life except in his head', she looked at him with sadness 'and now I see in yours'. Bert seemed about to speak but then just reached out and put his hand on hers. 'You have children Bert'. 'One' he replied 'just one' 'And your wife, where is she?' 'Left years ago, hardly a marriage really, you know - mistake really. And you?' 'I was happy for a long time', Lucie smiled at the memory, 'a nice man from Rouen some years after the war, but he is dead now and so,' Lucie shrugged. 'I am a grandmother five times. It is a strange thing, you live so many years and time is so long, then you come to something like this and it's like all the years are nothing.' She patted the back of Bert's hand. 'Anyway, a card would have been nice - at Christmas perhaps. Just something to tell me that you were still alive'. Bert nodded still unable or unwilling to speak, just nodded, his eyes dark and full.

By six o'clock it was all over. The past had been given its due. Tomorrow they would visit the beaches at Arromanches and the memorial at Pegasus Bridge, then they would go home. back to the wives remaining and the distant grown up children. To their quiet rooms where the truth about time sat in every corner and peeped out from every heavy framed photograph.

Lucie rose to go, but Bert held onto her hand. 'I must go' she put her hand on his wrinkled cheek. 'I am quite tired and it is a two hour drive back to Rouen.'

'You won't be staying at the farm?' asked Bert, surprised, 'There is no room,' she smiled 'they have guests, remember'. Bert shrugged 'Maybe it's not to late to send you that card.' She kissed him gently on his cheek, her hand was trembling but then she was a very old lady and it had been a long and emotional day. 'It is too late,' she smiled 'but send it anyway'.

He watched her walk away. Almost certain he would never see her again.

Nicole drove them back to the farm. Taffy, a bit worse for the wine, decided to go for a lie down but Bert said he felt fine and wanted to go for a walk. Nicole began to explain directions but Bert shook his head 'I know the way' 'Yes, yes of course you do' she smiled at him 'my grandmother was very glad to see you, you know, Since my grandfather died, she's been different, sad, she was very fond of you'. 'Yeh thanks love'. Bert crossed the farmyard, waved goodbye to the watching Nicole and went along the cart track now ribbed with the marks of tractor tyres, up towards the high woods. It would not be dark for a couple of hours yet and the early evening light illuminated the great wall of leaves with an unnaturally bright hue. Fifty years of growth hadn't changed it all that much. Not when compared to the things of man. He found the gully high up on the west side easily. It was before the group of three old oaks and after the pond. It fell steeply from the side of the forest track and resembled a large shell hole, probably the root cavity of some long ago rotted tree. Bert scrambled down through exposed tree roots and bracken, till he walked again across the dry crisp ferns at the bottom. When he reached the middle, he stopped and stood just looking down at the earth for quite a while. Almost imperceptible to all but the trained and knowing eye. The mound remained undisturbed, shallower now sinking away into the forest floor. Another 10-20 years and it would be gone altogether. Bert sat on a nearby fallen log to get his breath. He'd never been quite the same since that bout of bronchitis back in '89, As he sat he continued to stare at the mound.

'So boy you were a traitor as well as a bastard, eh. Well, well, that would have made a bit of a difference, wouldn't it now?' Bert laughed a dry laugh and as he stared at the mound, 50 years melted away and it was 10th June 1944 again.

Bert had gone for a walk in the woods to clear his head to think about Lucie and the previous night - he had never known a girl quite like her. He had never even thought about marrying a French girl or any other foreigner for that matter. He'd always assumed that he'd end up with a girl similar to the ones who lived down his street like Joan or Alice but it all seemed different now. He looked idly out over the valley, wondering what it would be like to live there, to see it in all its seasons, the reds of autumn the, whites of winter.

Jean Foucault came walking down the path, his wiry black hair stuffed into his beret and his eyes quick and contemptuous as ever. They surveyed Bert as he approached. 'I hear you have been with Lucie Marielle'.

'Whats it to you?' Bert disliked the resistance leader, for there was something about his disdain that went beyond what Bert accepted as one of the bitternesses engendered by war.

198

'I cannot understand why she would want to go with you but no matter. Sooner or later you will get killed by this war, people like you always do. Then I will take your Lucie?' He made an obscene gesture with his fist 'and when I take her she will like it well and we will laugh at your English manners'. He took an exaggerated bow, 'no doubt'. Bert took off his helmet and squared up. 'Come on, you foul- mouthed bastard'. Jean looked incredulous and swiftly kicked him in the balls. Bert slumped to the path in agony. 'Stupid little English man,' Jean spat at him, 'I hope I break your stupid little balls for good'. He kicked him in the ribs a couple of times and turned and walked off down the path whistling. Through the mists of pain Bert felt his anger rising, 'I hate you,' he thought, 'I hate you more than the Germans.'

Bert couldn't remember afterward whether he'd taken his gun out of the holster or whether it had fallen out during the struggle. He only knew that it was in his hand and for a marksman like him a very simple shot to make.

The sudden call of a bird nearby brought Bert back to the present. He looked at the mound again. It had taken him nearly two hours to bury the body to his satisfaction. He had been trained in the burying of weapons, parachutes, transmitters and the like so they didn't show a trace and he used that skill to good effect. By the time he had finished, his balls had stopped aching but his mind was no clearer. He knew he was on the edge of panic.

He should have gone and told them what he had done, what made him bury the body for Chrissakes? But Foucault was a big hero locally, there was a real chance the FFI would shoot him. And what would Lucie say?   He couldn't face her, he couldn't face any of them. Every time he tried to think it through calmly, his mind went blank. He just wanted to get away somewhere where he could pretend it had never happened. He could go North, He could go North tonight. Captain Loring had told them all on Tuesday. Those of them that wanted to 'see it through,' could be transferred to the 46th Tank pushing on towards Belgium forthwith.

Yes, he would go north and try to forget what he had done, the coward's act could be redeemed, the sour taste, sweetened. He must shake off the ghastly pall that hung over him and then he could forget he had ever been here, this valley, this forest, at all. 'Oh Lucie,' he cried as he dragged the final fronds of bracken into place, 'Oh Lucie'.

Bert looked at the mound again, in the fading light even he could not see it. The stain of guilt that had been on him for fifty years began to lift a little. If only he had come back before. How long had they known about Jean's true colours. 10 years?, 20 ? 'Serves you right, Bert me boy' he said to himself, 'serves you right for being such a coward.'

Slowly, wearily he climbed back up the gully. It took him much longer than it had fifty years earlier. Finally he stood on the track once more, waiting for his breathing to return to normal. In the valley below, above the rooftops of the Marielle farm he could see the river meadows unnaturally bright in the last rays of the sun. It was all so familiar to him this small valley. He'd gone away to forget but of course he hadn't, he hadn't forgotten a thing.

It seemed much further walking back down the track. His legs felt like lead. He was glad to hear the sound of a tractor behind him. Glad to see the smiling face of Luc, the grandson that might have been looking down from the cab. 'Hop up, Monsieur Morris, Then you will make it back in time for the soup'. Bert grasped the young man's hand with his wrinkled and shaking own. Once he was firmly seated, Luc let out the brake and let the tractor roll forward. Together they dropped down through the dusk.

VIAGGIO CON INVERNO

The train flickered suddenly out of the tunnel into the blaring sunlight. He shut his eyes for a moment waiting till the pain behind his lids faded. To his left the land rose almost sheer, grey and uncompromising, yet hardy summer flowers still waved there, reds and yellows bright against the craggy rocks. He looked higher to where the peaks could be seen, real mountains, still tinged with the snows of the previous winter.

Joanne stirred slightly but did not wake.

He looked out of the window to his right. They were passing through the section of the Cote d'Azur where the Alpes Maritimes reached to the edge of the Mediterranean, where the railway line wound its unlikely path through tunnels and along the edges of the rocks that crowded down into the sea. He remembered this place from a previous journey back in '70 or '71. He had been young himself then, only a little older than Joanne. Then the train had been packed to the rafters with Algerian and Tunisian immigrants, all fresh embarked from Marseilles and bound for a career of servitude amongst the fashionable villas and hotels of Cannes and St. Raphael. A happy smiling bunch nonetheless, unfazed by the cramped carriages and the interminable delays along the line.

He looked at the sleeping girl, snuggled up on his lap, pale hair in a loose spray across her cheek. People always look younger when they are asleep. Young girls especially with their mascara wiped away and blusher diffused to a gentle pink. Joanne looked about twelve again, soft and fresh, unsullied by the devices and rigours of adulthood. He smiled ruefully and stroked her cheek. The sea was still, mirror static, he stared out at the horizon trying to probe the very rim of the sea the place where it finally reached the sky. Horizons always made him thoughtful, pensive, they spoke of futures, things yet to happen, incomplete journeys, just out of view. Somewhere out there his lay but like the line between sky and sea, it was thin and indistinct.

He woke Joanne up as the train entered the outskirts of Cannes and ran along between the beach and the town. Although the October day was quite warm, the beach was totally deserted. Not even a dog walker or hardy backpacker to be seen. The umbrellas had gone for another year and only the metal outlines of the beachfront bars remained like some sketchy memory of what had been. Joanne looked across the curving bay of palm trees and sand to where the white wall of the Carlton hotel dominated the skyline. A smile crossed her lips

' Neat' she murmured 'absolutely cool'.

'This is Cannes' he told her, 'where they have the famous film festival'.

Her eyes widened 'Oh, will the stars be there now, like Brad Pitt and Johnny Depp' ?

No of course not,' he almost laughed,' the festival is in May'.

'Is it?' she frowned, 'what a shame. Do we get off here?'

'No, Nice is another 30 minutes further on'.

He had told her all this before he was sure. Joanne stood up and stretched and smoothed her white dress down across her thighs. Then she flicked her hair forward round her face and the girl became a woman again.

'I'm hungry,' she said as she sat back down, 'can we go to the buffet?'

'It's a trolley,' he told her, 'you'll have to search the train for it.'

'Give me some francs then,' She held out her hand. 'Do you want anything?'

'Get me a beer, I'm not hungry'.

'OK,' she tripped off down the train - tall lithe and graceful, turning the heads of the two young men in the end seats as she went.

He sat back and closed his eyes. The trip through France had been a nightmare. Night trains were always a grueling slog but this one had seemed more so. They had both drunk too much the previous evening - was it really only last evening - sitting in a bar opposite the Gare de Lyon.

Watching the car lights swirl across the Boulevard Diderot, he had tried to explain the insidious history of the broad wide elegant streets that Joanne admired so much (that he too himself secretly admired) but she had refused to believe him, refused to believe in a duplicity by authority that would extend to reshaping the landscape of a city.

'It's all too paranoid,' she had said with a shake of her carefully curled hair. He snorted but didn't push the issue.

Later Joanne had flirted with a couple of American boys just back from Venice, broad shouldered and even toothed. They were friendly enough, personable in that strange way that Americans can be whilst only asking endless questions and offering no answers or observations of their own, as if sharing your life with you. 'You did that? Hey that's really neat'. Childishly he had allowed himself to become irked by their attentions to Joanne and he had argued with her later on the platform. Joanne had sulked until she fell asleep.

So while she slept the sleep of the innocent he had remained awake feeling slightly nauseous, feeling the headache, the uncomfortable dryness of his mouth and anxiety grow in him until he knew he would not doze. Resignedly he watched the sleeping cities of Dijon and Lyon ghost by. If he couldn't shake this nervousness things would just get worse. The tense neck, the grinding teeth, the pointless sense of alarm were never far from the surface now, deep breathing, mind calming techniques worked for a while but he needed to let go. He needed as Eliot had so wisely said "to care and not to care".

He thought about Joanne and smiled, he had promised himself he would not get like this, would not load each event with unwarranted significance, each act with foreboding. She was traveling south with him and not in Paris with the American boys but he had seen the jealous contempt in their eyes. "Old man how dare you", it said, "How dare you take this girl." Well he would have to get used to it. He'd have to reach beyond all that now. Whatever he might try to do or say to justify or mitigate his actions he had been a teacher and she had been his pupil, he was 48 and she was 18. He must learn to be hated just as she must learn to be pitied.

When he was younger he had been exemplary in that respect, all those years. Sixth formers had come and gone, testing their sexuality, their desirability out on him, some serious, some contemptuous, some fearful, some committed and intense. All had been dispatched with a terse 'That'll do, Felicity' or 'Margaret, please go home and think about what you've just said.' Easy, really - slightly embarrassing but little else, after all, these weren't women but little girls. He had watched them grow up, watched them arrive on their first day barely twelve, mute and trembling as they walked along the main corridor to their first assembly.

Why had she been different, why had everything changed on the last day of the Spring term. Was it no more than that his life and esteem were at a particularly low ebb that fateful day? Approaching fifty he had begun to rail against the idea that the significant part of his life had already been lived, his children grown, his wife gone too. It seemed die was cast, the plot unwound, the denouement duly signalled with no twists or reverses in sight. Somehow it just galled.

Joanne came back along the train carrying a half baguette, a bottle of Perrier and a can of Kronenbourg. She handed him his beer and looked at him. For a moment he couldn't name the expression on her face then suddenly he realised it was pride. She sat down and snuggled her head against his shoulder. He smiled at her ignoring the blush that spread across his face and the eyes of the young men in the corner.

In Nice, they booked into an hotel near the station despite Joanne's protests that they get one overlooking the sea. 'They all cost a packet' he said. 'Besides I'm not lugging the bags all the way down the Avenue Medecin only to have to lug them all back again in a couple of days'. 'We could take a taxi,' she offered. 'Money is a funny thing, it goes quickly when you throw it around - if you want to run out somewhere about Rome than that's the way to go about it'. She sulked then but not for long. Soon she was showering and wandering naked about the room rummaging for clothes in her suitcase. He lay on the bed watching her feeling deeply weary, the remnants of alcohol in his system combined with the sleepless night. In a little while she would ask to be whisked off to the shops on the Avenue Massena, then on to some ultra lively bar and he would take her and his mind would love it but his body would groan and complain at him until wine worked its numb, short-lived joy.

She'd stay behind after the end of lessons with important questions. Her face bright and alert full of the brash confidence that pretty girls have, as if a world that has treated them so kindly so far will never let them down. He was used to handling this kind of situation but with Joanne he felt undermined from the start - a certain look, a gesture, he couldn't pin it down. She would lean into him when he was pointing something out to her, the feel of her firm young breast set his arm tingling, her thigh would brush his when she passed him in the classroom. In the beginning they had played all the secret games that illicit lovers do but he had always known from the first moment he kissed her, that day after English 5, that they would be found out, that he was just playing the game of secrecy for the sake of some remnant of decorum. It was a testimony to Joanne's maturity though, that five months went by, five months of meetings in obscure London pubs and little tourist hotels in the back streets of Bloomsbury before he was called into the Head's office.

He remembered walking down the long wide corridor of the main building, knowing it was for the last time and feeling - well excitement, rather than fear or relief - after all those years of clinging on to the edge of propriety and normality he had finally fallen off, floating away from the structures and rules that had shaped his life.

Joanne finished her preparations with a final and triumphant fluff of her hair. 'C'mon Geoff,' she said full of the satisfaction that her communion with the mirror had given her, 'let's go.' He got up slowly but could not avoid the dizziness. Joanne was by the door waiting. He took a deep breath and followed.

The next day the rainy season broke a day or two early. They sat on the bed and stared out of the window through the streams of water at the rain washed platform of Nice Ville station. Trains came and went, there was a brief scurry of passengers on the street and then all was quiet again.

They had planned to tour the marina area and gardens of Le Chateau but it was far too wet. He was secretly pleased, he was content just to lay back to the lulling sound of the rain and the swish of tyres outside and let the day drift. He felt her restlessness beside him. It reached across the room, intruding on his calm, his need for stupor.

'Joanne stop it'. he said conscious of his schoolmasterly tone.

'I'm not doing anything.'
'You're twitching , fidgeting - be still'.
'I'm bored' she said plaintively, 'I can't help it'.

He looked at her, he could sense the restless energy that was invisible to her, taken for granted. Of course she was bored, how could she be anything else.

'Lets go to a movie,' he said, getting wearily off the bed as she clapped her hands in glee.

Later in the middle of the night he awoke. The rain was still streaming down outside. In the bathroom a grey misty reflection stared back at him, like a photograph slowly losing colour and definition. What could she possibly see in him, the adrenaline rush that she had given his ego was running down. The idea that he was somehow ahead of the game seemed absurd, scepticism grew in the furrows of his forehead. He felt daft but also in awe of her. A fifty year old man -well forty eight anyway - in awe of an eighteen year old girl. You didn't need a masters in classical drama to see the stuff of tragedy looming. He went back into the bedroom. She lay like some pale sculpture in the mottled light, hands palm upwards, hair spread across the pillow, one breast exposed, he felt his breath in his throat. Whatever happened, he was closer to happiness now than he had ever been in his life. He could see the shape of it if not the detail. It was scary to be so close after all those years spent standing at the other end of the room.

In Florence the Arno was on the edge of flood. The arches of the Ponte Vecchio described a mere sliver of a curve at the water line and the sandbags were being put in place along the Lungarno Medici. They wandered through the already empty lower galleries of the Uffizi looking for the stairs. The first floor was crammed with the Renaissance's finest. Here Joanne was silent for a while, worshipping at the church of line and form, colour and perspective. He watched the intensity in her face.

'They say Botticelli was a complete failure in his day, that's sad don't you think,' she looked at him, looking at her, ' to create such beauty and be told that it's crap.'

206

'Masterpieces are often despised,' he told her, their greatness is offensive to people.'

'Because they know they can never aspire to such greatness themselves?'

'Perhaps, but maybe just because they don't like excellence? Not everybody does.'

She looked at him puzzled and was about to reply but he had already moved on.

In the market on the Piazza San Lorenzo, Joanne spent an age trying on shoes. In the end he left her to her own devices, went into the Medici chapels across the road and spent the time looking at the reliquaries of long dead cardinals, little pieces of finger bone or toe bone attached to gold chains like some grisly key rings, honeycombed with age and strangely pagan for Christian artefacts.

At twelve everything closed except the restaurants and bars, shopping on hold until a civilised hour. Back at the hotel he suggested that they too siesta but she said she was too excited to sleep and would rather make love. For a long time he toiled above her, her legs raised to his shoulders , sweating in the stale shuttered room with the constant whine of scooters echoing up from the street below. Then he mercifully slept until five when he was wakened by Joanne already dressed and made up with that heightened feverish look that too much make-up gives to a healthy skin. 'I want to go to that place we saw from the hill,' she said, 'the one with the verandas, overlooking the Arno.'

Six o'clock saw them sitting at a window table in an almost deserted restaurant. It was too early for the Italians to eat by some hours, the only other occupants were an American couple with a girl about thirteen collapsed in a sulky heap beside them who never spoke, only snarled giving everyone a good glimpse of some serious dental braces.

The Arno had carried on filling up though it hadn't rained all day, some of the sandbags on the far bank were already damp. Men with lorries came and went adding second and third layers of bags.

'Do you think the city will flood?' asked Joanne, winding a strand of spaghetti carbonara carefully round her fork.

'It might.' he said, ' It's happened before, back in the sixties'.

'Oh, that long ago' she replied.

It occurred to him then that the Sixties was as distant and unimaginable a concept for her as the Thirties was for him. The sense of time passing touched him for a moment, like a cold hand on the back of his neck, he shuddered, drank full from his glass and watched the brown Arno swirl.

'We'll run away 'said Joanne when he met her after school and told her what had happened. ' How romantic, ' he replied sarcastically, 'next you'll be saying two can live as cheaply as one, love is all we need to live on and somewhere there's a far away country where we could be happy without fear of persecution. A Utopia for lovers '.

' Well there must be, mustn't there - somewhere ' she said.

The simplicity of her idea was naive and charming and he thought little more of it then. It was only after weeks of verbal insults and threatening letters and about the time the summonses started arriving that he realised she was right.

Rome even in November was still warm. They had spent the day trekking between the Coliseum and the Vatican and up and down the Spanish Steps. Joanne's sprits seemed to take a higher turn in this warmer clime and she had been lively, vibrant and even witty all day. He noted with pleasure that some of his dry humour was rubbing off on her at last.

Now it was late afternoon and they wandered along the banks of the Tiber going generally in the direction of the hotel. The feeling of well being allowed them to wander on and on till they drifted out of the tourist area and found themselves alone on a path between the Tiber and a high crumbling Renaissance wall of some nameless Palazzo. He had just realised their mistake and turned back when suddenly from nowhere a group of small boys appeared and surrounded them yelling and jostling.

He shouted at them to go away though he knew that would do no good. Joanne, looked on terrified, immobile. She had no bag with her at his insistence and her thin strapless summer dress made it clear she had nothing stealable. So quickly the whole group had turned on him. He felt many hands reaching inside his coat and he grabbed at the one that was closing on his wallet. The boy whose hand he had grabbed leapt upon his back. An act of desperation, he thought. The boy was probably only about eight or nine but surprisingly strong for his size. The unheld hand had settled on his windpipe and was choking him. He knew the boy was not actually strong enough to do him any lasting damage. His wallet only contained about 14,000 lire in it, he should let them have it. They were only poor little kids after all. Then one of them kicked him in the shins and he felt his balance begin to go. "This is absurd", he thought but still he panicked. For the second time in a year his training failed him. He stepped backwards and smashed the boy against the wallside. There was a crack as a bone in the boys arm or shoulder went. The boy gave a wail and let go, writhing in agony in the dust. He turned to face the rest of them but already they were backing off, picking up the moaning boy, his arm hanging useless and running away down the path, glaring back at him from time to time.

'You all right?' asked Joanne beginning to shake a little eyes wide with fear and amazement.

'I'm o.k.,' he told her, dusting himself down but he wasn't - the sound of the crack echoed and re-echoed in his head, becoming louder each time. A deafening splintering that surely could be heard throughout all of Rome.

'I don't understand'. They were back at the hotel. Joanne bathed the scratches that covered his neck and hands. 'They were just little kids but they were prepared to take you on. Are they that hungry?'

'Those kids weren't malnourished I can assure you.' he rubbed the bruises on his neck.

'Then what makes them so desperate, so determined?'

'Oh the promise of a good beating if they come back empty handed I expect.'

Joanne shuddered. 'It's horrible, it's like out of some Dickens novel. Thank God you got rid of them.'

'Yes' he said bitterly 'but then I always was good with kids.'

He got up and took the suitcase from the rack.

'Are we leaving?' Joanne asked

'Yes,' he replied gathering up the first handful of clothes, 'I've had enough of this town, haven't you?'

The train to Brindisi left at midnight and though it was an extravagance he booked a sleeping car, he wanted above all to sleep, he wanted to feel better in the morning.

Once the steward had made up the beds he got up on the top one and went straight to sleep. For a long time the sound of the train could be heard in his dream, a slow and leisurely 'click-click' 'click-click'. He was travelling through a dark country into the light, the pin-point at the edge of his retina, the end of the journey. Suddenly it was very bright, suddenly it was a sunny summer day and he was walking along the main corridor of the school. The walk seemed much further than usual, the corridor went on and on. "I must go and see the head," he thought, "before someone tells him I'm here." As he walked on and on up the corridor, children came out of the classrooms, not many, one or two from each but there were so many classrooms and soon the corridor was full of girls trailing behind him. He looked for Joanne but couldn't find her, just a sea of expectant, curious faces. He finally made it to the end of the corridor and was about to open the Head's door when he felt a weight on his neck, then another. The girls attacked silently. He tried to throw them off but there were too many. He went over face down on the carpet and the kicking began. With it came a curious high pitched sound, too strangled and uncomfortable to be a laugh or a moan, something primal, unnerving..................

The sound stayed with him into wakefulness. The dawn was breaking, slivers of light broke free from the edges of the blinds. He lay there for a moment still bound to his dream. Above the rattle of the train he could hear the sound of the sea. He went quietly out of the compartment and stood in the corridor. He stood there for quite a while watching the dark sea move through the shades of sunrise to an iridescent blue.

He had only wanted to be happy - It hadn't seemed too much to ask but he hadn't got the singularity of purpose that the pursuit of happiness required. He simply wasn't bloody-minded enough and that was that.

He knew now he hadn't re-written the end of his play after all. This was clearly as all good theatrical scholars would tell you, merely a sub-plot.

As the ferry left Brindisi they stood on the deck and stared at the horizon.

'How far is it to Patras?' asked Joanne.

'Oh, about a couple of hundred miles, I think, it will take over a day to get there.'

'It's like stepping off the edge of the world,' she said her eyes full of wonder.

He watched her face so fresh and bright after a simple night's sleep.

She was so young, he thought, this was but the beginning of a huge escapade called life, the beginning of a long adventure.

An adventure that he had already lived.

Seeing how far she still had to go, how much of her journey was still unmade, he couldn't help but contemplate the inevitable shortness of his own but like the good teacher he was, he put his arm around her shoulder and pointing towards Greece, described what they would find there.

Underneath the Masts

Clive lived out near one of those radio masts that you can see from the trains that run up and down out of London Bridge station. I don't know which one, but I remember standing out in his garden during parties, looking up at it, watching the little red lights winking away above the chimney pots and TV aerials. I remember wondering what it was like to be up there, up above the city with the endless spidery network of lights spread out below.

'Windy.'

'What?'

Clive was standing beside me clutching a can of lager and a Rizla packet.

'Windy, might even blow you off if you didn't have one of those harnesses to keep you on.'

I didn't think I had spoken out loud. Maybe Clive had just followed my line of sight.

'What's it for?'

Clive shrugged, 'TV, I think. It's sending repeats of the Golden Shot right through us even as we speak. Left a bit, right a bit, fire.' Clive cannoned his empty Stella can into the back fence, startling a tubby black cat. 'Who knows what strange channels might be running in our veins.' Clive snorted, snorting being as close as he ever got to being annoyed. 'Heavy shit TV waves. They suck down the bad karma from all over the world.'

'Perhaps we should go in then.' I offered, wanting to escape back to the kitchen, beer and pointless conviviality.

'No point. It's too late. All that mindless, gormless nonsense is part of us now. We'll just have to live with it, try to avoid singing hemorrhoid commercial jingles aloud on the tube.' He sat down on a garden chair and began to roll a joint. I went in search of a stimulant of my own.

Clive had arrived obliquely into my world. When I moved into the Anerley flat share he was there, sitting in the lounge, listening to John Martyn's Solid Air. It took me a couple of days to realise

212

that he didn't live there. That he came and went according to some inner timetable of his own, offering beers and advice to whoever had the time or the inclination or failing that sitting around in the lounge listening to other people's records.

'Who's friend is Clive?' I asked after a couple of weeks
'He's no one's friend, well, rather he's a friend of the flat.' The other flatmates told me.
'Sorry?'
'We think that a long time ago he was a friend of one of the people who shared here. After they left he just passed himself on.' Sure enough, Clive would turn up, once or twice a week, wanting to see no-one in particular, suggesting that one or more of us accompany him to the local pub, or to his house to smoke some shit and listen to a better sound system than our feeble Amstrad.

So Clive was sort of tolerated more than welcomed. If he wasn't really anyone's friend, well he wasn't anyone's enemy either. If you were feeling lonely or at a loose end, then Clive was usually there to fill the void and if you weren't, well, he was quite easy to shake off. Mostly you just left him there in the lounge, reading your magazines and drinking your beer. I still felt bad about avoiding him though. 'Don't do to others what you wouldn't want done to you.' My old man had once advised me, one of the few things he had said that I had carried with me into adulthood. Not that Clive would have cared, but beneath the Buddhist calm one felt an emptiness in Clive, not loneliness exactly, but an air of resignation, of having given up. That was it – given up. He was a man without the slightest vestige of anticipation.

Clive's house was very big, yet he lived there alone. I wondered how he could afford to live in such a house. I asked him straight out one night as we sat listening to Roy Harper over the sounds of the buses revving and grinding their way up Beulah Hill. 'So, why don't you have anyone else living here?'
Clive snorted as if the idea was absurd. 'Flatmates are nothing but trouble. Surely you must have noticed this by now.'
I took his point but pressed on, 'But don't you need the rent?

Clive sighed. 'Money equals hassle. Keep it to a minimum that's what I say.

The other thing Clive kept to a minimum was housework. The living room was a modernist sculpture of uneven piles of LPs and magazines topped off with a smattering of audio cassettes, most with their hinges broken, a dusty guitar sat in one corner, long out of concert pitch. In the shadowy recesses, beyond the pale ring of light cast by the desk lamp on the coffee table, a small archive of Clive's life could faintly be seen; bent beer and coke cans, empty rizla packets, the foil cartons from indian take aways ringed with dried tandoori paste the colour of blood. Only the books seemed cared for, stacked neatly and orderly on precarious shelves, Tolkein and Kerouac, Hesse and Peake, Dore's engravings, Beardsley's pen and inks.

'So how can you afford the rent?' I pressed on with my line of enquiry.

'That's simple, I don't pay any.'

'How come?'

'I own the fucking house. Joke eh. It's all mine.'

'Really?'

'Uh-huh. Mum and Dad died you see, in a road crash, a stupid accident. He lost control and hit a skip, stupid. They were arguing I bet. They always were arguing about something.

'How old were you then?

'Twenty.'

' - and you've lived here on your own since then?'

'Yep.' Roy Harper ended and he replaced it with Loudon Wainwright singing a song about gays in a gym.... "Together they squeezed blackheads underneath florescent lights." Loudon sang. 'I love that line 'said Clive.

'No other family?' I asked.

Clive hummed and mumbled along with 'Unrequited to the Nth Degree.'

"Oh when I die & it won't be long

Oh you're gonna be sorry that you treated me wrong
You're gonna be sorry that you treated me bad

214

And if there's an after life I'll gloat & I'll be glad "

And for a while I thought he had relegated my question to the conveniently unheard, but finally, he replied. 'My sister lives in Norfolk, with some farmer guy, owns about half of it I think. She wears pearls and rides a horse, probably at the same time for all I know. Listen to this next track man, this guy has a real sense of how absurd people are, you know.'

Hassle free Clive may have been but he was often hard work, Clive talked when Clive felt like talking, but when Clive wanted silence he ignored everyone. His insularity made him dull, static in a way I found frustrating. I wanted more than introspection, I wasn't going to spend my time in contemplation and understanding when there was life out there to be lived. I wasn't going to let it all go by. But then I found that Clive could be very useful, for Clive had a way with girls. He didn't care whether they liked him or not, didn't care whether they talked to him or not, because of this he was relaxed in their company. He didn't try to impress them or flatter them. They liked that, it made them feel comfortable, because then they didn't have to 'perform' either. He'd just walk up to them and start talking as if he had already met them somewhere and was picking up on a conversation they had earlier. Hanging around on the fringes of this process meant you could share in this sudden intimacy without the risk of a stupid word and a likely rejection.

That said, Clive's choice of girls left something to be desired, they always seemed a little dog-eared and emotionally tawdry, with long nervous nicotine stained fingers and unexpected moods. Prone to anguish rather than tears, full of tales of bastard life and the treachery that was humanity, stories that erred too far on the side of self-pity to earn my sympathy. They wore ragged leather coats, had holes in their tights and chipped nail varnish. Girls named Jenny and Sukie and Sasha and Katie and one who everyone just called Mouse. Girls who made love desperately yet pitilessly, as if whatever kind of solace they sought there, it wasn't comfort or camaraderie.

Life, my life, whole months of it at a time, slipped by in a welter of routine. The workdays, dull and mindless, the nights, an amalgam of half formed hopes and heartburn from crap food and too much lager. I was forlorn and ennervated by turns. I lived on music and the hope of girls. Clive just lived on, without ambition, seemingly quite content.

Clive's house continued in its slow decline. The winter gales loosened roof tiles and water seeped into the rafters and ceilings. Every room on the upper floor smelt of mildew, stale, dank, forgotten.

Dirty pots and pans clustered round the kitchen sink, the dust got thicker, the curtains greyer. Cans scattered like aluminum mice as you walked. The carpets felt crisp beneath your feet. Fluff buds the size of macaroons stuck to your clothes when you sat on the sofa.

As his house crumbled so it seemed that Clive too had become dustier, more pallid, as if the neglect was rubbing off on him. He had rash on his cheek and a cough that he couldn't seem to shake. 'English winter.' He would say between rasps, though it was April already. I suggested a walk in the park, along the esplanade of the ruined palace down to the lake. Clive squinted at me as if trying to make me out. 'I don't think so.' He said finally and sat back down of the sofa.

The house was looking dreadful and I told him so. 'Why not give it a clean, you might find that missing King Crimson cassette.' I offered trying to sound flippant and failing. Clive looked at me flatly, contemptuously. 'You sound like a mother. I don't need a mother and I don't need to waste my time cleaning it just so it can get dirty again.' He stood put a hand on each shoulder and spoke to me in a concerned voice. 'Normal things, they seem so simple and easy to achieve but there's such a danger in them, believe me, there's such danger in normal things.'

'It might be what's making you sick.' I offered, while trying to extricate myself from the mother image.

'I'm not sick.' Clive took deep breaths to denote healthy lungs. 'I've just been staying up too late that's all. Living. You should try it.'

216

'I do, I just prefer to spend my time out of the vicinity of the remnants my previous months meals.'

Clive shook his head slowly in "know not what they do" mode. 'The trouble with you is that you're really quite normal. Oh you pretend not to be but underneath you just can't wait for it all, can you? The wife, the mortgage, the noisy kids. In ten years you'll be pushing them all round Tesco's, worrying about the mortgage rate with the only bright moment in your day the point when you fall asleep in the middle of the ten o clock news.'

'I don't want that.' I said a little dumbfounded at his outburst.

'Course you don't, but it's what you'll get if you go on trying to be normal.'

I avoided Clive a little more than usual after that. I had plenty of other things I could do with my time, other people to spend it with. Clive didn't seem to notice, or if he did didn't say, just came and went as he chose, though now, I noticed, the dust seemed to have settled on him as well and it drifted in the sunlight coming through our lounge windows for some time after he had gone.

Early that summer I met the girl who would take me away from the flat share world. Her name was Frances and she worked on the floor below in the vast office block that, like its employee's, had long lost sight of its reason for being there. It was a proper romance, with a proper girl, thoughts of forever and white goods. We went to Paris together then on to the South. When we got back our plans for co-habitation were already laid.

The night before I moved out of the flat, I dropped round to see Clive. He was sitting on the sofa, which had now collapsed slightly at the back making him seem a little hunched. Beside him was a girl in black with the thickest eye makeup I'd ever seen. They were staring at a rose light from a lava lamp that was resting on the coffee table where it stood like a lighthouse shining its distress beacon on the wrecks of empty coffee cups and full ashtrays.

I told him where I was moving to and suggested he might drop round sometime.

217

'Honor Oak Park,' he said, not taking his eyes off the lava lamp. 'Honor Oak Park, eh?' the way one might have said the moon.

He never came. Five or six months later I dropped by my old flat, a brief social call, my last as it turned out, as the remainder of those who I had called flatmates were due to move out a few days later. A new order was taking shape there. Clive was sitting in the lounge, sipping a can of Stella and reading the NME. 'Hi Clive.' I said. Clive nodded but he didn't look up. Clive, after all, was a friend of the flat and I no longer lived there.

A few months ago I was driving through the area on my way from an out of town meeting, traffic bound and already late home. I had only passed that way on a handful of occasions since I lived there. Yet it still seemed so familiar. How strange it is, I thought, the way that places we had been in every day for months or even years we hardly ever see again once we leave. So, on a whim I turned off the fume filled, crawling A214 and made the short detour into Clive's road. I don't know what I had expected to see or what I had expected to find. Everything the same I guess, silly of me.

Clive's house was a ruin. The roof had fallen in, the tiles tilting and slipping toward the gaping hole at the top, like some wounded reptile. Mauve budlia stalks waved from the bared timbers like joss sticks in a vase. The windows were roughly boarded with wood on which glittered gold and silver graffiti.

I stopped the car, walked though the rusty gate and peered in through the gaps in the planks. In a weird way I almost expected to see Clive sitting there, in the midst of all the desolation but there was no one, nothing, not even the long suffering coffee table, just puddles and mouldy leaves on the blackened floor.

As I was getting back in the car something up above my head caught my eye. I looked up. The lights from the TV mast blinked back at me redly, smugly. Still sucking down bad karma no doubt. For a moment my normal soul was full of sadness. I leant head in hands upon the roof of my Audi, but only for a moment, for I knew that anyone watching me might have noticed that I had about me an air of resignation, that I might just be a man without a single vestige of anticipation.

MATHURIN

As he entered his late 50's, the writer Jules Mathurin found that he had become world famous. His works had for many years provided him with a steady income, enabling him to travel, provide for his family and to take more care over the novels he wrote than would have been the case if his sales had been less auspicious. Nonetheless it was a jobbing existence and when sales were low Mathurin would work as a general handyman, fixing sinks, septic tanks, laying patios and mending walls, much as his father had back in the Auvergne. Then about ten years ago, his publisher Georges Verdon had appointed his son Gaston to run the marketing side of the business and Gaston had brought the publishing house, if not exactly into the still new 21st century, then he had certainly dragged it, finally, into the one that had just expired.

In the course of this 'makeover' Gaston had spotted something in Jules Mathurin's work that Mathurin himself had been unaware of – that the vein of cynicism, of bitterness, of ennui that ran through his work heralded the unbrave, acrimonious world of the 'noughties' as they were apparently known (or in some circles, Decade Zero). Jules Mathurin's back catalogue had been dusted off, given gaudy new covers and a publicity campaign to match. Gaston had done this without consulting Mathurin and the first Mathurin knew of it was when a significant amount of money began arriving in his bank account, followed quickly by a request from Le Figaro for an interview. Mathurin had phoned the Editions Verdon offices to be told that the amount of the bank transfer had not been an error and nor was the request from Le Figaro a hoax and that they saw a very bright future for his 'oeuvre' as they called it.

Mathurin put the phone down and contemplated the lake. It was early spring and the snows had only been gone a few days but already it felt as if life was bursting along its shores and the lake was already shaking off its grey hue for something blue. He had lived in Locarno for four years now, he supposed he would be seen as some sort of tax exile and by some no doubt as a traitor to France but he had simply liked the place. There was something out of touch about that part of Switzerland, squeezed between Italy, the mountains and the lake, something old-fashioned, His friends from Paris found it irritating but he found it comforting, like the Italian Swiss had looked at 'progress' and found it suspect and walked ever so slightly away from it. The tourists who came here in the summer were usually old-fashioned too – except for those who came up on the boat from Stresa, but they generally found the town disappointing and soon headed for the station and the mountain railway to Domodossala.

Mathurin did the interview with Le Figaro and two more the same month one with Paris-Match and one for a magazine called VSD. They all seemed to want to know how much of his books might be true. 'None of it,' he told them, 'it's fiction.' They gave him a look as if to say 'come on, we know better, we bet you lived at least some of it.' He said 'it's all fantasy – that's why I write – to live the things I wasn't able to or didn't want to.' After the articles were published Gaston Verdon rang him up and advised him not to keep telling reporters that his novels didn't reflect his life. Mathurin asked him why, considering it was true. 'Readers these days – our readers,' Gaston replied, 'like to invest in a complete package, to feel that the writer is embodying the narrator/the hero. It's not so much of an ask, is it?' Mathurin shrugged and agreed that it probably wasn't much of 'an ask' and promised to be enigmatic when it came to questions of that sort.

At first things didn't go so badly, the extra money came in handy, enabling Sabine, his wife, to fulfil her wish of sending their twin daughters, Mathilde and Laure, to a prestigious finishing school. Mathurin wasn't sure that such a school was the best place for them but Sabine was and so, it seemed, were Mathilde and Laure. Mathurin had become a family man fairly late in life, being 42 when the girls were born. He had doubted the wisdom at first, but he had come to find it one of the true happiness's of his life. Without it he knew that his later years would have been bleak and he feared for the fate of the man he had once been, the man who had been rescued by Sabine.

As was said, at first things didn't go so badly, but the invitations; to speak, to be interviewed, to endorse began to mount up. His mail box swelled ridiculously till eventually the post office refused to deliver mail to his house and told him they had created a post-restante box for him down in the central post office in the Piazza Grande. His e-mails became unmanageable too so he was advised to hire a secretary, which seemed absurd but he really was being snowed under.

Four women responded to the advert that he had placed in the Giornale de Popolo. *"Professional writer seeks administrator to handle interface with the public and manage general day to day affairs."*

He and Sabine spent a long time haggling over a suggested salary. Mathurin, saw no reason not to pass a generous amount of his growing surplus wealth on to the person who was going to free him up to write, to live. Sabine felt that if he made to post too financially attractive then he would not only get too many applicants but too many of the wrong sort. Sabine suggested that no figure be mentioned and that Mathurin once he had laid out the details of the work involved ask the applicant how much they thought they should be paid. Mathurin thought this was a little sneaky though it made sense. He agreed because he knew in the end he would pick the assistant by instinct, the instinct that had always helped him where people were concerned.

Four women applied for the job, Mathurin had spread their appointments widely throughout the day, not wanting to be rushed or to rush them. Although the work was fundamental and perhaps even a little menial, they would be responsible in some part for his reputation as an author and he wanted to them to be as comfortable as possible during the interview. Sabine showed them into his study and he could tell from a simple glance from her how she felt about each one. He had no intention of appeasing Sabine on the matter however, perhaps an act of petulance on his part but one he felt was somehow necessary. Katrin Voller was German-Swiss, originally from Konstanz, now living in Ascona across the Maggia, an Ascona now virtually joined at the hip with Locarno. Mathurin knew she would be efficient but she was also humourless, like Gaston Verdon. He told her he would let her know. The second applicant Marta Torres was a voluble Filipino catholic whose volubility had already distanced Mathurin from choosing her when she noticed the row of his books along the shelves and, realising that he was THE Jules Mathurin, rose abruptly saying she would not work for someone who wrote such sinful books. Mathurin pondered this for a while after her departure - the idea of honesty being sinful.

For some the truth is a plunge into enervating waters, for others it is a hand grenade waiting to explode. The third applicant was a local woman called Celeste Blesi, she was homely and practical and clearly had the approval of Sabine. Mathurin liked her and she was certainly at the top of his list - until he saw Giulia Azzario. With Giulia life came into the room, life in the form of an irrepressible energy, a spirit born of belief, an amused sprite born of knowing, a tousle haired, dark eyed Italian girl who filled every inch of his sombre study with the glory of who she was – no more – no false pride but no false modesty either. She was from Vicenza she told him where 'everything was stuffy and provincial.' She had worked in Venice for a while, like most of her young friends, but in the summer the heat and the flies made it unbearable and she had moved north. She was currently working in a bar in Minusio but it was closing. She was rusty with office procedure but had a Formazione Professionale in Business Studies and felt no uncertainty about her ability to take on the role required of her. 'How is your telephone manner?' he asked, though by now he was only asking questions now to justify his choice to Sabine later. 'People like the sound of my voice,' she smiled without pride or modesty, 'and I am always polite.' She asked about the salary and Mathurin added a number of Swiss francs to his original estimate. She nodded at this. 'When can you start?' He asked. 'I've got the job? She was neither surprised nor amazed, 'I can start on Monday.' They shook hands on the deal, her hand was surprisingly firm for such a delicate looking thing and then she left trailing the smell of summer fields and the room full of promise. Mathurin shook his head, had he really been stunned by what he had seen, he who had experienced endless glimpses into the human heart, privileged or otherwise – no – he had not fooled himself or been fooled by her – he was thankfully beyond that – and yet, a little happiness danced inside him, a happiness in the knowledge that he would spend some days at least in the presence of Giulia Azzario.

When she found out his choice Sabine told him he was an old fool and he had probably brought trouble on himself but whether that trouble would come from Giulia or from Sabine herself she didn't elucidate. They had been married for twenty years now and the exasperations she sometimes felt about him were beginning to show more and more, like those bits of metal that road workers put into paving stones to show when the paving was wearing thin and would soon crack or disintegrate if not replaced. If she wanted to replace him he wouldn't blame her. He felt the thinness too - in his soul, an emptying of his personality, ready for the long hard climb towards infirmity and death.

Sabine had been a late flowering love, fifteen years his junior, he had met her at Livre Paris, the Paris Book fair the year the German's had been the invited country amidst much reconciliatory rhetoric from Chirac and Schroder on the opening. Mathurin didn't attend every year but back then he was pretty much promoting himself on his own with virtually no support from Editions Verdon, so he went when he could spare the time and the cash. Sabine was working on the Hachette stand, all the big publishers invested in 'eye candy' for their stands while the men in suits with clipboards, the deal clinchers' hovered in the shadows. It reminded Mathurin of those girls who would try to thumb lifts from passing motorists while their boyfriend hid in the bushes. Sabine had been given the task of walking between the stands handing out leaflets and exuding sensuality. Mathurin was sitting at the Editions Verdon stand, next to a picture that explained who he was, waiting for someone to ask him a question, want an autograph or a photo or heaven forbid buy a book. Sabine smiled at him as she walked past, he smiled back touched by her kindness. She went on a few more steps then, as if she'd changed her mind, came back to the table. 'Would it sound sycophantic if I told you I love your books?' He read her name on her exhibition badge. 'Coming from a rival publisher, Sabine, not at all. 'Oh, I'm not an employee, I just do promotions. I work for an events company. 'Is there such a thing? I never knew.' Mathurin realised that the world of marketing was more shameless than he had imagined, with beauty and it's darker doppelganger sex as the true currency. 'You'd be surprised,' Sabine smiled ruefully, 'the things they come up with. I expect you are fed up with people asking you this but are you writing a new book? Mathurin looked at the woman in front of him, how old was she? 23, 25? But something was passing between them and he would be foolish to ignore it. He had no ties, his last relationship had ended ignominiously the previous September, so ignominiously that he had avoided returning to the fray, for fray it now seemed. However the clear blue eyes, delightful nose and winning smile of Sabine told him to take a chance. 'I am and if you would like to meet me at the bar during your break I will tell you all about it.'

So it had begun, good years, years with Sabine Belfort from Arras, the dour Flemish town that had risen from destruction at the end of the Great War, whose claims to fame were its underground tunnels and being the home of Robespierre who, Sabine assured him, was still a hero to the town. Mathurin had been delicate in his courtship of Sabine, allowing her to trust him, drawing her in without our being to fawning or attentive. He had made those mistakes, not everyone embraces unconditional love with equilibrium. One had to tread quietly and unobtrusively through the undergrowth that led to the prize, too quickly, too loudly and you would startle. When they finally became lovers it became clear to him that he needn't have been so cautious, she had been ready long before.

Mathurin knew things had changed between them over the years, that imperceptibly, slowly the relationship had settled into a routine, they were loving but made love less often, they were caring but it was a methodical caring – a practised habit – not without truth or honesty but without the passion, the depth of feeling that had passed between them before. As he reached his 60th year Mathurin, felt no yearning, no loss in this. Perhaps that was what old age gave you – a stillness that took you beyond ambition, beyond boredom, beyond desire. If Giulia Azzario had awakened something in him it wasn't that – desire, but there was the matter of the stillness. She made him feel as if he had embraced it too soon.

Giulia arrived punctually on the Monday morning, she was dressed more soberly than at the interview, which made Mathurin think that she too knew about the 'eye candy' effect and how to use it.

He would need to be careful.

Yet Giulia turned out to be exactly what he had needed as an assistant, not just wanted, because he hadn't known himself exactly what was needed, but she did. So much so that he could tell that Sabine was impressed and after a week or two she gave up giving Giulia arch looks and became almost friendly with her. Giulia's organisation was impeccable, she never forgot or missed or confused a thing. Her telephone manner was so warm and enticing that they received a visit for Gaston Verdon himself who pretended that he was on a whistle stop tour of his 'favourite' authors but Mathurin knew it was just to view that enchanting voice in the flesh. He took them both to an expensive lunch where Mathurin, presumably the reason for Gaston's visit, was virtually ignored. Mathurin would have been irritated but for the fact that Gaston's attempts at seduction were so crass and Giulia sidestepped them elegantly. Afterwards he couldn't decide if he admired her method or her refusal more. 'Sorry about that,' he had told her once they were back in the office and Gaston had jetted off to some more receptive clime, 'but he does pay the bills, so telling him what I think of him might have to wait.' 'I say no much more often that I say yes,' she smiled, 'so I've got quite good at it. 'I can see that.' He laughed and she laughed too.

The summer came and slipped away, Mathurin completed his latest work and gave it to Giulia to read. Two days later she said, 'It's very accomplished but I don't like it as much as some of your other work.' Mathurin was a little taken aback at this, he had tried to raise the level of his prose, to push his narrative in a new direction, Giulia's response suggested to him the he had failed. 'Do you know why you didn't like it? 'of course, because you tried too hard to impress everyone.' Mathurin shrugged at this, aware of the fact that the one person he had tried to impress had just told him it hadn't happened. 'Oh well, let's see what the world thinks of it.'

The world, at least the literary world, agreed with Giulia, "Lacking in his usual integrity," said one "Stylish, intriguing but very much a rabbit out of a hat," said another. The sales were excellent of course but Mathurin knew that if his reading public agreed with the critics then the shortfall would come with the next book. Gaston Verdon knew so too and sent Mathurin an e-mail encouraging him to return to what 'made him special.' The problem with that was that Mathurin didn't want to return to his old ways and apart from that he had absolutely no idea what made him 'special'.

226

The snows came early that year, dusting the upper slopes of Cardada, Cimetta and the imperious Sassariente. Mathurin took long solitary walks sometimes by the lake, sometimes in the town, starting from the Via Scazziga, where it ran cheek by jowl with the station platform and you could see the destination indicators (Zurich, Milan, Stresa). From there he would wend his way through the tiny streets, crossing briefly through the main street, thronged even this late in the year with tourists and students, until he arrived above the town, somewhere on the Via Monti that would wind up and up into the hills, from there he would contemplate the world as he saw it.

He had long ago given up believing that there was a meaning to the world, science had made it quite clear now that humans were a freak species living on a freak planet in the middle of a toxic solar system that itself was suspended in who knows what. Genetics had taken care of the concept of genius and natural selection had begun the long burial of blind faith and the afterlife. Although the concept of the afterlife had always seemed absurd to Mathurin - the idea that the human spirit went on forever - that said, the idea of nothingness seemed absurd too, but then he could believe in that. Growing old hadn't been as bad as he had feared and his long tussle with infinity, with nothingness, had come to stalemate. He had parked it somewhere in the recesses of his mind, it no longer sat in his shoulder like a malevolent parrot squawking terror into his ear.

Mathurin sat and looked at the lake in the gathering dusk, he reached into his memories. Should he write in a more autobiographical vein? He could see the value as art but was wary of the things in his past that he would have to revisit even if he obscured them fully from his readers, besides, his memories were like little hallucinations to him now, things that seemed less true with the passing years. These episodes flickered back, usually at night. Things he had forgotten flowed back to him. Details appeared that he had lost. He had long since given up assessing his life in moral terms or even in terms of failure and success. Even so, he wasn't proud of some of the things he had done, of the people he had been. He had done reasonably well considering his temperament. Had he done as well as he might?

Almost certainly not, but he hadn't expected that. So perhaps it was time to put the pieces together.

Towards the middle of November the snow that had misted the mountain tops came down to the lake in earnest, each morning a fresh heavy overnight fall kept the snowploughs toiling up and down the Via Monti and along the lake fronts. Mathurin told Giulia not to bother coming in, to deal with the e-mails from home and he would look to the rest. In truth the work had slackened off lately, the Mathurin vogue was waning and he also spent less time writing than he once had – he was digging deep now and the act didn't tire him so much as make him veer away from his subject. Inside the can of worms was another and then another. Had he really been that man? Was he still that man? That was the haunting thought. He didn't want to be – but was it that easy? He pressed on though, as the snow continued to fall and the ploughed snow was piled higher and darker at the side of the roads.

When you are writing a novel the characters involved have an unsettling way of taking over your narrative, minor characters become major and vice versa and the major ones having established their precedence in the pecking order begin to dictate how they should be treated – and worse – how they treat others. It can be fun, exciting, to be led in this way but it can also be annoying. It was annoying now and he kept breaking off, staring out the window at the frozen edges of the lake and the black silhouettes of the birds as they searched vainly for food. He went into the room that Giulia used as her office, sat in her chair which still seemed to hold her essence, an imaginary warmth, a perfume. The appointment book was open on the desk and he read the entries in her precise hand. He missed Giulia, she always filled the rooms with her breezy, happy energy, her simple but powerful loveliness. She had become important to him, he had no thoughts of trying to possess her but her presence made him happy, fulfilled a desire of sorts. In a couple of days the roads were finally cleared and Giulia's return restored his equilibrium though his struggle with words, with his memories eased only slightly.

Mathilde and Laure came home for the holidays, infected by the elites as he knew they would be, giggly and pompous by

228

turns, he found them irritating. He had realised some time ago that they lacked the hunger for knowledge that would make them truly clever and it no longer annoyed him -perhaps they all did – decade zero – when so much was available on the surface that you didn't need to dig to come up with things to keep you occupied. Sometimes he wondered if it wasn't all a slight of hand, a distraction, a magic trick by those in power – those in real power – to deflect from the way in which the world was being shaped, from the trench being dug between the rich and the poor, dug to make sure that crossing seemed impossible and should not be attempted ever again. Perhaps he should write about that but he knew he would need facts, proof and part of that magic was that there was no proof, only the brutal, obvious results of what had occurred, results that were easily blamed on the victims.

Even though she was closer in age to Mathilde and Laure than to Sabine, He could see that Giulia didn't like them. She said nothing and showed no animosity towards them but Mathurin knew. For their part Mathilde and Laure saw Giulia as no more than one of the servants, they were already comfortable with the elite's view of hired help. Though he felt guilty, Mathurin was glad when they returned to school. He would do his duty by his daughters but he could not admire them just because they were family or love them just because he should. He would not fail them and if they grew to respect life then he would welcome them into the small and shrinking coterie of those who did.

In February the bad weather returned, fiercely this time, the roads became impassable from one day to the next, because Gaston Verdon was pressing for Mathurin's next novel, a novel that was now progressing beyond Mathurin's early agonies, Mathurin really needed Giulia's help with the day to day. It was Sabine's idea that Giulia should stay over – Mathurin would never have suggested it – while travel remained uncertain. So Giulia, her presence, her warmth, her essence came to stay.

Mathurin preferred to start writing early before the practical demands of the day intruded, muddled his thoughts and jarred apart the trancelike state in which he preferred to create. He could edit and amend any time anywhere but the act of creation needed a sense of solitude, of isolation. After the second hour, as the light was creeping up from behind the Sassariente he would shake the tension from his neck and go down to the kitchen for coffee. Forgetting that Giulia was in the house he was startled to see her leaving the bathroom in a short white towelling robe. She smiled as she walked towards him rubbing her wet hair vigorously with a towel. Barefoot, her long brown limbs moved like a dancer across the carpet. Her robe as she rubbed at her hair parted slightly to reveal a full and lively bosom. If she noticed she did nothing to pull her robe shut. 'Good morning, Monsieur Jules,' she trilled and she passed by him trailing the aroma of sweet damp flowers as she did so. He replied in a whisper and turned to watch her walk back to her room; scrubbed, rosy, naked beneath the white towelling. The enervating valley that led between her breasts imprinted on his retina. What he had said about his feelings for her not being desire – shattered. He did nothing of course. He had convinced himself there was nothing he could do. He even complimented himself on his ability to cover up his 'confusion' as he called it, but it turned out that he was not even doing that. One night, sitting in the lounge, watching the lights twinkling on the far lake shore, Sabine sipping at her Kir Royale said, 'Your love for Giulia is beginning to show and I find it disturbing.' Mathurin was surprised, he stared at his Pastis and water for a while. It was not the content of Sabine's statement that gave him pause but her use of the word "disturbing". Like one might refer to odd behaviour in a public place or an unwanted noise in the street. The choice of the word irritated him, put him on edge. 'I do not love Giulia, so you have no need to be 'disturbed'. I admire her – she is admirable – you said so yourself. You have no reason to be jealous.' Sabine stifled a laugh, 'I'm not jealous – I'm not suggesting that you are having a relationship with her or that you are even intending to –' 'Good,' said Mathurin, 'she is, after all, just young enough to be my granddaughter.' 'As I was saying,' Sabine continued, 'It's not jealousy. I just don't want to see either of you hurt. I know you're not in love with her – yet – but you are in love with the idea of being in love with her and it is showing. If I can see it so can she. When I was her age the difference in years never stopped the old men, the rich and successful old men, from coming onto me. Most of them were objectionable – but not all – the authors especially seemed very attractive. She admires you, that is clear. Who knows what father figure fantasies lay hidden amongst the pressed flowers, poems and soft toys of her dreams. Don't encourage her.' Mathurin though still annoyed agreed to rein in his 'admiration', though more for Giulia's sake than Sabine's

By spring the novel was complete and Mathurin let it fester in his laptop for a week as he always did. He gave the book the title l'homme qui convient and the dedication 'To one who made it possible'.

As was normal once he had finished a book, he felt empty and restless. The weather was too foul for walking, so he decided to catch up with the novels of some of his contemporaries. He downloaded several works to his tablet and sitting in the hush of his library began to read. The problem with being a writer, a writer trained in the devices of writing, was that you were always aware of them being applied. However skilfully they were utilised you became aware of them and it had the same effect for him as if an actor in a play had broken character, shattering the suspension of disbelief, that sacred pact between the artist and the audience. That is not to say he did not enjoy them and in many cases admire them but he remained outside of them and he could never be fully absorbed by them. He was sure other writers felt the same about his books – at least he hoped they did.

After a week had passed he re-read l'homme qui convient, made a few minor adjustments and gave it to Giulia to read. He knew he risked an argument if Sabine knew he had showed it to her first, but Sabine would just say something like 'very nice dear'. Sabine had traditional ideas about being supportive.

Giulia took the manuscript home with her. Next morning she came into Mathurin's study, placed the manuscript on his desk and walked out without a word. Mathurin felt a little pang of fear. He had shown her Mathurin and she had left without a word. He waited until he could bear it no longer and then went into the office. She sat at the desk with tears in her eyes but they were not tears of horror or despair. 'You wrote this to please me didn't you?

'I wrote it to prove something to you - and to myself.' 'It's beautiful.' 'Beautiful?' Mathurin was perplexed, surely there was nothing beautiful about the raw ugliness of a life laid bare. 'The honesty is beautiful. Truth is beautiful. Could she really admire the dark man of the novel, just because it was true? She was certainly looking at him differently. 'It's – exciting. I feel you. The real you. This was what Mathurin had wanted – wasn't it? – to be admired by this woman, yet he felt himself instinctively backing away – had he really set out to seduce her all along? And if he had why? It was true what Sabine had said, he loved the thought of her – but beyond that? He was too old for a new life, a new plan even if he had wanted one – and he didn't. While he was pondering the best and least heartless avenues of retreat, Giulia stood up and kissed him fully, lips parted on the mouth and the damage was done.

For days afterwards nothing was said. What had passed between them was passed over. Yet whenever he looked in her eyes he could see the question in them but he had no answer so he stopped looking. There was an offer there, a promise so dazzling that the old Mathurin could not – would not have refused. That he did so now was not out of a sense of propriety or even of loyalty to Sabine – he wanted to be done with the magical attraction of women that had dominated and perhaps even afflicted his life. They had taught him love and hate, they had taught him hope and despair and he had given that lesson back to them – sometimes in spades but never with an easy heart.

To begin again? Even that thought was an anathema to him but to begin again with such a young woman? Sabine had been quite right, he should not try to be young, it was foolish to pretend to be young and yes – he had brought this trouble on himself. Besides you only began again out of desperate unhappiness, vanity or compulsive restlessness, none of these applied to him. He knew he should part company with Giulia, tell her it would be best if she left, he knew she would not argue though she would be upset. Still he delayed. He was not yet ready to leave the shadow of a young girl in bloom.

Then l'homme qui convient won the Grand Prix de Roman of the Academie Francaise and all hell broke loose. Mathurin had suddenly gone from being successful and known in certain circles to becoming a 'big winner', something a much wider public could understand; A cluster of paparazzi appeared around his gate, a fraction of those attracted to film stars but unnerving nonetheless, the requests for interviews flooded in, this time from literary journals as well as the magazines and newspapers. Giulia was inundated with calls and e-mails. Gaston phoned to congratulate Mathurin and agreed to send administrative support in the run up to the ceremony and two young assistants, Michel and Anais, arrived on the Milan train the next day. Mathurin had no time to write but that didn't matter as he had no will to write, the muse, which had gnawed at him the last forty years was silent, perhaps too shocked at what she had wrought. He stayed in his study as much as he could, asking not to be disturbed unless there was an emergency, still he knew he was the centre, the eye. of a strange kind of hurricane. The Prix Roman – his name would register in the same roster as writers such as Mauriac and Bernanos and Saint-Exupery - though there were many on the list that he had never heard of at all.

The day of the ceremony neared and Mathurin and Sabine were to be flown to Paris. Mathilde and Laure, who having always found his occupation a 'little weird', fully understood the concept of big winner, appeared and insisted in coming along too.

Michel, Anais and Giulia gave him a little drinks party before they left as they were staying behind to 'keep shop' as Anais put it. They gathered in the office and toasted his success. Mathurin saw no point in avoiding giving Giulia the credit she deserved for this and pointedly did so. Michel and Anais looked at her thoughtfully and toasted her too. Giulia blushed and gave him a look as if to say 'and-?' Mathurin looked at his watch and gave excuses about the need to pack.

Mathurin and his family had been installed at the Hotel Du Crillon, an hotel that Mathurin hated for its arrogance and the pathetic deference of the staff, the forelock tugging, humiliating level of subservience that was presumably considered necessary by the clientele. They drifted past him in the lobby, the duchesses and the hedge fund managers, the Sheiks and the oligarchs and he felt tainted even breathing the same air as them. Gaston Verdon was there to greet them. Mathurin bet he loved the hotel. While Sabine, Mathilde and Laure were out shopping, Mathurin appraised the room, a knowing mish-mash of art deco and Louis IV style, clever, elegant, designed to make the guest feel part of the history of France – in a superficial way. The hotel, Mathurin had heard, was now owned by the Saudi's like so much of the expensive end of the planet. Mathurin poured himself a Scotch, though it was much too early, and looked out of the window. Below him the Place de la Concorde bustled its way through another traffic clogged day. The air of the city was apparently poisonous now, though with the treble glazing and the air-conditioning, neither the noise nor the fumes reached him. Mathurin stared at the point where a King, a Queen and countless others had been executed; he tried to imagine the baying mob, the shuddering swish of the Guillotine blade, the smell of blood as it spilled out of the baskets and made the floor of the scaffold slippery. It did not take him long.

So the evening arrived and they were driven in limousines the short distance across the Seine to the Institut de France in the Quai de Conti. He had to admit the Sabine, Mathilde and Laure all looked lovely, but then the amount that they had spent in the Parisian beauty parlours and fashion houses he would have expected nothing less.

Inside the Institut there was a select yet determined crowd of people, mostly Academie members and their families, they were here for two reasons (if you discounted the free food and drink), to mingle with their rarefied peers and to share in the triumph of Jules Mathurin whether he liked it or not. Mathurin decided that he didn't like it, beneath the glittering chandeliers they came, in twos and threes, sniffing him out; radical or reactionary? one of us or one of them? All of them running their hands across his fame as if it was a flame that could warm them, ogling him like a curious artefact, trying to decide if it could be put to use or not. In the end Mathurin politely gave them all short shrift, left them in no doubt of his uselessness to them, gave a short almost insolent and certainly discourteous acceptance speech. His family meanwhile glittered with the glitterati and he was grateful at least they were having a marvellous time. Sabine in conversation with a well-known 'pop' philosopher whilst Mathilde and Laure had gravitated to the handful of younger men in the room, writers, Mathurin guessed, as that was the one

234

profession that seemed to get you admitted to the Academie under the age of fifty. Mathurin picked up a glass of champagne form a waiter, he didn't really like the stuff but he knew it was probably very expensive –so. Gaston Verdon came up to him smiling unsmilingly. Mathurin smiled unsmilingy back, resisting a sudden urge to punch him in the face. 'Jules. Jules, you do like to bite the hand that feeds you.'

'I thought that hand was yours.'

'- and it is and I hope to go on feeding you for many years to come.'

'As long as I keep churning out the words.

'as long as you keep doing what you love'.

But I don't love it any more, Mathurin thought, and the sudden realisation left him shocked, he had always wanted to write, he had wanted to earn enough so he didn't have to do anything else, he had wanted his work to be appreciated – but he hadn't wanted fame, but fame had found him and was riding on him hysterically, expectation cornered him, raising its hands in hope, asking him to emulate, to better his art and that thought was making him bitter. He could see it in all their eyes; in Gaston's, in Sabine's, in Mathilde and Laure's, in the sparking, loving eyes of Giulia Azzario and he didn't want it. As he turned away, Gaston said. 'By the way we are taking your office work in house, in Paris, save you the cost and the distraction.'

Mathurin froze, perplexed. 'Why?'

'Because the interest in you after this is going to triple, We need to be able to respond to that interest quickly. Michel and Anais will be on the team.'

'What about Giulia?'

Gaston gave a smarmy grin. 'Oh, she's on board, Michel and Anais were very impressed with her. She'll be joining us at Editions Verdon.'

'In Paris?

'Of course.

''She's agreed to this?

''Sure, it's a great opportunity for her. You focus on your next novel. Leave the rest to us.'

He was tempted to say that there would be no next novel but then he realised that would put Giulia immediately out of work.

On the journey back to Locarno the following day he tried to rehearse what he would say to Giulia when they met and as he did so he realised he did not know what he wanted to say. "Go, I wish you well", "Don't go, I think Paris is a bad idea for you." But he knew as he said that, that it wasn't true. He imagined her in Paris. He knew that Paris would enjoy Giulia – he knew that she would enjoy Paris in return and be successful there - though he feared for her. He remembered what Sabine had said to him about just being desired. Your confidence blossomed but in the end you felt more and more like shop window goods or even so much meat. He could tell her that he needed her with him but although it was true, it was not true in the way she would think and he could not say it. As it was she had already left for Paris on his return - on his desk was a letter written in her elegant hand.

Jules

I apologise for loving you. I see now that it is an embarrassment to you. You are a good man. I should have realised that. I am to begin a new life it seems. Thanks to you. Wish me luck,

Your loving G xx

A good man! He laughed. If only she knew. If he was good now it was because he was weary. The devil in him had weakened, had left him to sanctity. The room she had used as an office seemed hopelessly empty - he would close it up, use it as a storeroom, a place for unwanted and forgotten things.

He decided to write two further novels, to push his straining and creaking imagination through two more trials. Then he would be finished and Giulia would either be established in the world of Parisian publishing or not. They would not be novels he would enjoy writing but he would make them interesting and honest. He had many readers after all.

He spent a long time before winter set in sitting by the lake in the Alla Riva gardens, watching the restless flow of boats and water birds, trying hard to empty his mind - trying to live in the moment. He was reminded of a photo he had seen of Charlie Chaplin as an extremely old man, nearing the end of his vivid, tumultuous life. Shot from distance and from behind, it showed a small man sitting on a bench in his garden, distant and alone, clearly quite content with his melancholy - powerfully, intentionally alone, but somehow suggesting loneliness anyway.

As Mathurin sat there watching the sun slip down below the Gambarogno peaks he felt the weight of all he had known, all he had been, like a millstone on his shoulders. He knew now he would never shake them, these ghosts, these 'what ifs'. He knew that despite all his efforts he would never live completely in contentment with his waning life, his waning abilities – but at least things would be quiet. There were simple pleasures would be left to him, the joy of the sunrise, a woman's smile.

IT'S A SPRING DAY SURE

It's a spring day, as fresh and sunny as you can hope for, when Katie Swann and I go walking out along the cottonwoods down by the river at the edge of town. It's a small town, back when the idea meant something good. It's April 1912 and this is Crocker County, Kentucky. Katie Swann is fifteen years old, same as I. My name is Harry Puluvo and I love Katie Swann with as much heart and soul as you can have when you've only spent a mere fifteen years on God's earth.

Katie is dressed in her blue gingham pinafore dress with her hair plaited down her back. At the bend of the river where it winds down to the mill, I am overcome with the urge to touch her and I encircle her waist with my arms. She is all softness and sweet smelling skin against my rough serge suit and chemical pomade. 'Fresh' she mutters and raps my knuckles lightly with the birch switch she is carrying, a slow dreamy smile on her face. 'My momma says that boys who touch girls before their sixteenth birthday should be horsewhipped.'

'I'm sure that's true,' I tell her, squeezing her waist harder, spreading my hands wide like fans over her abdomen, 'yet it's a chance I have no choice but to take.'

'You are very sure of yourself, Harry Puluvo.' She links her fingers into mine but does not pull them away.

'Not at all,' I assure her, 'In fact I am trembling with awe at my good fortune.'

'Yes, you are lucky.' She nods and pushes my hands a little lower, only a fraction, mind. Still a long way from ... that place, but my mouth is suddenly dry. 'Still I guess I'm lucky too.'

'Oh Katie, I sigh into the dark hairs at the nape of her neck.

She lets me kiss her then, soft on the mouth, no slobbering, no tongues, no bumping of teeth. 'Nothing animal' she always says, just the breathy touch of lip, puckered and slightly moist, on lip.

'Can you feel it?' I ask her.

'Feel what?' she replies warily.

'My heart.'

'Beating fast?'

'No, in my mouth.'

She splutters our kiss away, laughing. 'Honest, Harry you do say the strangest things.'

I grin back, a little abashed that my joke has cost me the touch of her lips and the unacknowledged but unmistakable pressure of her pelvis on mine. But I'm happy that I can make her laugh because when she laughs, when she smiles, her face lights up in a way that stuns me. To know that people can be that vibrant, that alive, that luminous, that damn beautiful and then to think that such a person is kissing me, is laughing at my jokes, thinks I am 'swell' – wow. I guess it makes me a little nervous too. It's a big responsibility loving someone as special as Katie Swann. It's a high place to be for one so young as I. So it's no wonder that I get dizzy sometimes.

We walk on hands round each other's waists. We don't say much for a while, just let the first really warm air of the year drift by us, listening to the sounds and smelling the aromas of spring.

Soon we are in sight of the town. Once it had been on the very edge of the known world, back in the days before the restlessness in men took them across the Cumberland River and out into the wild lands of the west. The town had been bigger then, bouyed by the significance of being a last outpost. Now it was lost in the middle of a something much bigger and still a little bemused at its fall from grace. Katie and I wander up Main Street, just holding hands now looking very proper. We go into Steven's drug store, sit at the counter and stare at the shiny soda fountains, polished so bright. I order a large malted milk and two straws. Katie makes me promise not to blow. I promise but I blow a little anyway and she blows back. We giggle like a couple of kids which I guess we still are. It's 1912 and it's one of those perfect days that come back to me now and then, so full of promise and hope, still preserved with all its freshness, its pleasure intact. Like it meant something more than just a couple of people, not doing much but I guess when you don't spend that long alive then things like that can be significant. Me, I only managed nineteen years of it. That's when I ended up in France in a place called Chateau Thierry. I always used to call it Chateau Ferry but I am now aware that it is indeed pronounced Tee-erry. Dumb huh ? Nineteen years. So on that day, that perfect day a little math informs me that I had but four and a half years to go. More than Katie Swann though – she only had three.

I always thought that once I was dead I would know everything, but that's God's job I guess. I'm still none the wiser about a lot of things but my knowledge and understanding gets better. Over time a pattern emerges but the purpose remains as obscure as ever. Like what was the point of making two people like Katie and I only to blot us out just as we were starting.
Did we do something wrong?
Sure, I'd believe that of me, but Katie, not Katie.
I guess I stuck my neck out over in France. Hell I didn't care. Katie was gone. Life was not that great. I didn't care enough about it to keep it.
So I didn't.

Yeah I remember that day too, that last day, sure.

The smell of the earth at the edge of the trench, gouged and fetid, raw – moist like an open wound. I'm looking at the steps up. They're muddy and wet and don't look too strong. I'm worried that I'll slip and make a fool of myself in front of the other guys. Funny really, the things you worry about, 'cause I got out of the trench fine, absolutely no bother, then five steps later there's this explosion and everything goes black.

I don't know how long it is before I start to see light again. My senses are all mixed up. Once there was a time I could guess the passing of an hour almost to the minute but this is different. Anyway, just as it starts to get light again and it is more of an impression of light, not like the dawn coming, nothing like that, I hear Katie's voice, she's calling my name. I don't know that I'm dead yet so I think I'm dreaming. I call back and then she's there, well kinda, I can't see her, not like you can see people when you look at them, but she's there in my head. Yes she's there all right. 'Oh Harry, I'm so sorry.' She's almost sobbing. 'Calm down,' I tell her, but she just goes on saying 'Horrible, horrible.' In the end she calms down. 'I saw you die,' she says, 'You just blew apart. One minute you were there running, the next you were gone.'

'I've missed you,' I tell her
'Me too', she says
'Are you my guardian angel?' I ask her.
'If I am then I've let you down haven't I.'
'Can you see me?' I say
'Sort of, like I think I can.'
'Can I touch you?' I ask
'There's nothing to touch', she tells me 'not up here.'

I find that a bit depressing but not for long. It's hard to be unhappy for long when you're dead. Hard to hold any human type emotion, except for some reason - love.

'How come you're in France?' I ask her, after a while.
'I'm not,' she says, 'and neither are you, silly.'
'So where is this then?'
'It's everywhere.'
'So what do we do here, now?'
She sighs. 'There's nothing we can do except watch.'
'Watch what?'
'People, I've been watching you for the last year and a half.'
'Gee Katie, that's swell of you – you mean ever since …?'
'Yes, ever since.'
'So you don't blame me for what happened.'
'No, I don't. I was a little shocked and then a little angry for a while but then you sort of get to understand things. In kind of way you don't, maybe a way you can't, when you're alive. Besides it was all my fault really.'

I say nothing then.
'I've got to go,' says Katie after a while.
'Go where?'
'I've got to leave you for a time, there's stuff you need to understand, sort out in your head, get settled. It's all about getting settled, you'll see. But don't worry I'll be back.'

I was expecting a visit from some other folks or maybe some kind of head guy, something like that but I doesn't work that way. Thoughts come. At first I thought I was having them myself but they came too quickly out of nothing one after the other and after a while I knew this was the stuff that I had to take in. By the time Katie came back I understood all about being dead.

When she comes back for a long time we're just there saying nothing. I don't know what to say. I can tell she's waiting for me to start. So, in the end, I do.
'So you can see stuff on the earth.'
'Yeah, she says, glad that we've got going, 'Places, people, whatever you want I guess. I hurts a little at first. To see all those things going on without you – but you get over it – sort of.'

So I went to say goodbye to my folks.

If you want to go places here, you just have to think about them and you're there, well sort of there, cause you can't be seen and you can't touch anything. Katie was right. Seeing my Mom and Dad and my kid sister again made me real sad, especially when I saw how down my Mom looked.
There was this picture of me in uniform above the fireplace with this black velvet edging on it. I saw that she would look at it a lot and sigh. Then I'd feel bad that I got myself killed and let her down like that.
But as Katie also said you don't remain sad for long. It's as if those emotions you had like fear, anger, pride and even sorrow, go drifting off you. Not all at once 'cause I guess they were a big part of you, but over time. And love, like I've already said, is the feeling that never goes. Funny, isn't it?
Time is not the same here. In what feels like a few hours, down on earth, years have gone by. I first notice it in my sister. Almost before I know it she's grown and left home.
Now, when I think about the place where I died, I am surprised to see that the grass has all grown back and the trenches collapsed in. So I guess the war is over or moved on to somewhere else.
'Did we win? I ask Katie.
'Yes we won. A whole lot of people died though. So many that people are so shocked they say it'll never happen again.'
'I'm glad we won,' I tell her, 'glad to be on the winning side – well sort of. Damn though I never got to kill anyone.'

'You should be glad.' Katie yells at me. 'People who got to kill other people, even if they were in a war are treated very badly here. Killing is not considered acceptable, no sir, not under any excuse.'

'So what do they do to these people?'

'They let them be unhappy.'

'How?' I ask.

'Well, you know how it is when you feel unhappy but It goes away?'

'Yes.'

'Well for them it doesn't go away, I just gets worse.'

'And don't they ever get forgiven.'

'Not as far as I know – maybe.'

'And are there any other sins people get punished for?'

'No – as far as I can see the only sin is killing and the only virtue is loving – and that's that.'

'I love you Katie Swann.' I say 'I always have.'

'Even on that day? Her voice gets suddenly close in my ear. 'You didn't act like you loved me then.'

Don't punish me Katie.' I say defensively, pushing thoughts away. 'They haven't punished me, so you shouldn't.'

'What do you mean haven't punished you – you're dead, ain't you? Besides sooner or later we have to go back to that day. We have to see it again. How it all happened. Otherwise it will always be there, between us – that day.'

'What do you mean – go back?' I say 'We can't go back.'

'Of course we can silly – it's allowed.   Remember that day, It was a Saturday.' Katie's voice runs in my head and I find the mists parting. 'It's Saturday August 14th 1915, the day of your eighteenth birthday. You parents are throwing a party for you on your back lawn. In the shimmering heat of that Kentucky summer, we dance to your dad's old hand-cranked Victorola.

"Peg o' My heart", "Apple Blossom time", "By the light of the silvery moon".

All our High School friends are there.'

'I see it.' I say. It's like memory, only it's not 'cause I can see myself too. In my powder grey suit and high wing collar, lounged up against the beer table, watching Katie spinning through 'Skip to my lou' swirling from arm crook to arm crook as light as a butterfly. That day she's wearing her pigtail up in a braid and her neck looks so long and elegant. I can remember how much I wanted to kiss it. She's wearing this yellow dress that's quite tight round the waist. Harry takes another glass of beer and ambles across the lawn. He knows Katie wants him to dance but he can't and he doesn't want to try when all the other guys are doing it so well, twirling and leaping and clapping, big cheesy smiles on their faces whenever they do some clever footwork. Harry is glad Katie is enjoying herself though. He stops at the edge of the dance floor, not near enough for anyone to be able to grab him, to coax him on. I can see he's been drinking quite a bit. I never realised it showed like that even when you're not really drunk, even when you feel o.k.

'Do we have to go on with this?' I whisper to her.

'Yes we do.' Her voice is determined and near.

It's almost dusk when the party finally folds, the mauve translucent sky still humming with the heat of the day. Harry invites Katie for a walk down alongside the river, where it will no doubt be cooler. Katie seeing Harry a little the worse for wear ponders this offer, but as it is his birthday eventually assents.

We follow them as they walk arm in arm. They pause occasionally for a slow lingering kiss. Down by the mill race it is indeed cooler and they stand for a long time listening to the tumble and crash of the water as it forces through the sluice gates, spitting white high into the air.

Harry and Katie kiss for a long time. Harry puts his hand on Katie's breast. She squirms a little but leaves it there, quite likes it really, the feel of his hand softly kneading it, making the nipple start to swell.

'I can't watch.' I say.

'You must.' Her voice insists.

Harry suddenly reaches down and lifts up Katie's yellow skirt. Alarm bells ring inside her head as all the warnings, all the training (Never let a boy touch you there !,) kick in. She pushes Harry violently away, but Harry is six foot tall and of solid Kentucky stock and it is Katie who is propelled backwards, striking her back against the mill race rail, a rail on which twenty years of heat and damp and wood mites have done their worst.

244

The rail snaps with hardly any resistance and Katie is gone in the dark foaming water.

Harry stands for a moment stunned by the enormity of what has happened. Then ripping off his coat, dives into the churning foam after her.

'You tried to save me.' She says.

'Of course.' I tell her, 'what did you think ?'

'I didn't know that's all. There was no-one to tell me stuff like that.'

Harry and Katie are lost from sight now. The dusk has fled and it is deep and dark out by the old mill. Katie's body is already caught at the foot of the sluice gate and Harry never did find it, only gets to save himself by clinging to the mill wheel.

'The only reason I didn't let go – didn't let myself die then and there was that I still had a hope that you might have been swept clear and gone downstream - oh Katie, I'm sorry.'

'There, there, Harry it was an accident.'

'But it was my fault.'

'It was mine too. I didn't have to react like that. If I'd asked you to stop, would you have?'

'Yes.' I tell her.

'See, don't be so hard on yourself, Harry, you saw it, you saw what happened, plain as I and now we can be at peace with it.'

'O.K.' I say, 'if you say so.'

'I say so,' she says firmly, 'I say so.'

And so it is.

One day I think about my old house and am surprised to find my folks have gone. All the furniture is different and there's some strange electrical stuff in the kitchen, where the big wooden ice box used to be. In the lounge a thin, dark –haired woman is sitting on the sofa. 'Hello soldier boy,' she says to me, 'I guess you must be Mrs. Puluvo's dear departed.'

'What?' I say. 'You can see me?'

'It's a gift I have.' She smiles wryly. The word gift comes out like she has spat on the floor.

'Hell,' I say, 'what do I look like ?'

'Pretty much how you were when you died , I guess, late teens, early twenties, First World War uniform.'
'Is my face blown off?' I ask her.
'No, you look normal.'
'Just before I died then.' I tell her.
Then I catch up with something she has said.
'First World War?'
'Sure, there's a second one on now honey. Don't you get Radio America where you are ?'
'Who's fighting ?'
'Oh, it's pretty much the same sides.'
'The U.S. too?'
''fraid so.' She said.
'Where are my folks?'
'Place got too much for them, they moved over Scott County way to live near your sister, Becky.'
'Oh, I see, I'd better stop bothering you then.'
'No problem,' she says. 'ghosts or living folks, it's all the same to me. Come back whenever you want.'

I told Katie about the woman but she didn't believe me. I did go back but by then someone else was living there, a family. They didn't see me.

As time went by our parents turned up in the place we were anyway. It was great to be with them again, though strange after such a long time. Then our brothers and sisters turned up too. Though it wasn't like we were a family again. It's not that kind of close.

From time to time Katie comes into my mind and asks me things I can't always answer. She's disturbed by the passing of all the things she's known. Not the people, she understands about that. Not the places even but the way of things. 'It's like everything we understood, everything we believed in, everything we were about, is gone.' She says.
'I've been watching that too,' I tell her, 'the way things have changed. Old people see it, they moan about it, the way they always have, but nobody listens to them on Earth. Everybody

puts it down to the fact they ache too much or that they're angry 'cause they're no longer young or that they're just plain crazy but they see it and now I see it too. It's got to happen though. I can see that too. Hell, it's happening all the time really, every hour of every day takes us further away from where we started out, from that place that we called 'safe'. Though, of course, it only seemed safe, in our innocence, our trust.

Don't worry,' I tell her, 'things will work out o.k. Sure we're in another century now and lots and lots of things have changed but it's the things that don't change that are significant. Remember that.' I tell her. 'Look for these things in each new time. Things like friendship, like hope. Like how on bright, sunny days young people still walk hand in hand down by the river. That their eyes are still full of the happiness and optimism that living can inspire, sure, it will fade for them in time but each new spring will bring new kids and new happiness. That won't change for sure.'

'That's good,' said Katie and though I can't see her I can feel that she is smiling.

So every now and then we go back to that perfect day. That Sunday in 1912 and watch ourselves there, blissful and carefree on the edge of eternity.